SKY

WARRIORS

STEVE LIDDICK

SKY

WARRIORS

STEVE LIDDICK

TOP CAT
PUBLICATIONS

To Kiyo Sato

Books by Steve Liddick

<u>NOVELS</u>
All That Time
Old Heroes
Prime Time Crime
Sky Warriors

<u>COOKBOOKS</u>
Campsite Gourmet
Eat Cheap

<u>GIFT BOOK</u>
A Family Restaurant is No Place for Children

<u>MEMOIR</u>
But First This Message: A Quirky Journey in Broadcasting

Available in paperback on Amazon

You must learn what you are looking for
if you ever hope to find it.

CHAPTER ONE

The warmth of the springtime morning sun on Jeff Burke's face contrasted with the cool Pacific Ocean breeze tugging at the back of his dark hair.

It was Jeff's habit to arrive early at the flight school to enjoy a few moments of quiet before the pace of big city living intensified. Meanwhile, these calm moments helped to offset the gloom Jeff normally carried around with him.

"Good morning young man," Barney Lozares shouted across the pad.

Ferguson's Flight Service's chief mechanic was preparing to start his own work day as he rolled back the big door to the main hangar.

"Hey, Barney."

It was Lozares's crew's meticulous work on the aircraft engines that Jeff and his flight students relied on at altitude.

In the run-up area, the pilot of a blue and white Piper Cherokee was already reviewing a checklist in preparation for takeoff. Another early-bird's plane buzzed in the distance, converging on the traffic pattern for a landing on the mile-long asphalt runway.

"A couple of 'rat dodgers' already here," Barney said.

Jeff smiled at Barney's term for pilots grabbing an hour in the air before jumping into the rat race.

The early arrivals covered a diverse cross-section of the population, including students from nearby UCLA and USC, and those with the time and money to do whatever they pleased, whenever it pleased them.

Barney whistled as he went about his morning routine. The sound echoed against the hard-surfaces of the concrete floor and the corrugated steel sides and ceiling of the interior of the cavernous hangar.

1

Just then, the distinctive purr of a foreign sports car approached and pulled into the parking area.

"Your public is starting to arrive," Barney said.

Jeff ambled toward the trainer aircraft that were tied down next to the flight office.

Later in the day the ever-present so-called "hangar pilots" would come. They sported aviator sunglasses and flight jackets. They would toss out terminology and speak expertly of experiences they had heard from real pilots.

"Shortcutters" was another of Barney Lozares's expressions.

"They try to pass as pilots without putting out the effort," Barney had said with contempt.

Teaching others to fly had become more difficult for Jeff as personal problems spilled over into his professional life. It was distressingly common for him to jerk the controls away from a novice to show him once again how it should be done. Some of his students took it personally and began signing up with other instructors. Some dropped out altogether.

"Jeff, you've got three thousand hours in the air," the owner of the center told him after overhearing one of Jeff's explosive moments.

"You simply cannot expect them to do everything as perfectly as you do it the first time they try," Bill Ferguson said. "You can't let these kids be so concerned with trying to please their instructor that they forget to fly the airplane. It's dangerous—and we're losing business."

If Ferguson had not valued Jeff's experience, and if he did not have a story similar to Jeff's in his own life, the troubled flight instructor would have been long gone.

Jeff projected the quiet kind of strength that both men and women were drawn to. When he was Ferguson's chief pilot, his fellow instructors always brought the tough questions to him. That was before his life got complicated and he asked to be replaced in the top spot. Ferguson reluctantly moved Eddie Griffiths into the chief's position.

If Jeff Burke had flown airplanes in the same way he lived his life over the past eighteen months he would have crashed and burned long ago. What happened between him and his ex-wife ate away at much of the best of what he once was. Now he was working on the rest of it.

Jeff glanced at the ultra-expensive sports car in the parking area.

A blond-haired young man looked up from alongside a Cessna 152 trainer aircraft as Jeff approached.

"You must be Jeff."

"Must be," Jeff Burke said wearily, and a trace imperiously. He looked at the photo copy of his new student's driver's license on the clipboard. "And you're Arthur—"

"Pete," he said almost too quickly. "Pete Sunderland."

"Sunderland?" Jeff said, looking at his clipboard. "Of the defense industry Sunderlands?"

"Nice way to describe it. What do we do now?" he said, changing the subject with whiplash force.

Jeff noted the abrupt switch, took the hint that the family business was not his new student's favorite subject, and began to intone the elements of a pre-flight check with the delivery of one who had done it thousands of times before.

"It is critical before each flight to check all surfaces of the Cessna 152's metal exterior to see that they are operable and undamaged, to be sure the engine has enough oil, and the fuel tanks are full and moisture-free."

He reeled off statistics on the hourly gas consumption, payload capacity and cruise speed.

"I see you're on the schedule again tomorrow, Pete."

"I'm on the schedule every day."

"Really?"

"I want to get my license as quickly as possible, so I'm making a full time job out of flight training."

"Most of the students come in only once a week," Jeff said. "Some even less often. At that rate, it can take a year or more to get their license. If you stick with it, you'll have your private ticket in just a few months."

"What do you mean *if* I stick with it?" Pete sounded slightly offended at the suggestion that he might not.

"Some students don't finish the course after they find out how much work it takes."

3

"Trying to discourage me?"

"Nope. Just letting you know that flying an airplane is more than just a carefree romp in the breeze."

Jeff found himself becoming irritated with the young man.

Satisfied that he had covered everything, Jeff pointed to the seat on the left side of the aircraft and said, "Hop in. That's where the pilot sits."

"I thought you were the pilot."

"I'm the pilot in command until you get your license. But you're the pilot, so the left seat is yours."

The men belted themselves in. Jeff put on a pair of aviator sunglasses and continued his indoctrination.

He guided Pete through the procedure for starting the engine. The craft's gyro mechanism came on with a whine and whirred to a high pitch. The internal navigational system spun faster, until it reached operational speed.

"Clear," Jeff yelled through an open window for the benefit of anyone who might be standing near the propeller. A turn of the starter brought the 110-horsepower Lycoming engine roaring to life. The prop wash rushed past them.

"I'll work the radio until you get used to operating the airplane." Jeff said and pressed the microphone's button to notify the tower of their intention to taxi for takeoff.

They taxied to the active runway, passing aviation-related businesses and an assortment of buildings that housed private and business aircraft. Farther to the north of the airport, through the blue haze far beyond the glass-enclosed control tower, were the Santa Monica Mountains.

An occasional plane swooshed past them on takeoff or landing.

Pete pulled the trainer beside two planes already in the run-up area. Their pilots were going over printed checklists, working the controls, and giving their craft's systems a final check in preparation for takeoff. Pete did likewise.

Once the pre-flight check was completed, Jeff switched the radio to the Air Traffic Control frequency.

"Okay, Pete, move up behind the other planes holding short of the runway and wait for instructions from ATC."

When it was their turn, the controller's voice squawked through the small speaker above Pete's head *"Four-seven-echo cleared for takeoff."*

Pete pushed the throttle a little too far toward the firewall, causing the plane to lurch forward.

"Easy," Jeff said, again irritated at the young man. Pete backed off the throttle and the plane rolled smoothly into position between the large numbers painted on the end of the runway.

"Now give it full throttle," Jeff said as Pete nosed the plane down the runway.

With the engine's roar in their ears, the sweet smell of aviation fuel exhaust seeped into the cockpit. The two men were pressed back into their seats. The airplane's forward movement increased and the dotted line down the center of the runway seemed to beat a cadence as it passed beneath the accelerating Cessna.

"All right," Jeff shouted above the sound of the engine when they reached takeoff speed, "ease the yoke very slowly toward you."

Pete did as he was told, pulling back on the wheel. The aircraft also did as it was told.

"My god," Pete said, grabbing a look at the ground. "We're flying."

"Hey," Jeff shouted impatiently, "you're the driver. Keep your eyes on the road and on your airspeed indicator."

"Sorry. I guess I got engrossed in watching the ground get farther away from us."

"Well, don't get too fascinated," Jeff growled, "or the ground may come back up to meet us."

Far below, Pacific Coast Highway wound its way along America's western edge. They reached the shoreline, passed Santa Monica's brown cliffs, and turned inland over the Los Angeles suburb of Pacific Palisades. In mere moments their altitude had changed from two thousand feet above the water to just a few hundred feet over rough terrain that separated the seaside communities from the inland San Fernando and Simi valleys.

By the time they cruised through the misty coastal air above the mountains to a desolate area used as a practice zone, the Cessna had climbed another several thousand feet.

Pete followed Jeff's instructions through a series of simple climbing and turning procedures.

"We're high enough now to try a couple of stalls."

"You mean shut the motor off?"

"No. This kind of stall has little to do with the engine. It means you have slowed the airplane to the point where it is no longer flying. We do it so you can recognize a stall and recover from it."

"If you say so, boss."

"Slowly cut back the power," Jeff said.

Until the power had been brought back to idle, Pete had barely noticed the sound of the engine. The roar was replaced by a low hum and the whistling of air across the wings.

"Now, pull slowly back on the yoke . . . the wheel. Back . . . back . . . back," Jeff urged. "When the plane dips down, just ease the wheel forward."

The squawk of the stall warning became insistent. Suddenly, without notice, the bottom seemed to drop out of the world as the plane fell forward. The nose of the craft pointed directly toward the ground, the mountains rotating slowly beneath them.

"What the—"

"Push forward slightly on the wheel and add power," Jeff said, calmly.

Pete did as he was instructed and, as though nothing had happened, the plane returned to its previous speed and attitude.

"What was that all about?" Pete asked.

"That started out as a stall and turned into a spin."

"You mean I did something wrong?"

"You just needed to push forward. On the other hand, if a spin had occurred at low altitude on takeoff or landing at an airport, you'll find yourself in a hell of a fix. That's why you have to learn to recognize a stall and recover from it quickly."

"What would happen if I kept holding back on the yoke?"

"The spin would continue, you'd lose altitude at a frightening rate, and, eventually, you'd screw yourself right into the ground."

Sunderland's face lit up. "Yeeee-haaaaaaa! Let's do it some more."

"You actually want to do it again?"

"Sure. It was fun."

For Jeff, being asked to repeat the maneuver was a novelty. After their first stall, most of his students regarded it as a terrifying thrill ride. Even when they learned it was not a death-defying stunt, some would do them only reluctantly, in a white-knuckled sweat, grateful when it ended.

The Cessna climbed again to five thousand feet above the mountains. This time, Pete slowed the engine without being told. He eased back on the wheel until the warning horn sounded and the nose of the plane again dropped. Instantly, he relaxed pressure and the craft avoided the previous gyrations.

"It was more fun the other way." Pete said with a laugh.

Jeff looked at his watch. "Let's head for home." he said. Jeff was annoyed with his new student even more than his usual impatience.

The hour seemed to have gone by quickly. There were others on Jeff's training schedule, so the Cessna was aimed toward Santa Monica. They entered the traffic pattern and were on the ground in minutes, rolling to Ferguson's Flight Service.

After the engine had been shut down, Jeff said, "Pete, I hope you understand how serious learning to fly is."

"Why would you think I wouldn't?"

"Well, a lot of people look at flying simply as soaring high above the earth, free as a bird, doing as they please."

"You're saying there are rules. I understand that."

"Two kinds of rules, actually. There are man's rules and there are the rules of aerodynamics. Break one of the Federal Aviation Administration's rules and you might be fined or get your license suspended or revoked. But break one of the rules of physics and you can turn the Cessna and yourself into a twisted mass."

"I know that," Pete said, stepping down from the plane. "Look, Jeff, I'm not taking this lightly. I plan to be the best pilot I'm capable of being. But I absolutely insist on having some fun while I'm doing it."

"Fair enough. Sometimes I get a little impatient. Maybe I've been doing this too long."

"Bill Ferguson told me you suffered from that."

"What brought that subject up?" Jeff said, walking with Pete to his car.

7

"I asked him who the best instructor on the lot was. He didn't hesitate a second before recommending you. He also said you had a short fuse. I told him I was interested in an instructor's ability, not his personality."

"What else did Bill have to say?"

"Well, he made me promise that if I got discouraged I wouldn't just drop out of training without trying out another instructor first."

When the two men reached Pete's sleek sports car, Pete took a pair of sunglasses from above the visor and put them on.

"This is a Lamborgini Aventador," Pete said in comic imitation of Jeff's Cessna orientation. "It can reach sixty miles an hour in three seconds and is capable of speeds of more than 200 miles an hour. I have no idea how much gas it burns an hour and, frankly, I don't give a rat's ass. Note there are two leather-covered bucket seats. The one on the left is for the pilot. The one on the right is for a member of the female race, not always the same one."

"Do I sound that bad?" Jeff said.

"Like a summer camp counselor who believes if he has to sing 'John Jacob Jingleheimer Smith' one more time he will go mad."

"I've done that spiel a couple of times before."

"Jeff, I can see you are going to be a hard man to get a laugh out of."

"I've sort of gotten out of the habit." Jeff said, having a momentary flashback of events of the past few years.

As Pete Sunderland drove away, Jeff noticed a bumper sticker on the rear of the luxury sports car. It said, "My other car is a piece of shit too."

CHAPTER TWO

Jeff had pulled together a small world for himself after his divorce; an apartment on the beach at Malibu, a little orange kitty that could still get a laugh out of him, and a job that barely separated him from burnout. It often felt like a right-hander forced to write left-handed.

Although it had been many months since the breakup of Jeff's marriage, the hurt was still too deep for him to risk opening himself up to more pain by getting too close to anyone. He generally liked and needed people and knew that whatever was missing from his life was not just a twelve-year habit. Trusting was the hard part. The memory of that fractured trust often ran through his mind.

00

It was just before ten o'clock on that morning when Jeff pulled into his parking space beneath their Venice apartment building.

On a normal day it would have been much later before he came home. One of his students decided at the last minute to make the required cross-country flight with his instructor. It would be about a four-hour flight from Santa Monica to Phoenix in a single-engine Cessna trainer. The return trip would take longer into a headwind. Experience had taught him it would be easier to get a motel room at the Arizona end of the trip and fly back the following day, after a good night's rest.

Jeff let himself into the apartment to pick up a few items for the overnighter and to let Marcie know he would be gone.

He heard a sound coming from the second floor of their modest townhouse. Not a voice, exactly, though vaguely familiar. Not someone crying, he decided, as he climbed the carpeted stairs.

The sound became identifiably human as he approached the bedroom and opened the door.

One look answered the question. And a great many more.

Jeff could only stare at the entangled couple on the bed. They were not immediately aware of his presence. When they realized he was standing in the doorway, both spun awkwardly to attention.

"Jeff," Marcie screamed at him. "Goddamn you," she shrieked. Her face was mix of shock, fear, and shame as she grabbed the sheets and drew them around herself.

In that moment, the concept of past and future disintegrated for Jeff Burke. He had never been so vividly aware only of the present. All that had gone before suddenly lost its meaning. The *somedays* they once spoke of had dissolved with the opening of a door.

"Oh my God," she sobbed, burying her face in the blankets that lay in a twisted swirl.

The man was a neighbor and apartment complex handyman who had repaired leaking faucets and oiled squeaking door hinges. He had apparently been accommodating some of Marcie's more intimate domestic needs, as well.

"What can I say?" Marcie asked through her tears, unable to look directly at her husband.

"Not much left, is there?" Jeff said, his heart pounding. The sudden dryness in his mouth and a genuine pain in his mid-section made him truly understand what people meant when they described an emotional trauma as feeling as though they had been "kicked in the stomach."

The naked man stumbled clumsily across the bedroom to pick up his clothes, almost comical in his efforts to hide himself. He looked at neither of them, nor did they seem to notice him. He bumbled toward the door and was gone. Oddly, Jeff felt no anger toward the man. He saw only his wife, exposed, sitting on the edge of their bed.

"God, this is not something I planned"

"How long has this been going on?"

"It—I—about—a year. Jeff—I—"

"Are you in love with him?"

"No—I'm—no—." She struggled to speak but could not seem to find the right words, if there were any right words for such an occasion.

Jeff took a suitcase from the floor of the closet and sat it on the end of the bed.

"Please don't leave me, Jeff. I need you right now."

"Yeah," he said as he hurriedly stuffed things into the suitcase from his sides of the closet and dresser. "I can see that."

"Please don't do this," she pleaded.

"It seems to me you're the one who has done something. I'm not doing anything except leaving."

"Damn you," she said. "No, I don't mean that. I would never try to hurt you Jeff."

"You've been hurting me for a long time, Marcie. Now I understand why."

Jeff spent the next hour loading personal items into his car. Marcie stayed in another part of the apartment, too ashamed to face him.

As he prepared to leave for what would be the last time, Jeff looked at the wedding picture on the fireplace mantle. It showed a traditionally radiant bride and awkward bridegroom. In their final years together it was almost as though they had to keep checking with the photo to see how life was supposed to be.

The picture stayed the same without mercy.

00

Immediately after the split, no more was necessary for Jeff than the presence of his gender opposite. In recent months, however, Jeff had severely modified his personal criteria for someone he would care to share intimate time with.

Jeff had since become more confident of his own worth in the singles marketplace and more discriminating in his choice of partners. That decision immediately eliminated fully three-quarters of the available women. Those were the ones he referred to as "professional singles." They prowled the bars from Zuma Beach to Palos Verdes that were created for their ilk, with Marina del Rey the central hot spot.

Not that getting a divorce was ever a smooth ride, but for a young, single man to follow his natural longings, life in modern day Los Angeles was not only a lonely circumstance, it was a potential health hazard. He cringed when he considered his earlier lack of judgment.

Occasionally he found someone willing to perform her half of the ritual, but it was never fulfilling in the way it was supposed to be. There was never anyone he wanted to stay with him beyond the physical part. Mostly, when it was over, he just wished them gone. That troubled Jeff because he was not a man comfortable using others.

Jeff and Marcie had not gotten along well in their final years together. His wife had become increasingly critical of him. He could barely say anything that did not turn his words into a battle.

Jeff assumed Marcie was making him the dumping place for her own unfulfilled dreams. A simple "good morning" from him became a vehicle for argument. If he got up from his chair she demanded to know where he was going. If he stayed, he was "sucking all of the air out of the room." If he read a book he was "ignoring" her. If he tried to engage her in conversation he was robbing her of "alone time."

For awhile Jeff entertained the notion that things might have been different if there had been children. But he knew in his heart the end would have come either way. Kids would only have made them stay together longer. As it was, they should have parted sooner, before the hurts piled up, back when they might still have been friends. With children involved, the guilt would have been deeper and the young ultimately among the casualties.

If he had faced the situation directly he might have seen that what remained between them had less to do with love than with habit, tradition, and the expectations of others.

For most of their time together early in the marriage he allowed himself to believe they were headed in the same direction, hand-in-hand down life's pathway and all of that. Later the passion had cooled. But then passion always cooled, didn't it? He had believed they would grow old together. In their elder years they would take evening walks. They would play gin rummy at the dining room table. People would say how devoted they were to each other.

The marriage ended long before it ended, of course. That's the way it is with most marriages that end.

Typically, the young fall in love with whoever is nearest at the time and who most nearly meets the needs of the moment. Some spend the balance of their years together trying to turn each other into the person they envisioned when they still believed in Santa Claus, the Easter Bunny, and Happily-Ever-After.

Jeff's plan had been for them to make a life together, come what may. When the marriage fell apart, so did the plan. Jeff's *todays* became obstacles too large to even think about his *tomorrows*.

Still, the *tomorrows* kept coming.

CHAPTER THREE

Being Arthur Pedwick Sunderland the Third was far more complicated than simply putting three strokes behind the name Pete inherited from his father and grandfather.

For the youngest member of the Sunderland dynasty, having it all carried a high price, indeed.

"Try to get along with your father, Pete," Marian Sunderland had said to her son so many times.

"The only way to get along with him is to do everything he commands. I can't do that."

Almost from the moment of birth, Arthur III had rejected as many of Arthur II's mandates as he could safely get away with.

When his son reached the appropriate age, Pete's father did as all fathers do when they have the means and lack the patience for offspring who refuse to fall into line. The young man was shipped off to prestigious private schools, ostensibly to groom him to head the Sunderland empire.

"You're old enough now to be preparing to take over the business," the elder Sunderland said.

His father described his business as the "defense Industry." Pete called it "gunrunning."

"Not interested," Pete had told his father each time the subject came up. "Providing killers disguised as leaders with the weapons to murder their citizens holds no interest for me."

Early on, when time was still on his side, the elder Sunderland assumed that young Arthur would eventually come around and ascend to his rightful position in the royal succession.

"The business has given you an education and lifestyle that most people would die for."

"That's exactly my point," Pete said. "People *have* died for me to live like this, and I will not directly participate in such a thing."

"How would you like to have your allowance discontinued?"

15

"If that's what it takes to get through to you, then do it."

Pete knew very well that his father would never cut him off. His mother would not permit it. Plus, keeping his son in poverty would go against his father's carefully-crafted public image. And he surely knew that Pete would surely let the world know about it.

Sending the young rebel off to school had been a way to at least temporarily remove his son from his father's thoughts. School represented a socially acceptable storage place until that day when the boy matured or could otherwise be brought under control.

Marian Sunderland was the antithesis of her husband; sensitive and possessing a sense of ethics and justice. Merely by serving as a good example against the background of his father's poor one Marian had instilled those qualities in her son. For that, her husband would never forgive her.

The junior Sunderland viewed the family businesses as criminal, certainly inhumane. How his mother could be blind to her husband's nefarious enterprises was a mystery to him. The most profitable arm of the business was conducted off-shore, beyond U.S. law. The arm that could be considered "respectable" was providing war materiel to the U.S. military. It was unlikely that a man who influenced the major American political parties and helped finance state, congressional, and presidential elections would ever face charges. In any event, Arthur Sunderland the Younger renounced the methods used to maintain and advance the family holdings.

"I can't believe you could love a man like that, mother."

"Of course I love your father," she said. "He's my husband." As though that answered the question.

At about the age of twelve, the defiant heir had made a conscious decision to reserve a part of himself just for himself. To do that he would have to become as far removed as possible from that which threatened to suffocate him.

The name would have to go, of course.

But a nickname is something usually assigned by others. Most often it is a shortened form of a proper name. Sometimes it is based on a physical trait or momentous youthful event. Arthur the Younger chose not to risk the indignities kids so often inflict on each other. Arthur Pedwick Sunderland selected 'Pete' as the name to which he would respond. Eventually, by ignoring or pretending not to hear anyone who referred to him otherwise, the handle stuck. Even his parents accepted it, if only to distinguish him from his father.

A sense of humor was another of the Pete Sunderland's protective layers. If he could not change or endure a situation, he would permit himself to laugh about it. Charm was also in his personal defense arsenal. The resulting combination was called "leadership" by his supporters, "salesmanship" by his detractors, and "bullshit" by Pete, himself. By the time he reached college age, his camouflage skills were refined to an impressive degree.

Officials at the string of expensive schools Pete was eventually thrown out of, or not invited back to, endured his brand of humor for as long as they did in part because his father was rich and a prospective benefactor.

"Do what you have to do to make a man of him," Arthur II had told school officials. With his father's blessing, they did what they could to perpetuate Pete's misery.

Those whom the young man cared enough about to reveal himself to learned two lessons very quickly: People are not always everything they seem to be, and, having a lot of money does not necessarily mean you are rich.

Successful psychic survivors develop systems to separate themselves from those with conflicting agendas. Pete Sunderland devised a complex strategy to repel the alien side of his existence while still allowing him to enjoy the benefits of life at the seductive fringes of wealth.

"There is one positive side to having impossibly high expectations at home," he told Mike Higgins, a college roommate. "Everywhere else you ever go, life seems simple by comparison."

The relationship with his father aside, Pete was not without his personal successes. Social, scholastic, and athletic challenges came easily. Natural dexterity allowed him to excel in all the physical endeavors, including some that would not have had the approval of fathers of the young women he dallied with.

Once, when Pete and his friends were challenged at a bar by local rowdies, his reputation reached nearly legendary proportions. A group of bullying townies forced him to reveal his previously unknown proficiency in the martial arts. A hasty exit and the tormentors' complete recovery prevented any ugly repercussions.

Despite an active social life and a penchant for pranks, Pete made excellent grades in school. A confidant, engaging manner drew people to him. He had the ability to inspire trust, despite his own difficulty with trusting.

To create the illusion of self-sufficiency Pete took part time jobs all through college. He certainly did not need the money. In pursuit of normalcy he disciplined himself to use his meager income toward living expenses. Most of the money sent from home went into an investment fund.

Pete made a great effort to keep his off-campus activities to himself, but never assumed that any aspect of his life was out of his father's reach or surveillance.

"I've changed my major," Pete announced to his roommate.

"Again? That's the third time you've switched since I've known you," Mike Higgins said. "At this rate you'll be in college forever and never get home. Why?"

"You answered your own question, Mike."

A side benefit of reversing academic direction and holding down various jobs during his college career was that Pete managed to pick up many skills and interests. In six years, he had been exposed scholastically to structural engineering, economics, philosophy, American history, social science, and arts and humanities.

As a collector of occupational skills, Pete learned something about the dry cleaning, plumbing, construction, retail clothing and restaurant businesses. He had even sold vacuum cleaners door-to-door for awhile.

Having something to fall back on can be a great safety net. Even a claustrophobic can endure a small room much easier if he knows the door is not locked.

With college finally behind him Pete abandoned his practice of seeming to work for a living. Commitment to a job would have restricted his movements, and he needed plenty of room if he hoped to stay out of his father's way.

Pete's mother was an avid gardener. "Plants need a delicate balance of water and fertilizer to stay healthy," Marian Sunderland once told her son as he watched her work in her greenhouse. "Too much or too little of either will kill them and most should not be watered until they are somewhat on the dry side."

Pete's father effectively applied the dry plant principle to his son. He was given just enough of an allowance to let him live well, but not fly entirely free.

Pete's lifestyle was far better financed than that of a welfare recipient, a fact that gave him twinges of guilt. But being kept on the edge of reliance, he was no less shackled into a cycle of dependency.

Among the many endeavors that kept him interested and far from his father was a passion for backpacking. Hiking mountain trails could be a solitary activity or he could fall anonymously into an organized outing among people who did not need to know his family history. If anyone asked, he told them his name was Pete Summers and he was taking a year off from college.

By the time he approached his mid twenties, Pete had still demonstrated no interest in the family businesses, despite the elder Sunderland's efforts to swing them into the mainstream.

"I'm diversifying," his father once told him.

"You're trying to go legit while still hanging onto your dirty businesses," Pete fired back and continued to regard his father's approach to commerce as blood sport.

If Pete permitted himself any form of violence, it was the martial arts. Even that had a gentle philosophy behind it. As a fifth degree karate black belt Pete could easily defeat nearly any challenger on a physical level. His single practical application of the skill while in college left him with no further need to prove that to himself.

But the psychic war between a man with a pathological need to dominate, and a man fiercely avoiding other people's plans for him, had a grave side effect. With all his charm and apparent self-confidence, there were some serious weak spots in Pete's sense of who he was.

"It's hard to enjoy the dance when someone is shooting at your feet," was his own description.

To most of the young women who hovered in and near the Sunderland aura, Pete was regarded as a good catch. A flurry of spoiled, privileged young Beverly Hills and Bel Air society women saw him as a handsome fellow who could compliment the lives they were trained for. He referred to them as "debu-tramps."

Pete preferred to spend his time with women considered by his father to be of lower social standing. But he could never be sure of their motives either.

Thus, Pete's relationships on both sides of the invisible wall that separated Bel Air from the rest of the world were disturbingly impersonal. He feared that being born a Sunderland might be an accident of greater interest to a prospective friend than friendship.

Despite the few close associations he allowed himself during his college years, Pete had never known anyone he could be absolutely certain did not want something from him. The uncertainty created a pervasive loneliness. The more people he surrounded himself with, the more alone he felt.

In Pete's relationship with a formidable father, as with all confrontations between irresistible forces and immovable objects, there was the sense that someday something very large would have to happen and things would turn ugly in the extreme. Until that climactic collision, however, Pete's goal was to maintain the status quo, jumping through some of the hoops while avoiding the ones that were on fire; to balance what is, with what seems to be.

On Pete's twenty-fifth birthday something happened that changed everything.

00

"Mr. Sunderland," said the voice on the telephone. "This is Maurice Feinman, of the Beverly Hills law firm of Feinman, Pearce and Burns. I wondered if you could come to our office."

"You probably want to speak to my father—"

"No, this concerns you. It is about your grandfather's will."

"I thought all that was settled years ago." Pete had assumed that all matters regarding his grandfather's estate had been over and done with immediately following the old tyrant's death.

"Our firm is executor of your grandfather's estate. There are provisions in his will that apply to you this very day, your twenty-fifth birthday."

20

Pete drove to the offices of the law firm to learn that, among his many bequests, the old man had left his grandson twenty-five million dollars. He never told anyone about it before he died. Especially not his own son.

All hope that Arthur II would see his son succeed him had turned to ashes at the hands of his father.

In preparing their offspring for the difficult days that lay ahead, parents often overdid their messages of caution about the world they would one day face. The result was that even the most loving parents sometimes turned their young into victims.

By continuing at some low level of awareness to take the advice, the young often walked too carefully along a trail made so safe for them that they end up taking no chances at all.

Pete Sunderland's grandfather understood the concept well and reversed it to make certain that his own son would be prepared to survive in what the old man perceived as the cold business world he had created.

When Pete's father was just six-years-old his own father announced, "Today is the day you will learn to swim." He then threw the boy into the deep end of the swimming pool.

Arthur the Elder would allow none of the servants to come to his son's aid. The boy would swim, or he would die. His mother had passed away five years earlier, some said in self-defense, and was not there to protect him.

Arthur the Second did not die that day. But, in learning to swim, he also learned that he was utterly alone on planet Earth.

By withholding all positive emotion from his son, Arthur the Original had succeeded in producing an offspring who was equally at home as an honored embassy guest or a dirty street fighter.

For the benefit of those who had not yet gotten the word, or imagined that he had grown soft, Pete's father still occasionally had to demonstrate his proficiency at gutter survival. The man found that having a reputation for viciousness saved a lot of time.

Arthur Sunderland the Elder's attitudes toward his son became those of Pete's father toward his own son. The child of an abuser became an abuser himself.

In his sixty-third year, Pete's father was still busy visiting the sins of his father upon his heir. For all purposes practical and detrimental, Arthur the Second had become a duplicate of the person he despised.

But the cycle had been broken. It was detoured by the gentle example of Pete's mother, and further reinforced by the gift from his grandfather.

Orphans and those brutalized or barely tolerated as children often grew up to excel in high-level business. They seldom had concerns about how their actions might be regarded by people who loved them, because there were none. They developed a kind of shotgun mentality, blindly blasting away, certain to hit something that rejected, abandoned, or offended them in their formative years, back when they still needed and sought the acceptance of others.

Applied to big-league enterprise, excellence is sometimes defined and achieved under a different set of rules: fear as respect; revenge as a business tactic; sociopath as pillar of the community.

Behavior normally judged inappropriate in daily social or family relationships becomes admired by many. Even by those who had been taught not to offend or bring shame.

A conscience can be a terrible thing to overcome. Pete Sunderland's father suffered no such obstacle.

Pete's grandfather's bequest came as a complete surprise to Pete. But not nearly as much as it surprised his father. No doubt Arthur the Eldest had planned it that way. Advance knowledge of Pete's impending independence might have retarded the young man's personal growth. Plus, there was the likelihood that if Arthur II had known about it in advance, he would have time to fight the inheritance and continue his tyranny.

One of Pete's few memories of his grandfather was when he was twelve-years-old, shortly before the old man's death. He remembered only a humorless, shriveled remnant of a man who sat in an overstuffed chair in a darkened room and shouted demands for servants to bring him things forbidden by his doctors.

Only once did Pete recall his grandfather addressing him directly. "Be your own man, Arthur," he had said. Pete never fully realized what the old man meant until that day in the lawyer's office.

In his final days, after turning control of the Sunderland enterprises over to Pete's father, the family patriarch had taken steps to make at least partial amends. He gave his grandson the means with which to say a firm and final 'no' to the man the elder Sunderland had created, to his everlasting regret.

When he wrote his Last Will and Testament, Pete's grandfather buried the clause among dozens of others, thus remaining undiscovered until the proper time.

Knowing his own life was nearly finished, the old man apparently contented himself with the knowledge that Pete would become a free man a few years after he became a legal one.

The new-found independence gave Pete an entirely new outlook on life.

Though he had not lived to see the fruits of his plot, the old man must have smiled while putting together this double-edged conspiracy that was both a benefit for his grandson and a final swipe at his son. In truth, the elder Arthur did not like his son. A fact which, unquestionably, contributed to what Pete's father had become.

"Father and I have nothing in common," Pete had told his mother. "What do you imagine it is that keeps some people emotionally connected to another?"

Surely, he thought, there must be better reason for an abiding relationship than genes in common. Perhaps some trick of nature was at work, keeping mismatched pairs engaged in un-winnable games.

If his father were any other random citizen, Pete knew he would certainly never have sought out such a person. Nor was it likely he would even speak to an individual of his father's kind.

Yet, even after he learned of his emancipation, Pete continued to some extent to swirl around in that fruitless cycle, waiting for an emotional payoff that never came.

Marian Sunderland was the key, of course. Pete cared deeply for his mother. His parents lived in the same house. To see her was to see him.

Her occasional request to get along with his father threw the entire matter into a fuzzy realm, where father and son became a kind of organic Rube Goldberg device that seemed to function, but for no productive purpose.

Now that he was able to more nearly distance himself from his father's influence, Pete bought a luxury sports care and a Westwood condominium which he immediately moved into and out of the family's Bel Air home.

When he no longer had to depend on anyone to maintain the lifestyle he had become accustomed to, Pete did as every individual and society had ever done when suddenly released from oppression. He overreacted to the opposite extreme. After twenty-five years of relative compliance, there came a period of open contempt for his father. Pete enjoyed it for awhile, before the pendulum returned to a lopsided normalcy.

It may be argued that everything a person ever does, no matter how good, or how heinous, it is perfectly normal when viewed in the context of everything that ever happened to that individual.

If one subscribes to that logic, it was normal for a sexually-confused social misfit with delusions of grandeur and a malignant political agenda to carry a rifle to the sixth floor of a Dallas public building and assassinate an American president.

Following the same reasoning, both heroism and cowardice on the battlefield are normal if one considers the experiences that shaped those who stayed and those who fled.

While no jury in the world could be persuaded that Arthur Pedwick Sunderland III had been a deprived child, the sum of his experiences had produced a complex, undefined organism which, normal or not, answered to the name, "Pete".

CHAPTER FOUR

From the upper deck of his Malibu Beach apartment, no amount of squinting would bring Santa Catalina into Jeff Burke's view through the coastal mist. The island off the southern California coast would rarely be seen again before fall breezes came to occasionally clear the air.

To the south, a half-dozen beach communities were strung out along the coast toward the Palos Verdes Peninsula, hazily visible in the distance. There the land rose from the flat floor of the Los Angeles basin to a nubby peak, then fell sharply into the sea. Twenty-six miles offshore the earth again rose briefly to form Catalina Island.

At high tide the beach below Jeff's apartment had all but disappeared from view. Waves crashed with teeth-rattling savagery against wooden pilings on which the four-unit wooden apartment building rested.

There were scores of dwellings similar to his own from that point where Pacific Coast Highway met Old Malibu Road, down to the Malibu Colony several miles farther south. "The Colony," as it was known to locals, was a gated community-within-a-community. Its residents were the old and new rich, including luminaries from the business and artistic ends of the movie industry.

As Jeff arrived home, the shapely, red-haired neighbor who lived on the opposite side of his apartment wall walked up the wooden stairway. She held the arm of a man who looked hungrily into her eyes. Jeff had not seen him before. But then he rarely saw his neighbor's male friends a second time.

Though she would probably be considered beautiful by some, Jeff found the aspiring young actress unappealing. Her dress and hard bearing were as flashy as the flaming hair that fell across her shoulders.

25

Jeff's twenty-foot-wide, forty-foot-long apartment had a single bedroom and a bathroom at the road end. At the ocean end, a sun room with an enormous picture window framed a magnificent view of the Pacific. A sliding glass door opened onto a breezy wooden side deck to continue the panorama.

When not covered by the high tide, Malibu's beach was reduced to a narrow strip of sand mixed with surf-worn pebbles, shells, and the trash tourists left behind.

Boats under sail and power dotted the water in what Jeff referred to as his "front yard." Many miles farther out, an occasional tanker ship glided slowly past oil rigs that leaked marble-sized globs of sticky black goo that often fouled the beach.

The Pacific was blue to the horizon. Bright white clouds billowed into the lighter blue sky above. Wave after foamy wave slid over the beach and into the pilings below, churning up a briny mist of ocean salt and pleasantly sour seaweed he could smell and taste all the way up to his front row seat at nature's symphony.

From the deck, all of Jeff's senses were tweaked in a way that never happened anywhere he had ever been.

Why then, sitting in his favorite spot, was he feeling disturbed about his new student? What was it about Pete Sunderland that irritated Jeff and made him less patient than usual?

The rent on the Malibu apartment amounted to half of Jeff's take-home pay every month, but the calming effect on his damaged psyche made it worth the expense. He spent very little of his earnings on anything else and even managed to accumulate a small savings. His ex wife had not requested alimony, probably a result of her feelings of guilt.

Being at the beach, like some aspects of flying, allowed him to experience feelings he rarely permitted himself anymore.

If his life lacked zest, he could at least enjoy the scenery.

Jeff dabbled at being a recluse. He favored solitary activities, avoiding other people to the extent possible in a shared world. He lived with his best friend, a pampered cat about the same age as his divorce papers. They found each other when she was a tiny kitten. Someone had apparently dropped her off one dark Halloween night along Old Malibu Road rather than face their own responsibilities.

He had seen a flash of orange off to the side of the narrow roadway, just in time to swerve and avoid hitting her. When he opened the car door to investigate, she took it as an invitation to join him, jumped right in and climbed onto his shoulder. In one way or another she had been walking all over him ever since.

Since she was orange in color and it was Halloween, he naturally named her 'Punkin'.

Jeff's routine was simple. He took a weekly drive down the 405 freeway to visit his mother in Torrance. He spent eight hours a day at the airport and a few hours of judo practice several times a week at a Santa Monica gym. But for most of his leisure time he was stretched out on his deck or lazing about the apartment.

God bless this happy rut.

It had been a long time since he added so much as a close acquaintance to his short list, let alone a friend. Human contact in recent times was limited to people he worked with at the flight training center and students who passed through briefly on their way to becoming licensed pilots. Security in sameness; far safer to avoid relationships that threatened to become intrusive or permanent.

Through the closed glass door to the sun room Jeff saw Punkin clearly mouthing "meow" from inside.

"It's only a quarter till 'meow'," you spoiled brat.

Even though he understood the nearly human need of a seven-pound cat to control the actions of a 175-pound man, Jeff caved in and altered the dinner schedule by fifteen minutes. He knew she would try to push mealtime up by another quarter hour the next time.

After he and Marcie separated, Jeff often found himself speaking aloud when there was no one else around. He could not recall ever having done that in what he referred to as his "Other Life." In addition to Punkin's role as object of affection, she fulfilled the secondary purpose of helping to convince Jeff or anyone within range that he was talking to a cat, not to himself.

Punkin represented the only warmth Jeff allowed himself to feel for another being since the breakup of his marriage.

But, everyone needed something to love, and to love them in return. For the moment, Punkin filled at least part of the emptiness.

CHAPTER FIVE

Pete Sunderland absorbed every aspect of flying as though born to it. Jeff wondered whether his student had actually had some training, even although Pete's application indicated he had no previous instruction.

Jeff was impressed with his new student's coordination and quickness to learn. At the same time, he found himself irritated with the younger man.

"Line up your right wing with the mountaintop," Jeff said, talking Pete through a maneuver. "Keep it there as you make a turn around that point."

Hearing the instruction only once, Pete seemed to instinctively convert it to smooth action. With any challenge Jeff had created for him, Pete rarely faltered and never repeated the slightest flaw. Even if days went by before going through a maneuver again, Pete executed it as though no time had passed.

But, if Jeff lacked patience with students who had difficulty coordinating complicated exercises, he seemed to react equally badly to the very ease with which Pete progressed. If his young student executed a lazy-eight with absolute precision, Jeff made him run through it again. A flawless recovery from an accelerated stall still provoked something short of Jeff's approval. No banking turn around a stationary point on the ground was ever altogether acceptable. No approach to an emergency landing quite measured up. If Pete's skills threatened to overtake Jeff's exacting standards, the expectation was raised.

Pete seemed not to notice Jeff's brusqueness and what appeared to be a growing hostility. But Jeff's chief pilot spotted it.

Overhearing Jeff admonish Pete after a lesson, Eddie Griffiths said, "You're being pretty tough on the kid, Jeff. You can't forget that part of what we teach our students is confidence."

"I just want to be sure he's ready when I send him out to solo," Jeff had answered. "I don't want one of my students killing himself because I didn't drum something in him."

Even Jeff, who was usually hyper-sensitive to people, could sense that he was being harder on Pete than on any of his other students. But he didn't let up.

CHAPTER SIX

"Sunderland canceled his nine o'clock lesson this morning," Bill Ferguson said as Jeff walked into the flight office a little after 8:30.

"When?"

"Five minutes ago."

"Sonofabitch!"

Since there was no paperwork to catch up on and no drop-ins to fill the time slot, Jeff went to the pilot's lounge. He picked up a flying magazine and flopped himself into a stuffed chair by a window overlooking the taxiway.

For the time he had to kill before the arrival of his next student, Jeff alternated between reading about new aircraft he could never hope to own, and fuming over Pete Sunderland's low regard for the value of other people's time. The incident was also helping Jeff justify the irritation he had been feeling toward his student.

Later that afternoon, as Jeff returned from a lesson with one of his students, Pete Sunderland's red Lamborghini was parked on the tarmac. Next to him, a stunning young blonde woman occupied the passenger seat.

"Yo, Jeff," a smiling Pete shouted over the roar of a Cherokee 180 on the taxiway.

Jeff took his time in acknowledging Pete's call, hoping to make it plain that he was not pleased.

"Thought I'd bring Debbi by to see the place," Pete said.

Ignoring the young woman, Jeff said, "What happened to you this morning?"

"Something—ah—came up," he said, looking at Debbi with an amused smile. Her expression told the rest of the story.

Jeff tempered his anger.

"I sat here for the hour you were scheduled to be flying." Jeff said calmly. "When you cancel with no notice there is no time to

31

find a replacement, and the company loses the revenue for that hour."

"Uh, Jeff—,"

"There's no profit in that for Ferguson's Flight Service," Jeff said. "And it demonstrates very little respect for people in general and for me, personally."

"I didn't mean—"

"If you plan to continue flying with us in the future we would appreciate your extending simple courtesies."

With that, Jeff turned and went back into the flight office, leaving Pete and the young woman behind in numbed silence.

Finally, the young woman volunteered, "He had no right to talk to you like that, Pete."

"Debbi," Pete snapped. "Don't help. Okay?"

00

Every morning after Jeff's rebuke, Pete penciled in future appointments on the schedule for the date and time two weeks forward. There were no repeats of his cancellation, nor were there lapses in his consideration of others at the center. He seemed to have learned his lesson in courtesy as quickly as he was learning to fly.

Still, Jeff's patience with his talented student was in a delicate balance.

An hour of touch-and-go takeoffs and landings was monotonous work and physically tiring.

Jeff and Pete were completing what would be the last touchdown before ending the session. The Cessna was lined up perfectly with the runway numbers on final approach, about a quarter mile from the near end of the blacktop strip. Pete brought the power back to idle to let the craft glide to a landing as he had been doing for the previous hour. But Jeff suddenly decided the approach was not correct.

"Power! Power!" Jeff shouted.

Pete got the aircraft safely on the ground and veered onto the taxiway and contacted ground control for clearance to Ferguson's. He chirped the wheels when he brought the trainer to a complete stop. Only then did he turn angrily to Jeff.

"What the hell is the matter with you, Jeff?" Pete shouted so loudly and with such ferocity that Jeff was startled at the reaction, unlike anything he had heard from his student before.

"What do you mean?" Jeff asked, puzzled.

"If I do something one way, it's wrong. If I do something another way, it's wrong. If I do it the way you told me was the right way last week, it's wrong this week. Now what the bloody hell is going on here?"

Pete's words may as well have been a physical blow.

"I don't—I—" Jeff said, not quite sure how to react.

"Yesterday you told me I should reduce power on my landing approach. On the last landing today you were all over me for not using power on approach. Now which do you want, power or no power?"

Where he might normally have reverted to a self-protective mode, Jeff said nothing. He had no immediate response because he knew, without a doubt, that his student was absolutely correct.

Taxiing back to the trainer's parking space, Pete starved the engine of fuel, bringing it to a stop. Then there was silence. After a moment of reflection Jeff finally spoke.

"From the time I was eight years old I dreamed of being a pilot," Jeff said quietly. "When I was old enough I went to work at the A&P grocery store in my hometown and saved what I earned. When I turned sixteen, I started taking flying lessons. With my savings and what I made working after school every night and on Saturdays I was able to afford several hours of flight instruction each month. Pete, it took me a year to get my license. It took another two years to get my commercial license and instrument rating. You started last month. In a few more months you'll have your license.

"You're mad at me for being born rich?" Pete asked.

"As unfair as that sounds, I think so. It's not logical. You can't help being rich anymore than I could help having been of modest means as a kid. Until you called me down on it I didn't fully realize it was stuck in my craw and I apologize."

"I forgive you," Pete said.

"Just like that?"

"Yep. Want to know why?"

"Dying to know."

"Because I just popped off at you for pretty much the same reason."

"I don't get it."

"I stopped by my parents' house this morning and my father and I had a nasty go-around. Normally I wouldn't be so sensitive about things, but I was pretty well worn down by the time I got here. It was my old man I was really yelling at. I took it out on you and I owe you an apology."

"We were both kicking the dog."

"Human nature is a sonofabitch, isn't it?"

"Feel better now?" Jeff said.

"Much better, thank you."

"Good, because you're going flying again."

"Where are we going?"

Jeff opened his door and stepped out onto the pad. "*We* are not going anywhere, kid. You are. Time to spread your wings. You're on your own. Take it once around the patch and meet me here when you get back."

"You're sure I'm ready to solo?"

"I've never been more sure that someone was ready," Jeff said. He shut the door, leaving Pete alone in the cockpit, looking less confidant than he had a right to be.

Jeff watched Pete taxi back to the run-up area where he went through the procedure again, even though they had just flown for an uneventful hour. Then he took off smoothly and negotiated the pattern in what seemed from Jeff's observation spot to be a perfectly executed, by-the-book go-round followed by a landing that was indistinguishable from that of a thousand-hour pilot.

Jeff could see Pete's big smile from all the way across the parking area.

"Turn around," Jeff ordered as his student stepped out of the plane.

Pete did as he was told and Jeff pulled his student's shirttail out.

"Hey." What are you doing?"

"I'm trimming your tail feathers," Jeff said, taking out a pair of scissors and cutting a six-inch-square out of the tail of the shirt. "It's tradition."

"I'm glad I wore an old shirt."

Jeff laid the piece of cloth across the engine cowl of the Cessna. With a marking pen he printed "Pete Sunderland, 1st Solo Flight" and the date.

The two men walked to the flight office where Jeff pinned the cloth on the bulletin board with several other notices of that particular milestone in a pilot's flying career.

"Congratulations. You can't carry passengers yet, but you can practice on your own now," Jeff said. "You've done well Pete and I apologize again for being a jerk."

Pete started toward his car, then hesitated.

"Jeff," Pete said. "There's a party at my parents' place tonight. Why don't you come?"

Jeff looked surprised.

"What's the occasion?"

Pete looked at him blankly. "Occasion?"

"Yeah. You know, birthday, anniversary, divorce?"

"In Bel Air, a party is its own occasion. Will you come?"

"I'm not much of a party person. Frankly, I'm a lousy conversationalist."

"That's okay. Nobody listens to anybody at a Bel Air party anyway."

"What fun is that."

"The fun is in watching non-stop talkers saying absolutely nothing. It's a showcase of superficiality."

Pete wrote his parent's address in a small notebook. "I have seen four people in a group, all speaking at once, with none of them noticing there were no listeners. If you go in with the right attitude it can be a real honk."

"Will there be a big crowd?"

"Hoards of people. But you can get lost in it much better than in a small group. You'll enjoy some of them, too. Celebrities, good looking women." Pete tore the page from his notebook and handed it to Jeff. "You can bring someone if you like, but that would be a damned fool thing to do with all the women who will be there. Who knows, you might find a rich girl to marry so you won't have to risk your life flying with guys like me anymore."

"You wouldn't be offended if I ducked out early would you?" Jeff asked.

Pete snorted at the suggestion. "I'd consider it the mark of a truly sensitive person."

"It's been a long time since I felt very sociable."

"Come tonight and we'll watch the clown parade together."

Thus it happened that Jeff, the closet hermit and self-proclaimed grouch, agreed to do something totally against his carefully managed nature.

Jeff had treated Pete unfairly almost since the beginning. He now realized that while he was very sensitive to others, he was not entirely tuned in to himself. Now that the problem had been identified he felt disappointed in himself for having behaved that way.

When reconsidered in the comfort of his Malibu shrine to solitude, the thought of allowing Pete Sunderland to talk him into going to a party seemed pretty bizarre.

CHAPTER SEVEN

Jeff was unsettled by the fact that he found himself halfway looking forward to going to Pete Sunderland's Bel Air bash.

Until time to leave his seaside apartment, he would soak up what was left of the day's sunshine.

Jeff put on his swim trunks and a Led Zeppelin T-shirt, poured a glass of wine, and settled down in a deck chair on his beach overlook for some serious people watching on the sand below.

Jeff always eyed the procession more than usual at this time of the day in anticipation of the daily appearance of his favorite Malibu Regular.

A leggy, athletic blonde with a pretty face, long hair tied back in a bouncy ponytail, and a look of vulnerability, she sprinted rather than jogged past his apartment each afternoon. From the muscle tone her brief bikini failed to cover, he judged she also worked out. Certainly not with free weights like those used by the grunting, sweating male behemoths down the coast at Santa Monica's Muscle Beach. He assumed she had one of those high-priced, high-tech modern torture devices marketed as exercise machines.

Jeff looked forward to seeing her and enjoyed the fantasy that her prettiness might run beneath the surface.

The bikini-clad young woman's long legs glided her over the wet sand. Jeff knew she would run another mile or so up the beach and return for a second chance for him to see her.

He entertained the idea that she might actually be everything she appeared to be as she sailed by his observation deck each evening.

CHAPTER EIGHT

Managing a Santa Monica aerobics and fitness center was not an unpleasant job. The pay was more than adequate, the benefits were generous, and Stephanie Burgess was treated well by her employer. Still, it was unsatisfying.

Aerobics centers as portrayed on television and in the movies are places filled with beautiful, coordinated, sexy young women dressed in colorful, skin tight outfits. In truth, women who looked like that had little need to be in such a place.

With the outstanding exception of Stephanie, the classes were usually made up of groups of plain, clumsy, overweight, middle-aged women who apparently felt that the very act of signing up for exercises was sufficient to give them the bodies they desired.

During these half-hearted sweat sessions, the women burned off precious few calories. Afterward, many would reward themselves for having been so good by stopping off at Baskin-Robbins on the way home for a hot fudge sundae or other calorie-infused ice cream concoction. Their sloth produced no improvement in Stephanie's customers' physiques or in her sense of accomplishment. All of which made her college degree seem all the more a waste.

She and her high school sweetheart had eloped the night they both graduated from a small college near Buffalo, New York. Stephanie and Dennis Maxwell moved to Los Angeles six months later.

For the six years she was Stephanie Maxwell, her husband seemed to have few aspirations beyond driving a delivery truck.

At some point deep in her consciousness Stephanie realized that having children could be a complication in what had become an unstable marriage. Without mentioning it to her husband, she took the necessary precautions to avoid getting pregnant.

There was never enough money during those years. Compounding the problem, Stephanie's salary was higher than Dennis's. The result was unintended damage to her husband's eroded ego.

As hard as she tried to make the marriage work, a Peggy Lee recording her mother had often played at home kept running through her mind: "Is That All There Is?"

The final blow to their relationship was a literal one. During what would be their last argument, Dennis responded in the way underachievers with low self-esteem often do when they become frustrated and their status as a male demands the last word. He slapped her with such force that she slammed against a kitchen wall. He was immediately sorry and begged her forgiveness. But it was too late. Even before her cheek had stopped stinging, she was packed and gone.

Oddly, she did not immediately file for divorce, nor did she stop wearing her wedding band right away; in part because divorce seemed such an admission of failure and because her still-married status was a kind of protection against serious involvement.

She finally filed a year later, just to put it behind her.

Dennis did not contest the divorce. The dissolution was only as complicated as California law made it. She chose to return to her maiden name. The final decree arrived in the mail and she was once again Stephanie Burgess. To mark the occasion, she threw her wedding ring off the end of Malibu Pier. Then she went home and fixed a candlelight dinner for one, complete with an expensive bottle of French wine.

That night she cried herself to sleep.

When her father died Stephanie went back to Buffalo, New York for the funeral. Her four brothers had all moved away from home by that time. She had never been close to her mother. With her father and brothers gone there was no reason to stay in Buffalo, so she returned to Los Angeles and let time pass.

Occasionally she would run down a mental list of her personal attributes and compare them with what she believed were being sought by male singles. After rejecting the superficial and the unreasonable, she tried to work with what remained. Most of the men she met expected qualities in a partner that they, themselves, did not offer: faithfulness, loyalty, generosity, and most of the other good ones.

Stephanie more than adequately met the physical standard of beauty as defined by Playboy Magazine. But, despite everything a pretty face and fascinating figure were purported to represent, in reality they always seemed to attract the wrong kind of men. She was constantly surrounded by those who apparently saw her as their reward for being as wonderful as they believed themselves to be. Stephanie was in great demand by handsome, vacuous peacocks who worried far more about the look of their hair than the condition of their values.

She did not miss sex nearly as much as she missed closeness. Stephanie would have been content with a hug from someone she cared for. There seemed to be no good places to meet men of quality.

Though she enjoyed an occasional glass of wine, she was not really a drinker. She did not smoke and did not much care for those who did.

So much for going to bars.

She tried going to seminars and workshops in the hope they might be educational and provide opportunities for companionship. A wine appreciation course had been interesting and informative, but was filled mostly with couples and gay men. Fellow students in a small engine repair course turned out to be members of a lower life form who could not keep their greasy hands to themselves.

She even tried Sierra Club day trips. While she enjoyed the people she met and the places they went, the outings produced nothing more than one brief relationship and a few uninspired dates with men who turned out to be of the same ilk as those she had been trying to avoid.

Stephanie never felt the need to seek immortality in the form of children or other monumental evidence of having existed. But there was a growing feeling within her that she should be doing something that would leave the world, if not a better place, at least no worse off for her having been here. Helping fat, lazy housewives create a myth for themselves did not come close to achievements Stephanie had in mind.

She would drive to work every day by the same route down Pacific Coast Highway from her beach apartment at the lower, less expensive end of Malibu. She would often arrive at the center with no memory of traffic lights and stop signs. She was never completely sure whether she may have put pedestrians and fellow drivers in danger by her inattention.

Yet, as dissatisfied as she had become with her routine, Stephanie could think of nothing specific to replace it with beyond a vaguely-defined image of an interesting life outside of her job. And, of course, someone to share it with.

There was that one brief relationship during the nearly two years since Stephanie separated from her husband. He was a pleasant enough fellow, about whom she could not think of a single bad thing to say. Then again, she had nothing very good to say of him either. If he had been a color, it would have been a very dull gray.

Edgar was the controller for a large insurance company. Everything about Edgar was organized. His car was immaculately clean and waxed. His Century City apartment looked like the ones managers showed off to prospective tenants. Edgar even made love in a neat and orderly fashion and on a schedule.

They had sex at her apartment each Wednesday and Friday night. It was unfulfilling for Stephanie, both in its predictability and its execution. Then he would get into his car and drive back to his own apartment.

Peggy Lee was singing to her again.

Stephanie decided that her love life could do with much less efficiency and a lot more fire. If sex was to be nothing more than exercise, she got enough of that at the aerobics center and on her daily run on the beach. Her bedroom was no place for mere gymnastics.

She broke the news to Edgar as gently as possible and that was that.

Just as she remembered it, being alone was no fun either.

Stephanie's run for several miles up Malibu Beach every day compensated somewhat for her loneliness. The brief daily exposure to the sun added some color to her fair skin and some highlights to her blonde hair. It also occurred to her that she might meet Edgar's replacement along the way. She certainly would not find Prince Charming by sitting alone at home listening to the clock ticking her youth away.

There was one man she found interesting. She would often see him standing on the second floor balcony of one of the apartment buildings that lined the beach at the upper end of Malibu. He was always alone. As far as she could tell from that distance, he was tall and good-looking in a rugged sort of way. He seemed unaware of his appeal. So many of the men she had known preened and pranced and posed as if all eyes were upon them. She thought it would be nice to meet him, but never came up with an excuse that would not seem too bold.

She would just have to be content to see him as she ran past his beach apartment.

CHAPTER NINE

On the warm sand below, Jeff watched a mix of strangers and seaside residents of all shapes, ages, and rhythms who populated the beach. Most were in their late twenties to early thirties, at the very beginning of their adulthood and careers, still too young to know their limitations or to consider that they had any.

They had not yet learned what Jeff had come to believe, that security is an illusion, and confidence is an indulgence of those who do not know any better. He concluded they had little perception of failure at any devastating level and no comprehension at all of their mortality.

Factoring in personal experiences, Jeff determined that traits he once sought in a prospective companion were unreliable gauges. He decided that assessing the souls of others was an art best left to the innocent. Optimism was for the inexperienced.

The flaw in the reasoning, of course, was that Jeff had more than three decades behind him of being sensitive to others. His ability to read people, while obviously not perfect, sometimes had an unnerving effect on those he cared enough about to turn on his sensors.

How could he have gotten a clog in his own perception mechanisms where Pete Sunderland was concerned? Jeff had a moment of fear that his natural defenses against pain might also be shutting out good times. He wondered if the condition were irreversible?

For a short while after his divorce Jeff had concentrated on sheer numbers of sexual exploits. He concluded early on that quality control in relationships was too costly to the human psyche. Nothing personal, just an ego under reconstruction, thank you very much. No commitments. No apologies. No pain. He seemed to be running up a score. Or, perhaps, settling one.

Still, Jeff often speculated as he watched female members of the procession on the beach below whether one among them might be a match for his particular collection of needs and deficiencies, and he for theirs.

Surfers did not frequent Jeff's end of the beach. Something to do with an improper angle of the waves striking the shore. The famous Malibu surfing beach was around the bend, a mile down the coast next to the fishing pier. Jeff and his neighbors were thus spared the excesses of that particular band of career adolescents and their ragtag cadre of admirers.

Some of the usual passers-by, like fellow regulars at a neighborhood bar, had become a surrogate family of sorts. Except that in the comfort of his distant deck there was no need to care deeply for them or expect that they would care in return and disappoint him if they did not.

Jeff's relationship with the beach people was much like his relationship with the friendly cocker spaniel next door, to be enjoyed for a moment when the dog stopped by to have his head scratched, but with no real responsibility for the animal's longer-term care or well being.

If an amiable member of a compatible species happened to show up at Jeff's door or on his beach, he figured, fine and dandy. If not, in the unlikely event there was ever any room in his life for people, he knew where to find some.

Therein lay a dilemma that was causing Jeff Burke to doubt some of the things he absolutely knew for sure.

Grief is an odd phenomenon, whether it is for the death of a loved one or the death of a marriage. When it first strikes it seems the pain will never end. A mourner passes through stages that include denial, anger, bargaining, depression and, finally, acceptance. Each person who goes through the process makes the transition differently, in his own order, at his own pace.

Jeff had reached the point at which he could accept the end of his marriage, but not the manner of its demise. He did sense, however, that nursing the hurt much longer could qualify as self-pity and that any logical human being might soon have to find other excuses for his off-putting behavior.

Jeff Burke's carefully-crafted cynicism was eroding, threatening him with the loss of the bleak outlook he had grown so comfortable with. Some deep-rooted survival instinct seemed to be kicking in and he was enjoying less and less the role of uninvolved observer.

Maybe that was why he accepted Pete's invitation.

What should he wear to this high-class Bel Air wing-ding? Well, regardless of the dress code of the evening, Jeff would wear the dark blue suit that had hung idly in his closet in its clear plastic dry cleaner's wrapper.

Maybe they'll turn me away at the door for wearing a suit that's out of style," he thought, halfway hopeful.

Among the regulars were the dog walkers, the Frisbee throwers, and the catamaran jocks who crashed their craft through the surf to the calmer outer waters.

A well-known movie producer ambled by occasionally, perhaps between periods of inspiration in front of his beachfront word processor. The co-star of a new TV cop series stood in the sand, posing for the tourists, holding his stomach in as one who was hoping someone would recognize him so he could practice being aloof and then condescend to give them his autograph.

A vaguely familiar looking elderly couple from farther down the beach was among the Malibu Regulars. Maybe they had played characters in a movie he had seen. Or maybe they had been in the line next to him at the bank or the grocery store. They walked together as though they didn't know they were old and that only the young were allowed to hold hands like that and look at each other in such a manner.

Jeff was rescued from unpleasant memories when he saw her approaching in the distance. He rose from his deck chair and leaned on the railing. She splashed at the soft, sudsy edges of incoming waves that exhausted themselves on the beach and then receded into the offshore kelp beds in an ear-piercing hiss of bursting bubbles and tossing stones.

Jeff's Venus in a yellow bikini grew larger in his view, and he wondered again whether she might be a dancer. Her long legs stretched out with a graceful firmness, a distorted reflection of

47

herself on the wet sand beneath her feet. Yes, she had the legs and mid-section of a dancer.

She would run farther up the beach, then turn back in the direction from which she came to give Jeff a second chance to admire her.

Now that he was older Jeff noted that the girls of the type all the guys wanted when he was still in high school and college had, in fact, been a superficial lot. They seemed to believe that looking cool, and hanging out with a crowd everyone envied was sufficient. At that stage of their lives there was no apparent need to work at trying to be something special, because they seemed to believe they had already reached the pinnacle in the only world they knew. By the time adulthood overtook them, it was too late to change the pattern and fill in what was missing.

Now, two decades later, the women of that era appeared to have wised up to what they had missed when they were too busy exchanging precious bodily fluids with high school sports heroes to look his way and consider such a mundane quality as character. Many of them had since divorced, come out of their beauty-induced comas, and were now scouring the world for someone such as Jeff Burke.

A few minutes later he again caught a flash of yellow and a glimpse of her tanned body on the return trip.

As she approached Jeff's perch, he saw—or did he imagine—that she glanced his way. Then, astounding even himself, Jeff raised his wine glass, pointed to it and nodded. She looked away and Jeff assumed she had either not seen him or had chosen not to accept his brazen invitation.

But, about five paces later, Jeff watched the gracefully muscular legs go slack. Slowing to a walk, she changed course through the softer, drier sand, past a dark, cool, sea urchin and barnacle-encrusted maze of wooden pilings to the stairs leading from the beach to the apartments above,.

Meanwhile, his heart beating a little faster, Jeff walked to his linen closet, unfolded a towel from the stack, and threw it over his shoulder. Then to the kitchen where he removed a second goblet from an overhead rack. He stopped at the refrigerator for a bottle of young white wine and returned to the sun room where he filled the clean glass. He topped off his own glass in time to see her round the corner on the weathered wooden walkway. She slid the sun room door open and joined him inside.

As a veteran observer of beach fauna, Jeff had learned that the nearer they got, the less attractive they sometimes became. A toughness often showed through in the face and manner at closer range, or a lack of culture or elegance otherwise revealed itself.

Not this time.

"Hi," she said, after looking him over for a thoughtful moment. "I'm Stephanie Burgess."

She was even softer and lovelier at three feet from him than she had seemed from far across the beach.

"Jeff Burke," he said, taking the warm hand she offered in greeting and handing her the towel. She accepted it with a smile and an unforgettable whiff of a musky perfume.

She sat down on the offered seat beside Punkin, who looked at the young woman with great interest.

Stephanie took a small sip from the wine. Jeff noticed a slight wince.

"Not good?" he asked.

"Not bad, but fruitier than I usually prefer," she said with the trace of a pucker. "A New York vintner, I believe."

He checked the label and saw that she was correct.

"Huh."

He had found the bottle in a bin of odd-labeled wines at the grocery store where they were probably on sale because they had been on the shelves too long and the store needed to get rid of them.

"I'm afraid I don't know wines. Not much of a drinker. The label looked good. Nice colors. Pictures of grapes," he said, staring so intently at her eyes that she caught him at it.

"What are you looking at?" she asked, with a slightly uncomfortable smile as she dabbed perspiration from her face.

"Your eyes are green. I've often wondered as you ran by every day, but it's too far away to tell."

"Boy, that really sounds like a line."

"I didn't mean it to."

"You mean it's not a line?"

49

"Of course it is. I just didn't mean for it to sound like one."

Her laugh was a melodious chirp, which she coupled with a toss of the head and a flip of the blonde ponytail.

He noted that Punkin liked her and that Stephanie, to her credit, liked Punkin. He could tell because of the way she smiled when his small friend wound her tail around the visitor's ankles. Punkin performed a little half dance, half kitty cuddle routine that involved backing up, raising the tail straight up, arching the back and weaving her fluffy self through Stephanie's bare feet and legs, purring so loudly she could be heard above the pounding surf.

Punkin only did that when she liked someone. Jeff trusted Punkin's instincts these days more than his own.

"Do you often invite passers-by for a glass of wine?" Stephanie said, stroking Punkin's head.

"You're the first." he admitted. "I do my usual scouting in the usual places."

"With what results?"

"The usual," he said with a shrug, realizing how dismal those results had been.

"Sport trolling," she said, matter-of-factly.

"I'm sure that has been true at times."

"At least you're honest about it. Most of the guys I get involved with claim to be looking for a long-term relationship, when all they really want is a mother they can have sex with."

"Well, how about that," Jeff said, impressed with her candor, "a woman who admits to seeing a lot of men."

"I don't think I know you well enough yet to lie to you."

"Yet? You said 'yet'. Are we planning a future?" Jeff asked, refilling her half-empty glass.

"You don't know anything about me," she said, smiling and running her fingers through Punkin's fur. "How do you know you would even want a future."

"I know quite a lot about you."

"Really?" she said, skeptically.

"You're in your early thirties. Maybe a dancer. Something physical. Related to your profession? You were married, but aren't anymore. A fairly recent change of status, I think. No children. You don't believe you're looking for a permanent relationship, but you are. On a ten-scale of loneliness, ten being the loneliest, I would say you are a high eight.

It was apparent from her unsettled search of Jeff's face that Stephanie was not quite sure what to make of him.

"Close, but no stuffed duck, Sherlock." She took another sip of the wine and rubbing Punkin on all the right spots.

"You're college educated and a lot smarter than average," he continued, propping his feet up on the window sill. "But you play down brains because it sometimes gets in the way in this male-dominated world. Still, you don't like to be liked only for your looks and you find yourself surrounded by guys who don't care what's inside as long as the outside looks good."

She looked at him curiously across the wine glass.

"I was a late bloomer."

"You're very fortunate in that. If you had known from the beginning how you looked, you might have stopped right there, as so many do."

"On what do you base your observations?"

"Well, you have the figure of a dancer. But that wouldn't be enough to give you muscle tone like that without also lifting weights. You're not quite as tanned on that narrow patch of skin on the third finger on your left hand. The finger is still shiny from the metal, which indicates you took a wedding ring off fairly recently. If something were not missing from your life you simply would not be here. You have no visible stretch marks from child-bearing. You have the bearing of someone who has been to college. Anyone can tell you're no dummy. Your sudden silence tells me you're not crazy about having someone do this kind of appraisal."

Stephanie's wrinkled brow confirmed that her discomfort had deepened. When she rose from her chair and took a large swallow of the wine, he feared she was offended.

"Gotta go," she said.

"What's the rush? You only live about a mile or so down the beach."

"How did you know that?" she said.

"I figure you are about a fifteen minute run from here at the most. A half hour a day in the sun, considering your hair and skin coloring, would give you a tan about like that," he said, pointing to her lightly tanned arm.

"My coloring?" she said, holding onto the ends of her long blonde hair. "With a drug store on every corner in America, how can you be sure I *am* my coloring?"

Jeff reached across to where she was seated and took her hand in his. He ran a finger lightly across the yellow peach fuzz on the back of her arm. He had also noticed the thin blonde line running from just above the center of her bikini to her naval, but thought it prudent not to mention it.

He wanted very much not to let go of her hand, but she withdrew it quickly.

"Don't I at least get a grade on the test?"

"Okay," she said, with a slightly impatient edge. "I'm thirty-four years old. Not a dancer, exactly. I manage an aerobics and fitness center in Santa Monica. I stay in shape and I work out. I was married for six years, separated about a year ago. The divorce was final a few weeks ago. No kids, a bachelor's degree in communications, it's late."

"I have a couple of steaks in the refrigerator. Stay for dinner."

"Can't."

"You're a vegetarian? This is the night you wash your hair? You've got a boyfriend?"

"No, no, and none of your business," Stephanie said, handing him the glass. "Thanks. Bye."

The young woman who had been so friendly, suddenly turned hurried.

"Was it something I said?"

"You're a perceptive guy. You tell me."

"Okay, I will," he said gently. "I think I pushed some sensitive buttons. Maybe you need to go someplace safe and think about that."

The soft lips said, "Ridiculous." The green eyes said "Bingo".

"You're not my type, actually," she said, walking toward the door.

"Really? And how have you been doing with your type—actually?"

"Have a nice day," Stephanie said, handing him her wine glass.

"Will I see you again? I mean other than your daily run on the beach?"

"Never say never," she said, tossing him the towel and giving Punkin a final rub on her head.

"Look," Jeff said, hoping she would stay for even an instant longer. "I invited you up here for the wrong reasons. I'd like to see you again for the right ones."

"I don't plan ahead. Bye," she said, opening and re-closing the sliding glass door after her in almost a single motion.

And she was gone.

The apartment, so bright and cheerful only a moment before, had dimmed. The ache Jeff felt was all the more painful in air still heavy with Estee Lauder.

CHAPTER TEN

Jeff was not in a party mood, which was not unusual, since he detested the very concept. Most parties he had ever attended seemed full of people who drifted between conversational clusters with the single purpose of bringing the subject around to themselves. As the alcohol did its work, participants ultimately dropped all pretense of trying to find out about each other and blathered on pathologically about their own shallow lives.

But, what the hell. He had no other plans for the evening anyway. He had the weekend away from work to recover from any abuses he might subject his body to. And, as they say, he could check out how the other half lived. Bel Air was definitely home to the half that Jeff was not a part of.

The idea of going to a party after meeting Stephanie was even less appealing. Maybe Pete was right. Maybe he would meet the heiress of his dreams in Bel Air. Entire lives had been changed by the simple act of turning a corner or merely by looking up at the right moment. Or the wrong moment, depending on how everything turned out in the end.

Jeff had put some dry food down for Punkin to tide her over until he returned. Then he headed to Bel Air by way of the affluent suburb's back door. By taking the longer route through the mountains he avoided the dinner traffic that clogged the narrow coastal highway every evening. Turning off Pacific Coast Highway onto Malibu Canyon Road he took the winding cross-country route to the Ventura Freeway, then southward on the 405 to Sunset Boulevard.

As he drove, he promised himself he would be careful not to drink too much. It was an hour drive back to Malibu.

Jeff turned east at Sunset and cruised through the home territory of the rich and famous.

As he approached Pete's home he could see that the gray stone Sunderland mansion was, by far, the largest of the neighborhood's enormous residences. Nearly hidden from view by a thick hedge, the enormous house sat back from the street in the middle of what Jeff judged to be several acres of some of the world's most expensive, and exclusive, real estate.

He drove his Honda Accord up the paved circular driveway through a break in a row of tall, closely-planted Italian cedar trees. Luxury cars and limos waited for valet service or to drop off passengers. The closest things Jeff saw to an economy car was a small Mercedes sport convertible. He doubted that economy had anything to do with the owner's choice of transportation.

The conspicuous consumption made Jeff a little self-conscious about his working man's compact. Especially when the valet looked with disdain at the aging import. It occurred to Jeff that the young man's own car was probably of the same type and era.

As he stepped into the foyer, Jeff noticed that entry to the grand manor was only slightly more intricate than getting past airport security, though less intrusive and not quite as identifiable for what it was. About what one might expect at the home of a man whose enterprises, by his son's description, were of dubious repute.

Guests passed through what appeared to be a partially concealed metal detector with sensors imbedded in the sides and top of the entryway. Overly metallic visitors would trigger an alarm, heard only by a plainclothes security man standing off to the side, wearing a barely noticeable earpiece. Those were diplomatically asked to step aside and walk through yet another device that examined the contents of their pockets in greater detail. Jeff observed other security types standing around, holding hand scanners that could be used to search specific areas on an individual suspected of carrying a weapon. A very large man in a chauffeur's uniform stood back, apparently in the event less subtle measures became necessary. No one seemed offended by the precautions.

Jeff's name appeared on the guest list and he was granted entry without incident.

As he wound his way through the crowd he watched chattering people hand out hugs and air kisses. He heard a few "darlings" among the greetings. It seemed that Pete was right about this gathering rating high on the shallowness meter.

Many of the women wore outfits that looked more like costumes than dresses; what little girls who had played dress-up with their mother's clothes thinking it was high fashion. When the little girl grew up and acquired wealth, or acquired a husband with wealth, she went down to the exclusive Rodeo Drive shops and bought all the things she believed exhibited elegance. Additional proof, Jeff thought, that people with money do not always have class, and those who are dead broke can have all the class in the world.

Jeff did not see Pete Sunderland anywhere immediately.

It would be interesting to know, Jeff thought, how many people were there by invitation and how many, despite security precautions, had somehow crashed the gate. He had heard that to have a party of twenty people in New York City you invite one-hundred. But, to have a party of one-hundred in neighboring Hollywood, you need only to invite twenty. He wondered if that applied to Bel Air, as well.

In one corner, Jeff saw a well-known actor whose name he could never think of. He looked different out of his space ship and only life-sized. His ever-present smile must have cost a fortune. Some familiar faces were scattered around the big room; minor actors and actresses whose names he did not know.

Several politicians he recognized from the news media were holding animated conversations off to the side.

An aging, bejeweled movie queen held court. She wore too much makeup in a dated style she was too old for even when it was popular in the 1970s. Many facelifts made her look as though someone were standing behind her as one might pull the strings on a corset, tightening the skin on her face to stretch the wrinkles out. She tossed her head occasionally with a laugh heard throughout the large room. Her entourage took each cue and laughed along with her, apparently to further reinforce the belief that her every word was worthy of carving in stone.

Standing in a group was a spectacular blonde in a tight, low cut dress. She gave Jeff one of those warm, gooey glamour magazine model looks, where the face and head tilted down, as the eyes turned upward.

For Jeff on this particular night, the logistics of conquest and his lingering images of Stephanie were greater than his remaining energies could overcome. If this were point A, then point B seemed a long way off.

Besides, there was something about this one that seemed to shout that she would be no better than the rest in the short term, and no good at all over the long haul.

He went to an enormous mahogany bar and ordered a beer. He could still see her reflection in the full length mirror along the wall behind the well-stocked liquor shelf.

The party wound its way through rooms, hallways, and alcoves with high ceilings found only in homes built by people who give no thought to the costs of heating, cooling, or cleaning them.

A man brushed briskly past Jeff, indicating he was a person who was at work rather than attending as a guest. Probably the caterer, judging from the style of his tuxedo.

From behind him, Jeff heard the man say, "May I get you anything Mr. and Mrs. Sunderland?"

Jeff turned to see a distinguished looking older man whom he recognized from the newspapers and television news. The man had a presence that left no doubt as to who held the highest rank in the room. Beside him was a graceful older woman.

There were two other familiar faces with him. Pete Sunderland, with whom Jeff had spent over an hour in an airplane that very morning, and the world class blonde Jeff had seen earlier, whose major marketable skill seemed to be the ability to look down and up at the same time. He wondered what other talents might be in her repertoire. When he first spotted her, Jeff had not noticed Pete. Small wonder, with eyes and implied promises like that.

Jeff hoped the Sunderlands would go on their way and not notice him standing there. He would look in on Pete later, when he was alone somewhere.

As with most of his hopes in recent times, it was not to be.

"Jeff," Pete shouted, spotting his flight instructor across the room.

There was no escape, so Jeff slowly pressed through the crowd to join his host and get the ritual over with.

"Mother, father," Pete said, "Meet Jeff Burke, the man I spoke to you about. Jeff, my mother and father, Marian and Arthur Sunderland." Almost as an afterthought, Pete added, "And this is Paige."

"Hello Jeff," Paige said, extending her hand. "I'm Pete's fiancée." Jeff thought he detected a small change in Pete's expression. He also noted that the young woman was not the same one Pete introduced him to at the airport. It occurred to Jeff that Paige held onto his hand just a moment longer than was proper, considering the stated relationship to Pete.

"Mr. Burke," the elder Sunderland said, flashing a smile and shaking Jeff's hand, "my son has told us you are teaching him to fly an airplane."

"Call me Jeff, sir, and he is doing very well," Jeff answered, noticing Paige giving him the full eye treatment from just out of the view of the Sunderlands.

"Of course," said Arthur Sunderland. "He is my son, after all."

"That must be the reason, then," Jeff said.

"Frankly, Mr. Burke," said Sunderland, a chilly edge easing into his voice, "I am not in favor of Pete's taking flying lessons."

"Why is that, sir?" Jeff asked.

"I don't like the idea of my heir risking his life every day."

"He's at much greater risk driving to and from the airport than in an airplane, Mr. Sunderland."

"How so?"

"Far more occupants of cars die per million miles traveled than those who die in plane crashes."

"You don't say so," Sunderland said without enthusiasm.

"Pilots value their licenses," Jeff continued. "You rarely hear of a drunk or drugged flyer. Courtesy among pilots is the rule, where courtesy among drivers seems to be the exception. Planes are better maintained than cars and pilots are far better trained to fly aircraft than most people are to drive cars. Almost anyone can get a driver's license. But getting a pilot's license requires organization, coordination, dedication, and attention to detail. In other words, it takes someone special to become a pilot."

"I will acknowledge that my son is special, Mr. Burke," Sunderland said. "But I would still prefer to have him on the ground. I will be very glad when this latest notion runs its course and we can get on with his future."

Jeff picked up a trace of contempt in the old man's words and voice. Both seemed to be aimed specifically at Jeff. It was as though by applauding Pete's progress, Jeff was somehow responsible for his son's straying from his preordained path.

Arthur Sunderland was obviously an accomplished professional in the art of intimidation. It was also apparent, by his having felt the need to condescend to Jeff, that the elder Arthur was not feeling as much in control of this particular situation as he was accustomed to.

On the other hand, Arthur the Second might possibly be better informed than Jeff about Arthur the Third.

From the sound of it this could be another in a string of unfinished undertakings, and Pete may not have a good record for completing what he started.

"Pete has good instincts for flying," Jeff went on. "If he chooses, he can be a very good pilot."

"Mr. Burke, I hope you won't think me rude, but isn't that what one might expect you to say about a customer?"

"Pete is not my customer, Mr. Sunderland," Jeff said, trying not to show his irritation, which had reached an intense level. "He is a customer of Ferguson's Flight Service. I let the owners worry about commercial considerations. Pete is my student and my responsibility. I take his aviation education and his safety very seriously."

Pete was obviously pleased, both at his instructor's assessment of his flying ability, and at Jeff's apparent refusal to be cowed by a man Pete had described as one who made it his life's work to dominate all who entered his aura.

Arthur Sunderland muttered something in response, identifiable only as negative. Jeff was certain he had not changed the older man's mind.

Marian Sunderland finally spoke. "Mr. Burke, I commend you on your priorities. I believe you must be very good at what you do."

It was clear that she had a cutoff point where her husband's tactics were concerned.

"Thank you Mrs. Sunderland." Jeff liked Marian Sunderland immediately, although he wondered how such a woman could coexist with, let alone love, such a man as her husband.

In the unlikely event that Jeff were to spend more time around the Sunderlands, he suspected he might find out where the real family power was.

"Come with me, Jeff," Pete said. "Some people I want you to meet." On that pretext, Pete maneuvered Jeff away from the little group. Paige, apparently knowing which side of the cake the icing was on, elected to remain with the Sunderlands.

When they were out of his parents hearing Pete said, "I figured you needed me to help you separate the starlets from the harlots. Not that there's a lot of difference."

"Are these the only heiresses you have for me to choose from?"

"A dismal lot, aren't they? Well, at least you were able to show up in time to save my life. I thought I'd never get away from them."

They made their way through the crowd, inching toward a door that led away from the party.

"Your father is not pleased that you are taking flying lessons."

"For a very good reason."

Jeff stopped short. "Why is that?"

"Because it wasn't his idea. It's not part of the master plan."

"That plan being?"

"To control the actions of every living being on the planet, starting with me."

"An ambitious aspiration and hardly likely."

The quiet on the side of the door away from the gathering was startling.

"Don't underestimate him, Jeff," Pete said seriously. "When he can't bring an adversary around to his way of thinking, whether a public official, a political party, or a world leader, he provides their enemies with the means to destroy them. He trashes their reputations, their positions. I suspect he even has some opponents eliminated. The operative word here is 'control'. Then, after the enemy has been overwhelmed, he has nothing but contempt for them. In a fox hunt he would enjoy the chase, having the poor beast run terrified before him, but have no respect for the animal when it got caught."

"I thought he was in it for the money," Jeff said.

"Oh, he makes money no matter which side does business with him. Like a stock broker who profits whether he buys or sells a stock for you or a lawyer who gets his fee whether you win or lose the case. In fact, he usually sells weapons to both sides. But money is only part of the makeup of power. My father's prime motivation is to cause large things to happen. That done, he makes the one he conquered dance at the end of his string as a lesson to all who tried to resist and to those who might try in the future. A control freak out of control."

"Growing up in your house must have been, interesting."

Pete snorted.

"I've had a degree of success at putting myself out of his view, if not entirely beyond his reach."

"Maybe you're your father's son after all?" Jeff suggested.

"Could be," Pete said with a laugh. "Maybe it takes one to defeat one."

"I somehow doubt that your father thinks he is defeated."

"No much gets past you, does it, Jeff? No, he manages to make his presence felt. He forced me into the position of working at being myself. Most people get to do that without having to work at it."

"Looking around this house, Pete, it is difficult to see you as a victim of child abuse."

Pete stopped walking and looked at Jeff.

"Why? Because my bruises don't show?"

"I am curious about one remark your father made. He suggested you don't finish a lot of what you start. Are you going to be in that high percentage of student pilots who start out full of fire, then fizzle?"

"Don't pay too much attention to my father. I hardly think flying can be compared with skiing or tennis. I have a lot of interests. It's a kind of hobby of mine that I'll explain sometime. Besides, my father doesn't go scuba diving or backpacking, which is one of the reasons I do."

"Why don't you simply stay away from him?"

"You just met her."

"Paige?" Jeff said, surprised.

"Great screaming Jesus, no," Pete said, slapping his forehead. "My mother. I stay because I'm crazy about the old broad. Also, because she wants me to try to get along with my father."

"Where does Paige fit in?"

"Hey, if you ever find out, let me know will you?"

"You know, Pete, the longer I stay here, the weirder this place gets."

"See? I told you it would be fun. Follow me and let's get away from the fun."

Jeff trailed after Pete into the largest kitchen he had ever seen. The catering crew seemed not to notice the two men. Pete looked around, as though checking to be certain no one was watching. He motioned for Jeff to follow him into a large walk-in pantry.

"This will be our secret, okay?" Pete said.

"Secret? You don't want anyone to know your family has a food supply?"

The pantry smelled strongly of cheese, coffee, and of herbs drying where they hung in bunches from racks suspended from the ceiling.

When the door to the shelf-lined larder closed behind them, Pete walked to the far end of the room. He reached into a shelf, found a lever, and pushed the panel forward. A disguised door swung open, revealing a dimly-lit passageway. Pete motioned Jeff quickly inside and closed the door behind them.

Jeff noticed the narrow corridor had steel plating on the walls and ceiling and thick carpeting on the floor.

Pete said, "You never know when you might have to get out of the house fast."

The passage led the men to a spot adjacent to rooms they had just come from, taking an occasional turn behind a bookshelf or wall.

Color monitors hung on the walls where Pete and Jeff could see them. Unknown to the guests on the living room side of the hidden corridor, microphones and video cameras were concealed all around them. Recording devices were positioned on shelves beneath the monitors. Each screen was like a window to the adjoining room except that anyone watching from the hidden passageway could hear the conversation better than if they had been standing right next to those shown on the screen.

Jeff heard one man make a lewd suggestion to a young woman. He never got to hear her answer, but the girly giggle that echoed off the metal walls indicated she may have favored the idea.

The passageway finally came to an end at a heavy steel door. Pete looked through a small peephole before pushing the door open.

They stepped outside and found themselves standing in a greenhouse at the rear of the main residence. It was quiet and illuminated only by a full moon and distant security lights around the perimeter of the property. From the inside of the passageway the entrance resembled a vault door. But on the greenhouse side, the door had a weathered wood face. No one would ever suspect its purpose.

"What the hell was all that?" Jeff asked.

"It's a combination escape route and bomb shelter. Four-foot-thick concrete walls lined with heavy-gauge steel. It can easily withstand a terrorist attack, maybe even a direct missile hit."

"Either of which would seem out of place in Bel Air. I'll bet he didn't figure on your using it to get away from him."

"He probably doesn't know I know about it. I found it by accident when I was a teenager. Except for Hughes, the security chief, I doubt that any of those well-dressed thugs you saw out at the front entrance know about it either."

Pete sat some flower pots aside on one of the greenhouse potting benches and brushed away some loose soil to unveil yet another surprise. Lifting the top, there was a small sink and an adjacent compartment containing glasses, several bottles of liquor, and a mini refrigerator stocked with beer and wine.

"Jesus," Jeff said. "I can't remember the last time I was in a greenhouse with a wet bar. No—wait—never."

"I built it myself," Pete said, handing Jeff a beer.

"Pete Sunderland, the plumber?"

"One of the many skills I picked up while working my way through college."

"I find that hard to believe?"

"Which one? That I learned plumbing or that I worked my way through college?"

"Both, for that matter."

"Well, it was kind of a personal statement, a small way of letting me believe I didn't need the old man. Of course, I always knew I didn't have to take jobs, so I guess it wasn't much of a protest after all. I learned a lot, though. Want to buy a vacuum cleaner?"

"Secret passageway, hidden bar, a clandestine college career, is anything here what it seems to be?"

"There's more to most people than what they wear out front," Pete said. "And money isn't everything."

"Uh huh. It gives you a lot of freedom to do whatever you want. Or to do nothing."

"I've been thinking a lot about that lately. I figure it's time I do something productive."

"Wealth is a hard habit to break, isn't it?"

"That's part of what I have to find out."

Both men settled into cushioned Adirondack chairs with their drinks.

When people of very different backgrounds get together they often look for ways to communicate in a language that each understands. The words "How about those Dodgers?" have been known to bond otherwise mismatched people. The language of sports allows a minimum wage short order cook, for a moment at least, to be the equal of a world renowned heart surgeon.

Minorities, tech-heads, teenagers, soldiers, cops, and others who are out of phase, out of favor, or under siege often speak in invented languages and slang understood only by their breed. As they strengthen their brotherhood, they retain a sense of control over their environment. Others are let in only if they learn the common tongue.

In just that way Pete Sunderland was thus able to speak many languages. Pain, not necessarily of the same kind, from the same source, or of equal intensity, can also be a bridge between cultures.

For the rest of that warm spring evening, seated on dusty lawn chairs, Pete Sunderland and Jeff Burke found words common to them both in that semi-darkened greenhouse that smelled of fresh earth.

00

Driving back to Malibu it was hard for Jeff to keep his mind on driving. He was running the events of the day through his mind; most prominently, thoughts about Stephanie Burgess and their strange meeting.

Once again he wished that he had allowed her to remain a fantasy. By inviting her into his apartment he had made her flesh and blood. At least when he saw her from across the beach as a beautiful stranger he could have continued to imagine the possibilities. Having reality forced upon him had deprived him even of that.

It was after midnight when Jeff finally got back to his apartment.

Punkin met him at the door. She looked up at him pathetically and struck a pose which Jeff interpreted as the kitty equivalent of hands on the hips, one foot tapping. She made an impatient little sound roughly translated as: "Where have you been? You should let me know when you'll be late," and "what's a girl got to do to get something to eat around here?"

CHAPTER ELEVEN

Stephanie Burgess was lost in thought behind the Santa Monica Fitness Center's reception desk and did not notice when the owner walked through the front door and stood directly in front of her.

"Stephanie," Miles Peterson sing-songed softly, just inches from her face. "Where are you?"

"Wha—Miles—!" She snapped to attention. "I didn't see you come in. Did you say something?"

"I see you," Miles sang to her, "but you're not here. Is everything okay?"

"I must have been somewhere else. Sorry. I'll try to keep my mind on business."

"That's not why I asked, sweetie. I was just concerned."

"Oh, it's nothing. You know how you go over stuff in your mind and think what you should have said or done after it's too late. I guess I'm just flogging myself for the way I handled one of those coulda-woulda-shoulda situations."

"A guy, huh?" Miles said matter-of-factly.

"Ohmygod! Not you, too."

"Me too what?"

"Reading my mind. I met this man at the beach yesterday. He was very perceptive. He observed some things about me that were true, but it upset me that he could see them just by looking at me. Do I have a sign on my back or what?"

"Did he say something that offended you?"

"Not that I can think of."

"Did you like him?"

"How should I know if I liked him, Miles?" she said in a burst of frustration. "I just met him yesterday."

"Aha."

"What does 'aha' mean?"

"It means it wasn't what he said that upset you. It was your reaction to his being sensitive to you. Now, answer my question."

"Which one? I forget.

"Did you like him."

Stephanie looked at the ceiling and squeezed her eyes shut.

"Yes, dammit!"

"Aha."

"Please stop saying that."

Miles did a little crazy dance around the reception room. "Aha. Aha. Aha. That's it."

"Go away Miles and leave me to my self-indulgent whining." she said, her head bent forward, her blonde hair falling across her face.

"You like this guy and you're afraid of your own emotions."

"I don't have any 'motions," she said, moaning from deep within the recesses of her hair. "They all died."

"Well a couple of those little devils must have survived if you reacted like that to a guy. You're looking for love and when you think you may have found a likely prospect it scares the hell out of you."

"I just met the man, Miles. He's just someone I see when I run on the beach. Yesterday he invited me in for a glass of wine."

"Und how did you feel about that, fräulein?"

"Miles! Stop being my shrink."

"Then stop hiding from yourself."

"Is that what I'm doing?"

"Of course you are."

Stephanie groaned.

"What can I do about it?"

"Well, you could go and jump his bones before he gets away."

"That's fairly crude, Miles. Just like that?"

"Well, maybe not *exactly* like that, but something close. Whatever happens, you need to resolve this emotional block."

"Hmph."

"Nobody said life would be easy."

"But nobody told me it would be so hard." Stephanie said. She pounded her forehead lightly on the top of the counter.

"It's what happens during these hormonally active years that counts, Stephanie. You should get moving. Especially at your age."

"Look who's talking. You're the same age as I am. What's your excuse?"

"I only give advice, darling, I don't take it. Now get your lovely butt in there and wring some fat off those broads."

"That's another thing. I am an intelligent, educated, not unattractive, semi-liberated woman with great career potential–"

"With a terrific ass, if I might say so"

Stephanie frowned.

"Why am I here?"

"Because, my child, by getting these chubbies in shape for their dull husbands and boyfriends, you are doing God's work. Say hallelujah!"

"Thank you for sharing that with me, Miles. I've never thought of it in quite that way before. And I never shall again."

"If you see the guy again, find out if he has a friend for me."

"I love you like a sister, Miles. But if he has a friend for you, I don't want him."

"Bitch." he and cackled.

Miles was right, she thought. The question of what to do about it remained.

CHAPTER TWELVE

Pete Sunderland had taken himself off the calendar for a few days. He had not said anything to Jeff at the Friday night party.

After their solo flight most students intensified their efforts, building up time and experience toward the private pilot test. But Pete was penciled in on the schedule for this day and for the usual daily sessions for two-weeks in advance.

Jeff spotted the red Lamborghini next to the flight office as he walked toward the aircraft parking area. He could see Pete's blond head bobbing up and down among the airplanes across the pad. From as far away as the flight office Jeff sensed Pete's heightened energy level.

His student was doing a pre-flight check on a Cessna Skyhawk, bouncing from ailerons to elevators to wing tanks.

Jeff wondered why Pete was readying the larger, four-place aircraft instead of the smaller two-place 152 trainer. Pete spotted his instructor coming across the pad.

"Top of the morning," Pete called out.

"Where have you been?"

"I had something to think over and I've made a decision."

"Would a news conference be in order?" Jeff said as he approached the Skyhawk.

Pete jumped down from the step stool he was using to inspect the fuel level in the wing tanks.

"Let me ask you something."

"Shoot."

"Would you agree that the best way for a student to learn to fly would be to experience all kinds of weather and navigational situations and to encounter the widest possible variety of conditions likely to come up in a pilot's flying career?"

"Yeah, I'd say that."

"And by flying in and out of a lot of different airports, no two of which have exactly the same patterns or procedures, a student pilot would learn more in a few months than, say, during a couple of lessons a week for a year?"

"True. What's your point?"

"My point is that I want to be the best pilot I can be. To do that I am willing to lease an airplane and fly around the country and experience every flight condition known to pilotkind."

Jeff stared blankly at Pete for a moment. The he said, simply, "Have a nice trip."

"Okay. Here's the deal, I want to outfit a fully equipped plane with whatever gear we would need to live in rustic comfort along the way."

"We?" Jeff interrupted, "Excuse me, but you just said 'we'. That would suggest a 'you', and a 'me'. I don't remember saying I would be remotely interested in such a crazy idea."

"I want you to go along and teach me to fly as we go."

"Look kid. I have a job. I can't just pick up and take off on some half-assed adventure. Unlike some of us poor people, I have responsibilities. And I have a lot of shameless, sexist surveillance I have to catch up on at the beach, and a cat that loves me."

"Oh yeah. I forgot. You have a really terrific life here."

"Forget it kid. And don't try any of that vacuum cleaner salesman bullshit on me."

"You certainly wouldn't want to leave all that. I totally understand. And don't call me 'kid'."

"Look. My life may not be perfect, but it's manageable. It's taken me a long time to get it that way, and I like it—*kid*."

Pete became quiet. When he spoke again he switched from shooting down Jeff's objection, to totally agreeing with him.

"Yeah, you're probably right," he sighed and returned to his pre-flight routine, apparently resigned to Jeff's decision.

Even on such relatively short acquaintance, Jeff had learned that Pete was not one to give up so quickly.

"Maybe I'll ask someone else," Pete said, finally, not even looking up from checking the oil under the Cessna's cowling.

"Just for the sake of argument, who else, for instance?" Jeff said, teetering on the edge of the trap.

"Wally Dersham could probably get the time off."

"Wally—" Jeff said, then quickly lowered his voice. "Wally Dersham cannot find his ass cheeks with both hands."

"You'll do it then?"

"That's not what I meant." Jeff looked around the lot to see if any other instructors or students might be within earshot. "Look. The only reason Wally works here is because he's Ferguson's nephew. Okay? It would take you twenty years to unlearn the bad habits you'll pick up from him. That is if you are lucky enough to survive for twenty years."

"What's my alternative?"

"To forget the whole dumb idea."

"Well I'm not going to forget the whole dumb idea, so get over it. I'm going and I'd like you to come along."

"If I did go, what would there be to come back to?"

"To this very same job and your same old exciting life."

"Well, I'm certain Bill Ferguson would hold the spot open for a couple of months—a couple of months! Are you nuts?"

"Maybe, but that's beside the point. Yes, you would have your job again because I already asked Ferguson and he said it would be okay."

Jeff looked at Pete in disbelief. "You asked him without asking me?"

"I knew you'd be worried about your job, so I asked him. And he said yes. The economy is in a slump and things aren't that busy right now anyway. Besides, if he doesn't let you go I won't lease the airplane from him and pay the full daily rate. I'll go next door to the Grumman dealer and lease one of theirs. I mean, we'd put at least the minimum daily time on the Hobbs meter every day. Ferguson doesn't get that kind of use out of any plane on the lot."

"What about me? You think he'll be so grateful he'll just throw in a flight instructor for free?"

"Simple. I'll pay Ferguson the full instruction rate on top of the plane rental fee and I'll pay you a thousand dollars a week salary. I'll also cover the rent on your apartment for the time we're gone, and I'll personally pay all of our expenses."

"You mean Daddy will personally pay, don't you?"

"I'll ignore that because I know you're just so overwhelmed with the idea of a paid vacation, and you're basically being a shit. But you'll be okay when I tell you that, first of all, I have my own money."

Jeff did a comic double take.

"That's right, don't look so surprised. I inherited a ton of the stuff from my grandfather. In fact, my money earned more money while we've been standing here talking than you will make the rest of this year. Second of all, this would give you a good chance to stand back and really get a good luck at your thrilling life. And third of all, but not necessarily last of all, you will have so much fun you will pee yourself."

"Pete, look, I can't just—"

"Walk away from an offer like this?"

"There is no way I'll—"

"Turn down the chance of a lifetime?

"I'd have to—"

"Think about it for another thirty seconds?"

On points, alone, Pete had made the sale. But resistance often comes more from the heart than the head. The deal would not be complete until Jeff actually said the words.

At that moment, Wally Dersham pulled his old toad brown Toyota into the parking lot. Pete spotted him, but Jeff still had his back turned toward the parking area.

It was time to turn up the heat.

"This is a great opportunity for a freebie," Pete said. "Don't blow it."

"I have a nice routine going here," Jeff said, with no real enthusiasm.

Pete sensed Jeff had been worn down, but needed one more push. Pete looked over at Dersham, who was getting out of his car. "Good morning Wally," Pete shouted across the pad. "Say, Wally, if you have a minute—"

"My mom could take care of my cat," Jeff said.

"Never mind, Wally."

"My landlord would probably water the houseplants."

"That's a 'yes'," Pete shouted triumphantly." We leave two weeks from Saturday."

"Hold on here. I didn't say yes. Don't I have anything to say about any of this?"

"Sure. Jump in anytime."

"We'd need a lot of stuff." Jeff said, sagging against the aircraft.

"I'm a backpacker," Pete said. "I know of these things."

"Do you have any idea what kind of plane we'd need?"

"A Cessna Skyhawk with two NavCom radios, transponder, auto-pilot, and assorted newfangled doodads. Cessna Niner-Niner-X-Ray. You're leaning on it."

Jeff jumped back from the plane as though it were on fire. His mouth hanging open, he stared at the red and white four-place craft. Apparently, over the course of his flying lessons, Pete had been listening more closely than Jeff realized when his instructor described various aircraft and their purposes. The 172 was the very plane Jeff would have chosen. The Skyhawk would be small enough to be responsive as a trainer, yet large enough to carry camping gear for two. Plus, at 140 miles-per-hour, it would have enough speed to cover a lot of territory. The 180-horsepower Lycoming engine would give it enough power to get to altitude without taking all day about it. It had sufficient technology on board to prepare Pete for his private license as well as to give him a head start on his commercial ticket and instrument rating.

Pete handed Jeff four doubled-spaced pages and an outdoor equipment supply catalog.

"It's a list of all the gear we'll needed," Pete said. "I've already ordered everything. If you can think of anything else, just speak up."

Jeff looked over the neatly itemized inventory. Pete had, indeed, thought of everything.

"Come on Jeff, say yes. If you don't say yes I'll have to stand here looking cute until you do. Don't make me show you my dimples."

Jeff looked at the plane, sighed, and began to consider the possibilities. But the idea was still too new to jump right into it.

"Look here mountain man. I enjoy the out-of-doors, but I don't see myself sleeping on rocks and twigs for a couple of months."

"When we get tired of living under the Cessna Hilton we'll find comfortable motels and live like the capitalist swine from whose loins I sprang. We can stop anywhere we like, stay as long as we want, fly as much or as little as we care to." Arms outstretched, Pete swooped, birdlike around the front of the aircraft. "Maybe we'll even get lucky now and then."

"For a moment let's entertain the fantasy that I might be interested. Not that I'm going to do it, mind you. Let's say my curiosity has been stimulated to at least consider it."

"What else do you need to know?"

"Who's the honcho? Who would be running the outfit?"

"In matters of flying, you are the undisputed boss man. Otherwise we're just two guys on vacation."

"None of this employee-employer bullshit?"

"Absolutely. Complete equals," Pete said, smiling. "Buddies, even," he added with a stupid grin.

"Buddies?" Jeff said with a scowl.

"Well, okay, maybe not buddies, but amiable traveling companions."

Jeff looked at the Skyhawk again. He glanced at the purple wall of pollution building toward them from downtown L.A. Then he looked through the mist toward the Santa Monica Mountains to the north. Pete watched as Jeff seemed to be imagining a life beyond the smog and the hills, to places he had not yet seen.

"Two weeks from Saturday," Jeff said, quietly.

Pete knew he had closed the deal.

CHAPTER THIRTEEN

Punkin was sound asleep, but she alerted when the chime sounded at the side door to the apartment. Since Jeff rarely had visitors, the ringing came as a surprise. But it was nothing compared to his astonishment when he opened the door.

"Hi," Stephanie Burgess said.

Jeff could only stare, open-mouthed.

"Shocked?" she asked.

"Pleasantly flabbergasted." Jeff said, unable to think of a stronger term to describe his delight, though he knew there must certainly be one.

It was earlier than her usual appearance at the beach. She was dressed in jeans, T-shirt and tennis shoes instead of her standard bikini.

"Didn't recognize me with clothes on, right?" she said, somewhat shyly, Jeff thought.

"I'd recognize the eyes and perfume anywhere."

In fact, he had smelled her perfume at the grocery store that very afternoon and nearly whiplashed himself turning around to locate her. As it happened, the wearer was a birdy, tight-lipped old lady pulling a small two-wheeled shopping cart. He wondered whether women who looked like that should be legally permitted to smell like that.

"I have a present for you," Stephanie said, handing him a brown paper bag that had taken the shape of the bottle it contained.

"You hate my taste in wine," he said with a laugh, reading the label on the California Chardonnay.

"Call it my contribution to your wine education," she said. "And my way of apologizing for turning weird on you the last time. You were right, of course. I did have to go think about some things in a safe place."

"What did you decide?" he asked.

"That there is no such thing as a safe place. Anyway—" She turned, as though to leave.

"Don't go," He said, extending his hand to her. When she hesitated, he added, "Please, don't leave."

Stephanie paused for only a moment, then reached slowly out to him. With a dancer's grace she allowed herself to be led into the apartment, then into his arms for a kiss that promised the fulfillment of everything that had been missing from both of their lives.

"You were wrong about my being an eight on the loneliness ten-scale," she said. "I'm a full ten."

She buried her face in his chest and he put his arms around her, one hand gently on the back of her head, as she sobbed the kind of quiet sob that shakes the entire body and aches all the way through.

Not needing to ask why, Jeff held her there until long after she stopped crying, afraid the feeling might never return.

Jeff had also been deeply affected.

"We don't really know each other very well," Stephanie said.

"Moving too fast for you?"

"Probably."

"We obviously like each other. That's a good start."

It occurred to him how much he wanted to introduce this young woman to his king-sized waterbed. Instead, he took her by the hand and guided her to the living room where they curled up together in a large, overstuffed chair and held onto each other for a long time, talking very quietly.

Punkin walked along the high back of the chair, purring loudly, looking down at them.

Then, without a word, each apparently deciding the time was right, Jeff gathered Stephanie up in his arms, carried her to the bedroom, and closed the door behind them. For all the farther the pair moved from each other for the rest of the afternoon, a single bed would have been more than adequate.

Even when Punkin stuck a yellow paw under the door and used every trick she knew to get their attention, they would not come out, nor did they seem even to notice her.

Later, as they lay together on the huge bed, Jeff told Stephanie of the planned flying trip. He explained that his reason for agreeing to Pete's idea was that he could think of no better reason at the time to stay in Los Angeles. Stephanie had changed all of that and he told her so.

"I'll call Pete and tell him it's off," he said.

"Wait. Not just yet."

Puzzled, he asked, "Loose ends?"

"Not the kind you may be thinking of. My mother is having major surgery and could use my help. She asked if I would come back to Buffalo while she recuperates. I told her I'd have to think about it. I was going to say no. But now that this has come up I'll call and tell her I'll come. It will give me a chance to get to know her better now that we're both adults. I would be there for most of the summer."

"Pete and I will be gone for a couple of months. That would get us back here again around the same time."

Wrapping herself around him again, she said, "I would miss you."

"Then we'd better make the most of the time."

Punkin was meowing for her supper and pawing under the bedroom door again. But she would have to wait a little longer.

00

The next day Jeff told Pete about Stephanie. Pete had a moment of panic. "You mean you're not going?" he said as he finished his pre-flight check.

"I'm still in," Jeff said, logging the Hobbs meter reading. "I'm just not as enthusiastic about it as I was. Since Stephanie is going back east for awhile, it's still a go. If she were staying, I'd probably back out."

They prepared to taxi for takeoff. Pete requested ground clearance and pulled the Cessna onto the taxiway.

"You're very lucky." Pete said. "I wish had someone I could feel that way about."

"Don't give up. She's out there somewhere."

"My problem is I'm never sure if it's me they like, or the Sunderland money."

"So, find a nice girl who is as rich as you are who is having the same problem—and is as crazy as you are."

"If one exists. You don't happen to have her address, do you?"

Jeff smiled. "Well, I may run around in circles, but not in those circles. However, if I do happen to crash into her Ferrari or Rolls Royce by accident, I'll be sure to put you two in touch."

"Seven digits," Pete said quietly.

"What?"

"Her telephone number has seven digits. Ten if she's in another area code. There are thousands of combinations. I haven't been able unscramble them or I'd have called her long ago."

Jeff said nothing, having just broken the code himself.

CHAPTER FOURTEEN

Stephanie and Jeff agreed to take it slowly. After such a long time alone, each admitted to being afraid the other might grow tired of the relationship. Neither wanted to believe that, but neither wanted to take any chances that something might change the way they had come to feel about each other in the short time they had been together.

The slowdown lasted one day. Half the day, really, since the subject didn't come up until just before noon. Not counting three calls, of course, including one where Jeff picked up the phone to make a call. Although it had not rung, Stephanie was at the other end of the line. The coincidence generated such heat that Jeff estimated he may have set a new land speed record covering the distance between their two apartments.

They were nearly inseparable. Even Punkin seemed to be feeling a bit neglected. But she liked Stephanie so much she showed no resentment toward her for the attention her human was paying to someone else.

Jeff caused quite a stir among his fellow flight instructors when he was reportedly overheard whistling.

"No, I'm not crazy," Eddie Griffiths said. "I actually heard him whistling."

"Are you shittin' me?" Bill Furgeson demanded.

"No, I heard him too," Wally Dersham said. "I couldn't hardly believe it myself."

Several other witnesses were produced and questioned. Those who had not been present at the time of the alleged whistling remained skeptical. Never in recent times had there been as much as a rumor of a positive emotional demonstration from Jeff who, until lately, threatened to give gloominess a bad name.

Bill Ferguson was the only one bold enough or tactless enough to mention it.

"You in love or something?" Bill asked Jeff one morning on the flight line.

Although not accustomed to discussing his personal business or revealing his feelings, Jeff happily admitted to having a new friend who made the sky seem bluer.

"Good." Ferguson said, with a smile and a wink. He never mentioned his talk with Jeff to anyone, and did not bring up the subject again.

CHAPTER FIFTEEN

At Jeff's suggestion, Pete had signed up for ground school early in his training. After learning the rules and regulations, airport procedures and something of aerodynamics in the classroom, Pete had taken the Federal Aviation Administration's private pilot written test. He passed it easily, so that part of the process was over with.

"We'll have you take the flying and oral parts somewhere along the way at an FAA testing center—maybe St. Louis," Jeff said. "You'll be fully licensed before we get back to Los Angeles."

Busy with preparations for the trip, Pete had penciled in only one more session during the few days before their departure.

With just one day remaining until departure, Jeff arrived at the airport to find a white stretch limousine parked beside the Skyhawk. Its trunk and rear doors were open and a tall, hardy looking man in a dark uniform and chauffeur's cap was helping Pete unload its cargo. It was the same man Pete had seen at the party; part of the Sunderland security force.

Jeff heard Pete say, "That goes on the rear seats of the plane, Hughes."

Stacked between the limo and the Cessna was every wilderness item available for camping utility and comfort. Far more gear, it appeared, than would possibly fit into the cargo bay.

"What's all this?" Jeff asked.

"It's the stuff we'll need. I thought we'd take it with us today for a shakedown cruise."

"That's an awful lot of weight?"

"I'll spread it out. Everything will fit just fine. In fact, we are still short of the maximum allowable weight. I checked the manual and everything is distributed properly."

Pete obviously enjoyed the project.

"Actually, I had made one mistake," Pete admitted, packing some of the gear into the small cargo door and the rest on the rear passenger seats and floor. "I forgot to deduct the weight of the cartons this stuff came in, so I had some extra pounds to play with. Since we're allowed two passengers, but there will only be the two of us, we've got weight to spare, so look here."

Sitting on the rear floor were two motorized devices with wheels. At first Jeff thought they must be power generators of some sort. Pete freed one of them from the strap that held it, hefted the mystery package to the ground and unfolded it. The mechanism resembled one of those child's transformer toys that looks like one thing in its compacted form and becomes something completely different when extended.

In this case, the items were small motor scooters.

"Perfect for those remote airports that don't have convenient taxi service or rental cars. One for you, one for me."

"I thought you said 'rustic' comforts."

"Well, not too rustic. We're not savages, you know."

Climbing into the plane, Jeff said, "Let's see how she rides."

In the air the Skyhawk was less responsive than a 152 because of its larger size and the extra weight. But the craft handled well and Pete adapted quickly to any differences.

When they returned to the airport, Jeff looked over the gear again, completely amazed at its quality and the amount of thought Pete had put into it.

"I have to say, Pete, I'm impressed."

"How did you like my delivery truck?"

"It may be the very first practical use of that monstrosity," Jeff said.

"In another ten or fifteen years it will have surfboards tied on top."

"I assume your father knows about the trip. What did he say?"

Pete chuckled. "He said I was pissing my life away."

"And what did you say to that?"

"Bye Dad."

"What was Paige's reaction?"

"I don't know. I haven't seen her lately."

"Not even a goodbye to your own fiancée?" Jeff said.

"She'll have to start the wedding without me."

Everyone on the airfield seemed to know about their upcoming trip. For weeks, Eddie Griffiths had been providing a daily countdown. "Twelve days and counting," the chief pilot would say; "Eight days and a wakeup," he would shout across the pad.

With departure now just a day away, Jeff could see envy, even a trace of resentment, on the faces of some of the other staffers. That someone else should get to fulfill their own long-held fantasy was a green-colored dream for those who had to stay behind.

"Some of us have to work for a living," instructor Andy Grossman said with a baring of teeth that so many people try to pass off as a smile. Andy had a wife, three kids and a four-bedroom albatross in West Covina that separated him from his own lost hopes.

By the time Andy's responsibilities were behind him there would be no time left for himself. There would only be bitterness over what he never got to do. The door that was closing on him would be locked tight. He had become so accustomed to choosing other people's priorities over his own that he was not fully aware that his resentments bordered on hatred of his family and, at that moment, of Jeff Burke and Pete Sunderland.

00

Jeff drove Stephanie to Los Angeles International Airport. They said their goodbyes and she boarded her plane to Buffalo. They each said the separation would probably do them good.

Neither believed it.

Despite having met only a few weeks earlier, there was no denying they had reached a pleasant level previously unknown in their singleness. After the initial heat of their first meeting had moderated, they had gotten to know each other better. They told each other everything about themselves. There would be no surprises later.

Both admitted openly that they were half terrified of what the other might do, or fail to do, that might make their deepest fears come true once more. Two people at war with their experiences. All the while, each was consciously trying not to blame the other for injuries not of their making.

Jeff promised he would call often from along the way.

As difficult as it had been to let Stephanie go, it was also hard for Jeff when he dropped Punkin at his mother's house on Saturday morning with her kitty toys, litter box, cat food, and food and water dishes.

"She'll probably never forgive me for abandoning her, Mom." The words were barely out of his mouth when the little yellow kitty jumped onto the sofa beside Mrs. Burke, turned around the required three times, flopped down, and fell sound asleep. She didn't even wake up when Jeff left for the airport.

00

It was late morning when Jeff got to the airport.

Pilot error is the main cause of airplane crashes. One of the most common mistakes when the appointed departure time arrived was that a pilot's anticipation often overruled his common sense.

Jeff always taught his students that when the weather is bad, even if the girl you are trying to impress gets pouty, the flight must be canceled.

This was not such a day.

The weather was better than they could have hoped for. The sky was clear and a slight northwesterly crosswind was blowing across the runway.

Just as Pete had suggested, Jeff brought only his grooming kit and a few changes of clothing of the casual and grubby variety. Should a more formal occasion arise, Pete had said, they could always buy whatever they needed. Jeff had made it very clear from the beginning that Pete could pay the agreed-upon salary, the travel and living expenses, and the rent on his Malibu apartment. But if personal items were needed, he would buy them himself, just as he always did.

His small stack of personal gear at his feet, Jeff leaned on the Skyhawk and waited for Pete to arrive. He wondered again whether he was doing the right thing. Bill Ferguson had assured him he could step right back into his job when he returned. Jeff suspected Bill approved the trip because he thought it might be a good way to rejuvenate a burnout.

As usual, Pete was fashionably late. He arrived in the same limousine that had delivered the gear, driven by the same walking wedge of a man he had first seen at the Sunderland's party.

"Thanks, Hughes," Pete said, grabbing his bag and bounding from the limo to the pad as the enormous shining symbol of wealth glided quietly away.

"Well, here we are, Jeff."

"And where is that, Pete?"

"At the gateway to a bold new adventure," Pete said, with his self-assured smile.

"Do you think you'll be able to survive in the wilds, without your overdeveloped driver?"Jeff said. "What's his name? Huge?"

"Not Huge. Hughes." And he's much more than a driver. He's my father's chief of security. He has a Master's in History, wrote a book on chess, teaches anti-terrorist tactics at USC and he's a hell of a lineman at staff touch football games."

"He looks like the entire line."

"When you've made as many enemies as my father has, you surround yourself with muscle."

They climbed into the Skyhawk. It was different this time. They were not going to the practice area for training. They were flying into the unknown. The prospect was both exhilarating and a little frightening.

After their run-up, Air Traffic Control gave them clearance for takeoff.

For Jeff, leaving a city that held so many unpleasant memories was much like dining at a restaurant with a crabby waitress. Her only smile came at the very end of the meal, when she handed the customer his check and wished him a nice day. By that time, a generous tip or a fond farewell were out of the question.

STEVE LIDDICK

CHAPTER SIXTEEN

About a hundred miles east of Los Angeles, not far from the City of Palm Springs, a break in the mountains separated the Los Angeles basin's cities and suburbs from the deserts of the American southwest.

"All the air from the L.A. basin squeezes through that opening at Banning Pass,"

Jeff said. "Sometimes the winds get up to killer velocities. You often hear about trucks being overturned and motorists getting blown right off the road."

Even traveling at 11,500 feet above sea level, well above the highest point of the mountains on either side of the gap, they could feel some turbulence buffeting the Skyhawk.

"Pilots setting up to land at Palm Springs Airport often get the thrill ride of their flying careers."

"Looks like a lot of smog comes through here from Los Angeles," Pete said, fighting to keep the wings level.

Winds carrying pollutants into and beyond Palm Springs spread the blight across the desert where it mingled with the airborne garbage generated by other cities along the way.

Once past the enormous natural wind funnel, Jeff and Pete dropped down several thousand feet.

Along the way, Jeff occasionally threw Pete a training problem to solve. The men kept reminding each other that the line on the chart was drawn in pencil and could always be erased and redrawn if they took the notion. Neither felt pressured to follow a rigid schedule. They agreed that the idea was to enjoy the ride and to stop and smell the roses.

By late afternoon they spotted a small Arizona dirt air strip and decided it would be a good place to stop for the night.

The sun had moved closer to the horizon behind them. Both men were tired from being tossed roughly about the cockpit by a gusting tailwind and desert thermal updrafts that affected their high-winged aircraft so much more than one with a low wing.

As they cruised past the airport to scope out the landing conditions they could see several faded white wooden buildings with rusted corrugated metal roofs.

"This will be a little tricky," Jeff warned, noting the angle of the sun. "You want me to take it down?"

"I've got it," Pete said, going over in his mind how to land a ton of aircraft on sixteen-hundred feet of dry dirt.

Following standard strange-field entry procedure, Pete maneuvered the Skyhawk into position, dropping down from cruise altitude. A quick check of the windsock indicated a westerly breeze, and a landing straight into the sun.

Pete seemed unconcerned at the prospect of a bumpy ride into nature's high beam while executing the hardest part of flying an airplane.

"Like patting your head and rubbing your stomach at the same time," Jeff said.

"While playing a tuba," Pete said with a cackle.

Yucca, cactus and other desert scrub growth became more identifiable as the plane continued its descent to pattern altitude. In moments they found themselves on the downwind leg where Pete adjusted his speed, let down some flaps, and swung easily onto the base and final legs.

With less than two-hundred feet remaining until touchdown, the air became unexpectedly calm. The plane had stopped its bumping and gyrating, leaving the blazing sun as the remaining challenge.

The plastic windshield, with microscopic scratches caused by a thousand cleanings, compounded the harsh glare. Pete had to rely on the view out the side windows to help position himself as they sank toward the near end of the runway.

Fifteen feet off the ground, Pete eased back the yoke, flared the Cessna, and held it there, floating just off the surface. With the stall warning screaming in his ear, the craft settled to a gentle landing as the wheels neatly connected with the dirt strip.

The touchdown was louder and bumpier than Pete was accustomed to on Santa Monica's nearly mile-long blacktop runway. A rough surface offered the advantage of slowing the plane more quickly because of increased tire resistance.

"Good one," Jeff said. "Let's park it by the largest hangar. I think I saw a water faucet over there."

They parked next to the big building for protection from any winds that might come up in the night that would make the craft bounce and strain against its tie-down ropes.

When Pete starved the engine of fuel and it coughed to a stop after so many hours of continuous roaring of 180 horses in their ears, the sudden silence seemed intense.

"I don't think we should fly that long anymore," Pete said.

Jeff agreed. "Kind of defeats the purpose of a leisurely trip. How about if we keep it down to, say, no more than three hours a day."

With no other humans in sight, the pair spent the next hour setting up camp and assembling food and cooking gear for the evening meal.

Pete had brought some beef to barbecue over the campfire for their first night's dinner.

"Until we get to the next place where fresh meats are available," Pete said, "our cuisine will be limited to meals that come out of an envelope."

As much as possible, they made preparations for the following day's travel so they could get an early start. Pete filled canteens from the faucet next to a hand-lettered "O.K. TO DRINK" sign. He rounded up dried cactus and other woody materials from the surrounding scrub to get a handful of charcoal briquettes started. Jeff placed food, water, sectional charts, and other reference materials they would need in flight the next day to within easy reach in the cockpit.

By the time they finished their travel housekeeping duties, the sun had dipped below the horizon. Their dinner sizzled on a folding grill over the campfire.

Darkness came quickly. With little moisture in the soil to hold the heat of the day, the temperature dropped noticeably. They put on jackets and sat down to talk about the next leg of the trip. If they followed their loose plan, they would be in a town the following night that was large enough to have facilities where they could have a bath and a soft bed.

"I figure we'll be out of here by the crack of dawn," Jeff said.

"I was thinking more like the crack of noon," Pete suggested.

"Some mountain man you are," Jeff said between bites of steak.

On days when a specific destination was planned, an early start meant they would be able to take their time getting there. They could stop for a hot lunch at an airport restaurant along the way and still make it to any proposed destination with daylight to spare. They could even get in some practice on maneuvers in the air along the way, and on the questions likely to be asked in the oral part of the upcoming license exam.

"Do you miss Stephanie?" Pete asked, settling down beside the sizzling fire.

"Oh, yeah," Jeff said. "And it scares the hell out of me. I thought I had forgotten how to care about anybody. How about you? Do you miss your girlfriend?"

"You probably mean Paige?" Pete said, and tossed some wood onto the glowing charcoal embers. "No, I don't miss her. I couldn't wait to get away from her. I didn't even tell her I was leaving. And she's not my girlfriend, even though she goes around introducing herself to everybody as my fiancée. Don't know where she got that idea. I've been going along with the joke because it keeps everyone happy and off my back."

"It sounds like a communications breakdown," Jeff said, the light of the flames flickering against the faded white hangar.

"That is the basis of my entire relationship with my father. Paige is the daughter of Milford Lambert, of Lambert Technology, a large developer of computer software. In addition to equipping half the third world's armies with the tools of war, my father decided to improve his image. So he got into computer hardware. So, naturally—"

"Computer software and computer hardware sounds like a good match. "If you're talking about technology."

"Now, see, Jeff, you get it. We've only been talking for two minutes and you already know what I'm talking about. I've been telling my father the same thing for years. Why can't he get it?"

"Just say 'no' Pete. Watch me. Tongue against the roof of the mouth—nnnnnnnn—and push—ohhhhh."

"Do you kick a grizzly bear in the nuts? It would just piss him off. I don't take it too seriously, though. Being financially independent has made a huge difference in how much importance I give to my father's demands."

"Well, maybe a marriage of the princess of softness and the prince of hardness would work out," Jeff said with a grin. "Like those medieval unions that brought peace to European countries."

"A marriage of mechanics and electronics. You know what that is, Jeff? That's a robot. My father wants a robot. That way he can program his own son to do what he wants. No, if I ever marry, it won't be Paige. She gets around too much, if you get my drift."

"I noticed she has a wandering eye."

"As with most matters that concern me, it's my father's doing. He makes certain Paige is invited to every gathering, outing, dinner—everything. He's putting the pressure on. 'Time for a man to marry and settle down if he isn't a goddamn faggot'."

The campfire created an illuminated circle, dimming toward the outer edges, then absorbed into the desert night.

"So, why haven't you gotten married?" Jeff asked, stifling a snort.

"Oh, Christ. You're not going to start in on me, are you? Anyway, who would I marry? The only ones I attract are the kind with no money, who want mine, and those who do have money and treat marriage like a business merger."

"Okay, let's drink to Pete and Paige, Incorporated," Jeff said, lifting his canteen in a toast.

"I'll never get married," Pete said. There was glum finality in his words.

Well, there it was. Jeff could see it coming. When someone says how passionately opposed he is to marriage, it usually means he would very much like to find a permanent someone, but is frustrated in the search for Ms. Right.

"In my business, we have a technical term for that," Jeff said. "It's called 'bullshit'. If the right one comes along, you're as good as snared."

"Maybe, but I'm real particular, you know."

93

"Well, she'll have to be basically attractive," Jeff suggested.

"Right. She doesn't have to be a movie star, but I don't want a dog, either.

"Reasonably intelligent, and a woman who is motivated, though not necessarily highly skilled, in the amorous arts."

"Very little hands-on experience, thank you very much. I'll teach her everything she needs to know."

"Now there's a chauvinistic double standard if I ever heard one,"

"Hey, if I wanted somebody with experience, I'd marry Paige, even though it would break the hearts of the entire Los Angeles Rams backfield."

"And she's gotta have class."

"Money would help, too," Pete said, emphasizing the point with upraised fist into the night sky.

"You already have money—oh, right."

"Exactly. If she has money, she won't need mine."

"Maturity," Jeff said. "She's got to have that."

"Yeah. Somebody in the family will have to be a grownup," Pete said, laughing uproariously at his own joke.

"A good looking mother-in-law."

"Huh?"

"That's what they say," Jeff said. "If you want to know how she'll look in thirty years, look at her mother."

"Oh God. Thirty years with the same woman. I can't imagine that."

"My grandparents were married sixty-three years when Pappy died," Jeff said, pained at the memory. "When my dad died, he and my mother had been married thirty-two years."

"I know a guy who's been married thirty-five years," Pete said.

"See there. It is possible."

"To four different women?"

"I had a wife once," Jeff said. "I caught her playing house with a neighbor."

Jeff kept thinking of Stephanie and how comfortable he had been with her.

CHAPTER SEVENTEEN

From a surface temperature of eleven-thousand degrees, the sun's rays striking the quiet Sunday morning desert dawn had dwindled to a meager forty-five degrees where the two campers slept. An occasional droplet of dew slid down the surfaces of the Skyhawk and from equipment scattered around the campsite. A pair of mocking birds protecting their nest had a terrified hawk on the run in midair.

As quietly as they had inhabited the darkness, creatures of the night returned to their hiding places as the desert day shift came on duty. The denizens were a match with their surroundings in this harsh place where blending in was vital to survival.

Jeff slept with his head on an inflatable pillow propped against one of the Cessna's landing gears. Pete was asleep a half-dozen paces away, his face covered by the flap of his sleeping bag. Neither man stirred when a jackrabbit wandered through camp. Nor did they hear a car pull up behind the hangar, or its driver who walked slowly and soundlessly to where the men lay sleeping.

Only when an object passed between Jeff and the warming sun did he roll over to investigate. As he did, he came instantly awake and alert at the sight of a very large man looking down at him. The visitor wore a western style hat and a pair of super-sized brown leather cowboy boots. Back-lighted by the sun, the surprise guest's face was dark and unrecognizable.

The big man moved around into the full light where Jeff could see his face and the badge pinned to the front of a Monroe County Sheriff's Department jacket. The name tag worn over the caller's left breast pocket spelled out "Charles Benson, Sheriff" in white lettering.

"Mornin'," he said, keeping his voice low.

"Good morning sheriff. Any problem?" Jeff asked sleepily.

"That's what I stopped by to find out," the sheriff said, making a half turn to send a brown stream of tobacco juice into the dust.

A buzz from Pete's direction continued until Jeff finally threw a boot at the lump, jarring the snoring man awake.

"Lemme alone," said a voice from somewhere deep in the folds of the sleeping bag.

"We've got company."

That brought Pete to a sitting position, where he got an intimidating view of the lawman looking down at him.

"Good morning," Pete said. "Everything okay?"

"Seems to be," Benson said.

Pete rubbed his eyes. "This strip is on the chart. Not marked private—"

"The airport is open to everybody, son," Benson said. "I'm just making sure things are all right. The owner lives a couple of miles away. I look in on the place when there's something unusual. We don't get many planes from out of the area."

By that time, Pete had pulled on his boots and was on his feet. "How about some coffee, sheriff?" he said and stirred the campfire's coals he had covered with ashes and dirt the night before.

"I believe I'll take you up on that m'boy," Benson said. He removed an enormous cud of tobacco from his mouth and flung it into the desert scrub.

Adding some small pieces of wood he had scrounged the night before and set aside for the purpose, Pete had the small fire restarted in minutes.

By the time the coffee water boiled, Pete and Jeff had filled Benson in on their plans and everyone was on a first name basis.

"You didn't seem too concerned about our being here, Charlie." Jeff said.

"If you'd been bikers or living in an old rusty van I'd probably have been worried. But people who fly airplanes are generally a better class of folks."

"How do you figure that?"

"I don't mean that in a snobby way. Pilots are usually people of some means, as opposed to some ragtag band of losers who might be a threat to the health, property, and lives of the folks who pay my salary."

"I guess you get some of that kind, too," Pete suggested.

"Now and then. But most people who happen by are pretty responsible and respectful of the rights of others."

"I don't know Charlie," Jeff said. "After living in Los Angeles all these years, we're pretty desperate men."

Benson smiled the smile of one who had first-hand experience with desperation. "Desperate for a breath of fresh air and some elbow room maybe," he said.

"Nothing like a clear morning in the desert to remind us of that," Jeff said.

"No, I don't worry about people like you fellows. It's the disenfranchised itinerant that causes trouble. The most dangerous animal on the face of the earth is a man with nothing to lose."

Pete tossed some more woody chunks on the campfire.

"The only way to change it," Charlie continued, "is to help bring everybody into the winner's circle. If you make sure every living soul has a chance to build a life he'd be reluctant to give up, he won't risk it by violating your rights or taking your property."

"Sounds simple enough in principle," Jeff said.

"Putting it into operation is where it gets tough," Charlie said. "Too many elements at work against it. There are those who profit from those who don't have much. People like that are a lot like a forest is to a lumber company. They're a resource. The exploiters don't want that taken away from them. Entire industries depend on keeping things just the way they are. We have an economy that relies to a large extent on manufacturing and selling the tools of destruction."

Benson took another sip of coffee.

"So, even if we hate our jobs building those things, and even though it doesn't make any sense, it's a routine we got used to. We're not in a hurry to stop doing what we make our living at. Defense spending during World War Two got us out of the great depression. Trouble is, once we got on our feet again, we never developed anything big enough to replace the tools that saved our skin. Those businesses still sustain us, so it is in our best interests

97

to have a few enemies around to arm ourselves against. The Russians have come in real handy for a lot of years."

Pete and Jeff looked at each other. Pete would not have been anxious to volunteer the fact that Charlie Benson was talking about his family's primary enterprise.

"The welfare system is another," Charlie said, taking another sip of coffee. "The people who actually get welfare payments are the least of the system. Where it gets expensive is in the administration of the money. Hell, most government bureaus are set up that way. They either require you do something, or keep you from doing something. Isn't that a hell of a notion? If it's not prohibited, it's mandatory. Either way, the bureaucrats have to generate a lot of paperwork as evidence of how much we need them."

"Let's not forget the law enforcement industry?" Jeff suggested.

"A perfect example," Benson quickly agreed. "If there were no crooks, I'd be out of work. So would the people who made my gun, badge and patrol car. Don't forget the jailers, courts, lawyers, bail bondsmen and on and on—"

"How do you turn something that big around?" Pete asked.

"Why, you tear it down and start over."

"Whoa." Jeff said. "You sound like a 1970's radical liberal."

"In the 1970's, that's just what I was."

"No way, Charlie." Pete said.

"I lived in a commune two miles from here," Charlie said, waving out across a slight rise in the landscape. "There were a dozen more just like me. Peace, free love, smoking dope, LSD trips, tie-died clothes, Jimmy and Janice on the eight-track, lousy hygiene, no money, no responsibilities, no nothing. The whole hippie program."

"How did you get to where you are now?" Jeff said.

"I grew up. I realized that when you get something for free, somebody else has to pay for it. One day it came to me that it wasn't right. So I got a job. Then I got a better job and earned the respect of enough of my fellow citizens to get this job. Before I knew what hit me, I had become one of those people with something to lose."

"And here you are," Pete said, taking a selfie of the three of them, "fighting for truth, justice and the American way."

"You've got my vote," Jeff said, adding fuel to the fire to get their breakfast started.

Benson rose slowly to his feet.

"Well, fellas, I'd best hit the road. There are a couple of leftover Saturday night drunks to let out of the tank and some locks to be checked here and there."

"It's been an education Charlie." Jeff said, shaking the big man's hand.

"I want you to take my address," he said, fishing around in his jacket pocket for a business card and handing it to Jeff. "Drop me a postcard from along the way. There's enough of the hippie left in me to appreciate your free-spirited junket. I'd like to know how you boys are doing."

Pete and Jeff walked Charlie to his car. With a final wave, he was gone in a cloud of desert dust.

After breakfast, Jeff poured water from his canteen onto the campfire and refilled the container from the faucet.

"Okay," Jeff said. "Let's move out. We're burnin' daylight."

CHAPTER EIGHTEEN

A young woman in her late twenties looked out from under her wide-brimmed western hat, across a rolling expanse of northeastern Colorado. A herd of horses frolicked nearby. She smiled as they ran off youthful energy. At the same time she wondered whether she might be wasting her own youth by remaining at the ranch when most people her age had long since gone out on their own.

She loved the lifestyle and her close relationship with her parents. But there was a growing sense, despite four years away at the University of Colorado in Denver, that she had never really left home. Maybe it was because here she was insulated against unknowns that were avoided simply by doing nothing.

Perhaps it had something to do with the fact that on their trip from Ireland to Colorado, her great-great-grandparents on her father's side of the family were met along the way by a welcoming committee made up of her mother's full-blooded Lakota Sioux ancestors.

In the century-and-a-half since that unfriendly confrontation between her forbears, most of the natives and immigrants had learned to get along with—or avoid—each other. Her mother and father took inter-racial harmony to an uncommon extreme for the region when they married.

The one child they produced turned out to be a jet-black-haired, blue-eyed pleasing blend of fair Irish colleen and Native American princess. She shared the best of her parents' other traits, as well; the pleasant disposition of her mother, the irreverent humor of her father, and the alert intelligence of them both.

Aside from her slightly darker skin and somewhat diluted native features, other signs of the young woman's Indian heritage were subtle, though purposeful fashion touches. She routinely wore a symbol of the ancestry she shared with her mother: a Concho belt, a piece of Native American turquoise jewelry or a headband which, when seen in the context of her appearance, would serve as an introductory statement for those to whom the realization might come as a shock later.

So attractive was she in looks and personality that any initial aversion to her ethnicity by those she met usually passed quickly, swallowed up by the power of her confident, easy laugh. But, just enough of the time, there would be a nearly imperceptible reaction by some that she could only compare to a cloud passing across the sun.

In high school, the boys she dated were white, as were several lovers after she went off to the university. If the men in her life thought any differently of her than of the Caucasian girls she went to school with, it was never hurtfully obvious. She wanted to believe that their interest in her was not mere curiosity. But somewhere in the deepest reaches of her being she harbored the suspicion that being both white and Indian meant that she was neither.

Aside from there being no man in her life, she could not think of a compelling reason to leave the ranch, although it sometimes seemed an indulgence to stay.

As with all of her thoughts, she shared with her parents the growing awareness that the time might be near when she should evolve to another phase of her life. As always, they encouraged her to follow the course that was best for her, wherever that might lead.

She might already have moved on if she could have brought into focus the form her future should take.

CHAPTER NINETEEN

Pete and Jeff had zigged and zagged throughout the southwestern states before heading northward. They landed at interesting places as the notion struck them, purposely avoiding large cities. They took a breathtaking flight high over the Grand Canyon, flew low over desert buttes, ate buffalo burgers, bought western hats at roadside stands, and buzzed a nudist colony.

In the air east of the Great Divide, Colorado would soon turn into Nebraska and South Dakota, with a few craggy spots along the way.

"The population is thinning out," Pete shouted above the engine's roar.

"That's the best news I've heard all day," Jeff said.

As expected, their meandering had given Pete valuable experience in a multitude of weather, flying and landing conditions. Occasionally they dropped down to cruise the lower elevations for no better reasons than to vary the routine and to see what folks were doing down there. Periodic stops had given them a chance to tune in on hangar talk at small town airports and to observe local customs.

At least one hour of each day had been devoted to practicing specific maneuvers. The Skyhawk did not cover much ground during those times of climbing and circling, but Pete was becoming well prepared for the private pilot flight test he would take with an FAA examiner when they arrived in St. Louis.

Jeff would sometimes reach over and cut the power to idle to simulate an emergency engine failure. Then, Pete would put the Skyhawk into a glide and run through the procedures for restarting the engine, at the same time picking out prospective landing sites on the ground. Reacting quickly to possible trouble soon became automatic.

00

The miles between them and Los Angeles slowly piled up. It had been five days since they left Santa Monica airport. Although they were still within easy flying distance of their home base, as the crow flies, they somehow seemed far away from it.

"I never thought I'd say it, Jeff, but this is getting pretty dull."

"Up here above any breezes there's not much work to flying."

"I've already learned to do this part."

"Patience, kid. We'll probably make Pierre, South Dakota by this evening. That should be enough excitement for you."

Occasionally, ranch houses, if they could reasonably be called ranches, were visible as dots on the ground. Smaller dots were stables and other outbuildings.

At that altitude, cattle, horses and all but the largest vehicles were too tiny to see except where afternoon sunshine stretched out their shadows to a size visible from high above Colorado.

For every hundred or so scattered buildings, there was a wide spot in the road brazen enough to call itself a town and be shown on the map.

Just then Pete sensed, rather than saw, something off to the left side of the aircraft. Perhaps the monotony of flight had created a kind of mental template. When an almost imperceptible change of scenery overlaid the image that had been burning into his mind with intense sameness, the slight difference caused Pete to glance off to his left. There, close enough to read its numbers, was another single engine plane traveling in the same direction, inching its way past them.

"Check this out, Jeff."

"What is it?" Jeff said, startled after such a long lull in conversation.

"Aircraft off the port side."

Jeff leaned forward to look past Pete.

"At this range they surely know we're here."

Jeff turned on the NavCom radio and switched it to the air-to-air frequency.

"This is Skyhawk Niner-Niner-X-Ray. Bonanza eight-four-Zulu, do you read?"

A female voice answered. "This is eight-four-Zulu. Where've you been? We've been calling you for five minutes."

"We just now spotted you. Is this your home territory?"

"Yes. You?"

"Passing through from Santa Monica, California. Headed for Pierre, South Dakota."

Pete slowly narrowed the gap between the high-winged Skyhawk and the low-winged Beechcraft Bonanza until the two planes were about even, the Cessna slightly higher.

"Don't get too close, Pete."

Two people were visible in the cabin of the four-place plane, though the men could only make out the face nearest to them; an attractive young woman who was working the radio.

"I'm Sandy," said their neighbor. "Melanie is driving."

A second female voice called, "Howdy," she said, hollow against the background roar of their engine.

The men looked across the empty space as the Bonanza's pilot leaned toward her passenger side window, giving the men a wave and a heart-stopping look at the beautiful face that went with the voice. Even from that distance they could see that she had auburn hair, and facial features unmistakably Native American.

"Whoa." Pete said, grabbing the mike from Jeff.

"I'm Pete Sunderland. The ugly one here is Jeff Burke. Two bachelors traveling down life's skyway."

The women laughed and talked between themselves. Then Melanie took over the radio.

"Single, huh?" Melanie said. "In that case is there any rush to get to Pierre?"

Jeff thought he may have noted a trace of seductiveness. Pete was absolutely certain of it.

"Not necessarily," Pete radioed back. "Why?"

"How'd you like to join us at the ranch."

Jeff and Pete exchanged a quick glance and a nod.

"What the hell," Jeff said off-mike. "Flexibility, right?"

"Lead the way eight-four-Zulu," Pete said, without hesitation and put the Skyhawk into slow flight to give the Bonanza the lead.

The planes held their course for a few minutes longer before the flirting flyers were heard from again. "The ranch airstrip is at seven o'clock. See it?"

"Got it," Jeff said, spotting the long east to west runway below. "After you."

Private rural airfields for the average single-engine aircraft usually had grass or dirt surfaces and ranged in length from 1,200 to 2,000 feet. Anything shorter left too little margin for error. But what lay below them was a hardtop airfield that rivaled even Santa Monica Airport.

A large letter "P" made of stones painted white was off to the side of the runway to indicate the airport was private. It was only open to the owners and those specifically invited to land there.

"Jesus, Jeff. Look at that runway."

Jeff whistled in admiration. "The taxiway would make a better airport than most airports. These are not ordinary ranchers."

Pete made a wide, full circle to the right to let some space build up between the two planes. That would allow the girls time to get on the ground without feeling crowded by a tailgater.

"Runway two eight is the active," Melanie announced over the radio. "You can make a straight-in approach. Nobody else around but you and us. Daddy is already on the ground."

"Daddy?" Pete and Jeff said in unison.

"You'll have to behave yourself, Pete. Daddy's home." Jeff had an even better reason for behaving himself. He planned to call her that evening.

A mile east of the field, with the Bonanza already on final, Pete turned the Skyhawk back toward the airfield. He lined up the approach just as the girls turned off the runway to taxi to the main house.

"A pretty fancy spread," Pete said, as they neared the field.

"That Hughes helicopter down there would strain even your wallet," Jeff said. The chopper sat in the heliport circle next to the ranch house, its blade tethered. "And that Learjet would tear hell out of a million dollar bill." The expensive bauble occupied its own neatly marked space. Nearby sat an assortment of special purpose planes for business and pleasure. A mid-wing Piper crop duster and an aerobatic Aeronca Champion were lined up along the runway. They could see a large swimming pool behind the main house.

The Skyhawk whizzed past pastures and paddocks filled with dozens of horses. Even from several hundred feet in the air it was obvious they were blooded animals.

Several cows stood in a barnyard beyond the stables.

Pete was not immediately certain whether his wheels had actually touched the runway. The surface was so perfectly smooth that the Skyhawk had been on the ground for several hundred feet after he cut the power before he realized he was no longer flying and the plane was rolling to a stop.

Impressed with the size and quality of the facility, Jeff said, "Pete, I think we're among your people."

Pete shot him a dirty look.

At Melanie's direction, Pete pulled the Skyhawk into a parking space in front of the ranch house. A large, hand-carved wooden sign over the gate leading to the house said "Stafford Ranch, Julia, Melanie, and Hubley Stafford, Owners." Pete shut down the engine just as the two women stepped out of the Beech. A young Indian boy attached tie-down chains to the Bonanza, then to the Skyhawk.

"Hiya guys," Melanie shouted, as she walked toward them and offered Pete her hand. "I'm Melanie Stafford."

"You certainly are," Pete said, unable to take his eyes off the young woman.

"I'm Sandy Neilson," said her friend, reaching out to Jeff.

Both were in their late twenties and both, as Jeff's fisherman grandfather would have said, were "keepers".

An older woman with dark skin and distinctly Native American features waved from the porch.

"Mom," Melanie shouted to the woman, "they followed us home. Can we keep them?"

The woman laughed and shook her head in agreement.

"I'll bet she's heard that before," Pete said.

"Only about puppies," Melanie said, with a charming western twang. "You're the first strays I ever found at nine-thousand feet."

Melanie's mother waited on the porch for the foursome to join her.

"All right, boys," Melanie said, "what's the story here? Vacation? Business? Pleasure?"

"Yes," Pete said as they walked to the main ranch house. It was obvious Pete had claimed Melanie as his own. It was equally apparent that he was her choice.

The men explained the reason for their trip. They learned the girls had been college roommates and stayed friends in the years since. Sandy was a frequent visitor to the ranch.

"Mom, we ran across these fellows on our way back from Pueblo," Melanie told her mother. "I invited them for dinner."

"I'm Pete Sunderland, ma'am. This is Jeff Burke."

"I'm Julia Stafford. Please call me Julia. Glad to have you boys join us," she said, ushering them into the large house. "Come in, have a drink, and take a load off your feet."

"We'll pass on the drink, Julia," Pete said. "We've got a few miles to go yet."

"What? It will be dark in a couple of hours," Julia said. "You can't have dinner and get very far in the time that's left." She led the guests through her huge kitchen where she had been sewing. "Why don't you stay the night. We have plenty of room for visitors. Besides, we've already heard all of my husband's and the girls' stories. Frankly, the place could use a little new blood. How about it?"

Pete glanced at Jeff, who nodded.

"We'd like that," Jeff said, taking the seat Julia offered him at a large breakfast nook. "We're not on any special schedule, and Pierre will still be there."

Julia Stafford's kitchen was not fancy or pretentious. It was a warm reflection of the woman, herself. Neatly pressed linen curtains with flowers on them hung at the windows, dozens of cookbooks lined specially built shelves, and there were colors and smells that could turn the dreariest day bright and cheerful.

"Innkeeper," a voice boomed from the foyer. "How about some service out here."

"We're in the kitchen, Hub," Mrs. Stafford said, moving her sewing box to a side table.

They were joined by a distinguished looking white-haired man in his late-fifties. Dressed in a suede western cut jacket, expensive lizard boots and a large silver buckle on his belt, he was every inch the affluent gentleman rancher.

"I wondered whose Skyhawk that was," he said. "Howdy boys, I'm Hub Stafford."

"Daddy," Melanie said, "this is Jeff Burke and Pete Sunderland."

"Good to meet you fellas," he said, shaking their hands robustly. "Pete, are you any kin to Arthur Sunderland?" Stafford asked.

"My father," Pete said without enthusiasm."

Jeff was certain he detected a moment of distaste in Hub Stafford at the mention of the elder Sunderland's name.

"His people approached me about buying one of my companies a few years back. Been awhile. We didn't do any business, I do remember that. Anyway, I'm a horse breeder these days. You in the family business, Pete?"

"No way, no how, sir," Pete said, wishing the subject could be changed without offending his host. "I guess you might say I'm still looking for something of value to do. About time I got on the giving end instead of the taking end."

Sensing Pete's discomfort, Jeff volunteered, "He's at the awkward age."

"Got any ideas?" Stafford said.

"A few," Pete said, "none of which involve making money."

"I understand perfectly, Pete," Hub said. "About ten years ago it came to me that I was rich in possessions, but my soul was raggedy-ass poor. I had to do something about it, so I liquidated everything. Got a shitload of money, too. Excuse me ladies. Still got most of it. Went into the horse business for the fun of it, but even that makes money. The difference is that now I'm one happy sumbitch."

Clearly, it would be impossible not to like this wonderfully profane man.

"How about you, Jeff?" Hub asked. "What business are you in."

"I teach confused young playboys how to fly airplanes." Jeff said.

"Found your calling, huh?"

"Well, it pays for the groceries and that's all I really care much about at this point in my life, Mr. Stafford."

"Call me Hub. If you don't mind an observation, it sounds like you and Pete are each looking for pretty much the same thing, something worthwhile to do with yourselves. Welcome to that fraternity that suspects there's more to life than money and power."

"What happened that changed your mind, Hub?" Pete asked.

"The 'what' had been troubling me for a long time. I remember exactly when I made the final decision. I was looking out of the big window of my twenty-second floor Denver office. For some reason, all that pollution, the overpopulation and everything else that's wrong with society today smacked me right in the face. Right then I realized that Julie's and my life on the ranch and my life in business were a serious mismatch. I can tell you boys it hit me the way born-again Christians say they got saved. Hallelujah!"

"Funny," Pete said. "A man we met on the way here dropped in and you kind of dropped out. For pretty much the same reasons. You and Sheriff Charlie Benson would probably have a lot to talk about."

"Let's drink to breaking free of our bounds," Hub said, and all raised their glasses.

"While we're toasting," Hub said, "here's to our guests. As my Irish grandfather would say: 'May you live as long as you want to— and may you want to as long as you live'."

"Hubley Stafford," Julia said, obviously embarrassed. The girls howled without reservation.

"One good thing came out of my years in business," Hub said. "I met Julia while calling on a client in Colorado Springs."

Julia chuckled. "He needed help spending all that money."

"And you and Melanie have both done a helluva job of it," Hub said, with a bellowing laugh.

"Thanks for reminding me," Melanie said. "We want to run over to Denver and do some shopping."

"And I had to open my big mouth," Hub said.

"Speaking of conspicuous consumption," Jeff said, "why do you have an airstrip that's better than most commercial airports, Hub?"

"Now and then we get ants in our britches. We like to jet around, shopping in places it would be too hard to get to any other way. Melanie and I are both checked out in the Lear and the chopper, so we keep it up. Can't land a jet on a short dirt strip."

When they first arrived Jeff and Pete had noticed a small house nearby, possibly for ranch help. Probably where the small Indian boy lived who tied down the Skyhawk.

110

The Staffords could certainly afford a cook. But they learned that Julia did all the food preparation herself. The spread she set out was on a par with the Ohio farmhouse cuisine Jeff's grandmother and the other farm wives prepared for hungry field hands after a hard day's work when he spent his summers there in his teens.

"Too goddam much lace and frilly shit in here," Hub said, glancing mischievously at his wife. "Let's go into the den where a man can put his feet up on furniture without women yellin' at him."

If the kitchen mirrored Julia Stafford, the den was the architectural and philosophical reflection of her husband. Scattered about were a mix of Native American artifacts, sculptures, and original paintings of horses and Indians. Massive Ponderosa pine poles ran the width and length of the room. Rifles of all calibers and eras hung from racks on the walls and in dark wooden gun cases. Trophy heads lined the dark wood-paneled walls and knotty pine ceiling. The only covering on the polished hardwood floor was an occasional animal skin rug.

"I call this dad's 'morgue'," Melanie said. "I've been trying to talk him into giving these poor creatures a decent burial."

"At least I don't hunt them anymore," Hub said.

"He'd have you believe it was because his consciousness got raised," Melanie said. "But it's really because he's too old."

Hub Stafford swatted his daughter playfully and winked at his guests.

After an hour of exchanging each others' stories, Julia Stafford said, "You girls go ahead and show these fellows to the bunkhouse."

The men followed Sandy and Melanie.

The guest accommodations were reminiscent of ranch hand quarters. Though not elaborate, they were certainly a giant step up in comfort and décor when compared with campsites of the previous week. The same thoughtful touches seen throughout the main house were present in the rooms set aside for visitors. Julia Stafford's warmth was everywhere.

Pete and Jeff tossed their gear on their assigned beds. When they turned to leave, Melanie and Sandy were standing side-by-side, arms linked, blocking the only door out of the room.

"Think of this as your home for the next couple of days," Melanie said.

111

"Couple of—"

"You're trapped, boys," Melanie said. "No way out of here 'cept through us, and we ain't movin'."

Pete looked at Jeff, who nodded. He reached into the pocket of his jeans, took out his keys to the Skyhawk, and tossed them to Melanie. "I give up."

"God you're easy." Melanie said.

"Yeah, but I'm not cheap. You sure this is okay with you, Jeff?"

"I threw my calendar away before we left L.A."

The girls whooped for joy.

"Watch it, Melanie," Jeff said. "He's only interested in your father's money."

"Is that true?" Melanie asked in mock shock.

"Yes it is," Pete said. "If not for that, I'd be gone quicker than a snowflake in Tijuana."

"I don't get it," Melanie said, feigning a pout.

"You see," Jeff interrupted, "Pete's got this thing about women being after him only for his money."

"So, as long as Daddy stays rich," Melanie said, "I could at least be on your list of possibles?"

"My short list," Pete said, taking both of Melanie's hands in his and looking into her blue eyes.

"I think I'm gonna be sick," Jeff said to Sandy.

"How about you, Jeff?" Sandy said. "Do you have a thing about money, too?"

"Yeah," Jeff said. "You got any?"

"No. Mel's the rich roommate. I got through college on a scholarship."

"Football?" Jeff said, and took a punch to the arm.

"Money isn't real important to me beyond the basic needs and a few comforts," Jeff said. "Besides, my mother always said 'if she's a nice girl, she won't care what kind of car you drive'."

"Pete," Melanie said, stroking his hair. "I don't care what kind of car you drive."

"Melanie," Pete said, "I drive a Lamborgini Aventador."

"I don't care."

Pete and Melanie found a lame excuse to go off on their own.

"Why are you still living at home, Mel?" Pete asked. He, who was not that long out of the nest himself.

Taking no offense at the question, Melanie said, "It's something I've been asking myself a lot lately."

"Not afraid of the big bad world, are you?"

"Afraid? Not really. Apprehensive, maybe."

"You were away at college."

"It's strange," she said. "Academia is billed as a place to broaden one's look at the world. But I felt more like a spectator than a participant. It was pretty cloistered."

"Like a convent?"

"Well, I'm not a nun, if that's what you mean," she said with a twinkle in her blue eyes.

"Thank god. I was about to ask for the keys to the Skyhawk."

"I don't think I'm ready for you to go just yet."

"Oh, you're probably just like all the other girls. You'll toy with me and, after a few days, throw me away and I'll leave here feeling so—used."

Melanie wrinkled her brow. "Have there been a lot of other women?"

"None I've cared about. You?"

"No, there haven't been any women I cared about either," she giggled.

"That's encouraging," Pete said. "This could work. This could definitely work. You didn't answer my question."

"There have been a few men in my life. Nobody I'd want to be buried next to."

"Could I ask you a personal question?"

"What could be more personal than asking about my love life?"

"Why do you wear Indian jewelry?"

"Because I'm part Indian. Didn't you notice?"

"Sure I noticed. But you're part Irish, too. You don't wear a shamrock?"

Melanie gave that a moment's thought before she said, "I guess because being Irish is less of a concern among people I meet than being Indian."

"Never having met any Indians before today, there must be something I've missed."

113

"If you had lived as a white male in these parts, you might not feel inclined to have your arm around me."

"All I see is a more or less attractive young woman."

"More or less?"

"More, actually."

"I'm a twenty-seven-year-old spinster, you know."

"I'm a thirty-year-old bachelor. My dad suspects I'm gay."

"Are you?"

"Well, I'm crazy about my mother," Pete said. "I lived at home until not long ago and once, in college, I was on a decorating committee. Also, I love Broadway show tunes and I'm a big Judy Garland fan. I guess you'll have to draw your own conclusions."

Putting her arms around Pete's neck, she kissed him so softly and she smelled so good that it was as though he had never been kissed before.

"Wow." he said when she finally let go.

"That was the Melanie Stafford Sexual Orientation Test."

"How'd I do?"

"You can't tell for sure just once. It's a series, really."

"Can anyone do this?"

"Not with me, they can't."

"When can we continue the test? Is it a long series? When will I get the results?"

"I'll let you know." she said, kissing him again.

While Pete and Melanie examined the natural selection process in greater detail, Sandy and Jeff were taking a walking tour of the horse paddocks.

"How long have you known Melanie?" Jeff said.

"Since our first year of college."

"And you've stayed in touch ever since?"

"Funny, isn't it? We're so different, yet so much the same. We're both a little crazy and we both see the world as a bit off-center. We met in line when we were signing up for freshman classes. We hit it off from the beginning and roomed together all four years. We've talked on the telephone at least once a week ever since. Mel flies up in the Lear to get me every summer and I come down here for a couple of weeks. How about you and Pete?"

"We're finding we have many things in common," Jeff said.

"Two peas in a pod?"

"No, he's a pea. I'm a bean."

"Sounds like a partnership that doesn't look right at first glance. Just like Mel and me."

"It didn't start off smoothly for us at all. I resented his being of the privileged rich after I'd had to work so hard to get everything I have. I pretty much got over it, although the rich kid thing comes through now and then and I have to smack him down. Pete's one of those guys that no matter how pissed you get at him, you end up laughing."

"Did you notice how Pete and Melanie just naturally assumed that they were a couple? Why wasn't it you and Mel, or Pete and me? They just flowed right into it. Do you think they have built-in money sensors?"

Jeff had noticed the same thing.

"I think they have built-in 'lonely' sensors," Jeff said. "Pete picked it up when we were several hundred feet apart in the two airplanes."

"What did you sense about me?"

"That you're one of the prettiest women I've ever seen, and one of the nicest."

"Okay, I'll take it from there," Sandy said. She sat down on his lap, put her arms around Jeff, and kissed him.

To his own surprise, Jeff did not fight it at first. In fact, he rather enjoyed being with this bold young woman.

"Wait." Jeff said, muffled by a pair of lips on his own. "Sandy."

But Sandy did not wait. She continued the kiss until she felt Jeff's body go slack. Only then did she break her embrace and say, "What?"

"This isn't right."

"It sure feels right on my end," she said, breathing hard in her excitement.

"It would be real easy for us to get involved, Sandy," Jeff said. "But this is what I've been doing for a couple of years and it's gotten me nowhere."

"Oh, crap," she moaned, rolling off Jeff's lap and flopping herself down beside him on the hay bale, still holding his arm, her head on his shoulder. "You have a girlfriend, right?"

"Her name is Stephanie and I like her a lot. I don't know where it's headed, but I'm happy for the first time since I split up with my ex-wife."

"A wounded war veteran, huh?"

"On the losing side. But the prognosis for my recovery looks good."

"I was in that war, too, you know," Sandy said.

"A divorcee?"

"Divorcee? God, what a horrible word," she said, her face twisting into a grimace. "A leper? A typhoid carrier? A child molester? A divorcee?"

"Ex-wife. Ex-husband. Those sound kind of harsh, don't you think?" Jeff said, "How about 'former spouse'."

"'Widow' would be nice. I could have killed the sonofabitch when I found out he was sleeping with his secretary."

Jeff sensed that although the treachery was long past, the anger would be some time in fading. He had a lot of experience in that particular arena.

"There's some dignity to being a widow," he said. "It's like it wasn't anybody's fault. Like something perfect was cut short in its prime."

"Yeah, perfect," Sandy said.

"How long since you split?"

"Two-and-a-half years. Or, to put it another way, one Chevrolet dealer, a CPA and a ski bum ago."

"Anyone warming up in the bullpen, if you'll pardon the analogy?"

"No. All the men I meet are married, creeps, crazy, gay—" Sandy looked at Jeff and added, "or involved."

"God. Where were you the last two years when I was so miserable in L.A.?"

"Being miserable in Missoula, Montana."

"You're a great girl, Sandy," Jeff said, putting an arm around her shoulder. "I'm enjoying being here with you. But Stephanie is the best thing that's happened to me. I'm terrified of living like that again."

"Well, if it doesn't work out," she said, looking up at him, "you can always think of me as a spare."

"If it happens for you the way it did for me, just about the time you completely give up on ever finding the right person, there he'll be. Mr. Right, his very own self."

"I think I have already pretty much given up. Stephanie is a lucky girl."

"We're both lucky. We might never have found each other. It will happen for you Sandy," he said, giving her a little squeeze. "I promise."

Sandy just rocked back and forth and moaned her disappointment.

00

Everyone gathered in the Stafford kitchen for breakfast the next morning.

When Julia Stafford had a chance to get Melanie off to the side, she said to her daughter, "You like Pete, don't you?"

Without hesitation, Melanie said, "he's the one, Mom."

"Well, it's a little soon, but I'd say go for it, kiddo."

Jeff and Hub took a walk among the assortment of aircraft, just the two of them. Jeff had something he wanted to talk to the man about.

"Hub, your expression changed a little when Arthur Sunderland's name came up."

Hub looked around to see if anyone might be within earshot.

"I didn't like the man," he said. "Nothing I could put my finger on right away. But he just didn't seem like the kind of guy you could trust. It made me dig into his background. I didn't like some of the businesses he was in."

Jeff nodded. "Arthur the Third in there would agree with you."

"Pete doesn't like the man either?"

"What is there to like. The man is a killer by proxy."

Hub seemed astonished that their assessment of Pete's father was aligned.

"You see, Jeff, I built my businesses different from the way most entrepreneurs do it. I hired the right people for the job and I let 'em alone. In a way, they became partners in the venture. I paid 'em good and shared the profits. They rewarded me with hard work, honesty

117

and loyalty. Those people were family to me. I couldn't turn all that over to a man I thought was a thug."

As they walked back to the house, talking with Hub Stafford made Jeff even more aware of what he had been missing in his narrow life in the city.

The girls decided an aerial tour of the ranch was in order. With Melanie at the controls of the Bonanza and Pete next to her in the front passenger seat, the four took off for a spin around the thousand-plus acres. When they returned they saddled up horses and repeated parts of the tour on the ground, laughing and joking until their voices were raw. By the end of the ride, the men were raw in other places, too.

After they put the horses away Melanie said, "I want to share my secret place with you guys." She led them up a ladder to the enormous hay storage loft over the stables.

"Don't look down," Melanie said as they climbed higher, along the underside of the metal roof, and made their way carefully across enormous wood beams that ran the width of the building, high above the barn floor.

At the far end of the manmade cavern, they came to a flat, enclosed interior wooden structure that was the granary, for storage of feed and un-milled grains grown on the ranch.

"Follow me," Melanie said. She jumped off the edge of the storage cubicle, landed in the soft hay fifteen feet below and rolled out of the way of the others who were laughing all the way down. They rolled in the hay like children, kicking up dust.

They spent the rest of the afternoon lying quietly in the hay, enjoying each other's company. Beams of sunshine poked through openings between the wide boards in the side of the barn and made long, streaming shafts through airborne dust.

Pigeons looked down at the visitors from the rafters and made their distinctive swooshing, feathery sounds as they occasionally flew about. Their soothing coos sounded far off, though they were no more than twenty feet away.

Pete and Jeff told the girls about their decision to make the trip and what they hoped would come of it.

"What do you guys want to do when you get back to L.A.?" Melanie said.

"I don't think either of us knows yet," Jeff said. "We're still working on that."

"One thing I know for sure is that money isn't everything," Pete said.

"Oh Christ. Here we go again." Jeff said, winking at Sandy. "Only people who have money say that."

"Well, it's not everything," Pete said. "Some people are hungrier for a kind word than for a meal."

"Having given poverty a fair try," Jeff said, "let me just say that having money is better than not having money."

"But there are things you would do for free that you wouldn't do for any amount of money, isn't that true?"

"I don't follow you."

"You would mow some little old lady's lawn for nothing, but you wouldn't mow lawns for money. You would volunteer to serve meals to the poor, but you won't go to work in a restaurant for wages."

"How does that prove money isn't everything."

"Because money is not a consideration in helping people in need. Giving is the important thing. My point is that there are people out there who need someone to care about them, to be on their side, more than they need anything else."

Having endured nearly two years of being alone and hating it, Jeff could hardly find fault with Pete's premise. He also realized that he had never seen Pete as he was seeing him now.

"Practical application please?" Jeff said, egging Pete on a bit more.

Pete sighed and rolled his eyes.

"Somewhere there are people who could benefit from what we know."

"I don't believe it," Jeff said. "Pete used the word 'we' again. The last time he said 'we' were going to do something, the next thing I knew I was sleeping on spiny deserts and squishy meadows. Be careful ladies."

"What are 'we' going to do, Pete?" Melanie asked, snuggling up to him.

"Mel. Don't encourage him." Jeff cautioned. "You know how he gets."

"You know," Melanie said, "for some time now I've been thinking it's time I leave home and do something worthwhile."

"Any idea of what?" Pete said.

"No, and 'rancher's daughter' is not a recognized career field."

"Too bad. I'd hire you in a heartbeat."

"If you keep talking like that, dude, I'll never give you your keys back."

The day had gone by too quickly.

When they returned to the ranch house, Melanie's mother pulled a stem of alfalfa from Pete's hair. "Is that hay in your hair, young man?" Julia Stafford said.

"Yes ma'am," Pete said. "I believe it is."

"Have you been in the hay mow with my daughter?" she asked with a mischievous smile.

"Well, yes ma'am," Pete said, pointing to a giggling Jeff and Sandy, "but we had adult supervision."

"I'll phone the reverend." Julia said teasingly and shouted, "Hub, put on your good suit."

00

Early the next morning there was a blue mood around the breakfast table. The visit had been a pleasant surprise from the start. Leaving was difficult, for Pete and Melanie in particular. Jeff had an idea that it could be a beginning rather than an ending.

As they stood beside the Skyhawk preparing to leave, Jeff said to Sandy, "Let me know how you're doing." He gave her a peck on the forehead.

"That's the kind of goodbye kiss you give a little kid," she said, wrapping her arms around Jeff's neck and giving him a grownup kiss full on the lips. "I'm *not* a little kid, Jeff Burke. You might want to keep that in mind."

"You boys are welcome here anytime," Hub Stafford told them as they prepared the Skyhawk for flight.

Pete and Mel held hands to the very last. Jeff had to wrench his partner free of the starry-eyed young woman.

"You can run, Pete," Melanie said. "But you can't hide."

"I would never hide from you."

"Good, 'cause I'd hate to have to hunt you down and nail your hide to the wall of Dad's den."

The men climbed into the Skyhawk and it chugged to a smooth start.

In minutes they were aimed at South Dakota.

00

They had been in the air for some time before Pete took a piece of paper out of his shirt pocket and looked at the ten digits written on it.

"What's that?" Jeff asked.

"It's the combination I've been looking for," he said, showing it to Jeff."

Jeff saw the telephone number Melanie had given Pete.

Pete looked at the paper for a long time. Without a word, he folded it carefully and put it back in his pocket.

Jeff had only recently found the combination himself.

CHAPTER TWENTY

If it had been their intention merely to cross the country, Jeff and Pete could easily have done so in just a few days. Despite Pete's desire to spend more time with Melanie, the men decided to continue their journey as originally planned. At least until Pete took the private pilot test in St. Louis.

Cruising high over South Dakota, Jeff was checking out the sectional chart.

"There's a medium-sized town called Buffalo Valley just ahead. It's has an airport and a Flight Service Station."

"Good," Pete said. "I could use a little break. Maybe we could find a motel room."

"We just spent two nights with all the comforts. You got soft again at the Stafford's ranch. You can take the boy out of Bel Air, but you can't take Bel Air out of the boy."

Pete ignored the dig.

"There's the airport just ahead," Jeff said. "There's a restaurant on the field and a motel within walking distance."

Few airports are conveniently located in city downtown areas. Small strips in particular lacked the accommodations of those closer to larger metropolitan areas.

"Let's hope the motel doesn't smell like its previous guests," Pete said.

The men had agreed that until they reached towns small enough to satisfy their desire to avoid crowds, yet large enough to support comfortable sleeping quarters with sanitary facilities, they would continue to camp out and use airport washrooms to clean up.

When Pete tried to contact the airport's Automatic Terminal Information Service system on the radio, all he was able to get was static.

"ATIS is out of commission," he said. "We should check with air traffic control."

Jeff took over the microphone. "Buffalo Valley tower, this is Cessna Niner-Niner-X-ray. We are five miles southwest of the field. Requesting airport information."

"Niner-Niner-X-ray," came the response, "if you had checked your sectional chart you would have seen the ATIS frequency. You can find that information there."

Jeff and Pete looked at each other. Jeff keyed the mike once more. "This is Niner-Niner-X-ray. Your name, please?"

The operator apparently considered for a moment whether, or how, to respond. When he did, he made certain that when he exhaled in exasperation it went out over his radio. "The name is Hickman, Niner-Niner-X-ray," said the man in the tower, without losing the sneer in his voice. "Did you understand my last transmission? Over."

"Oh, I received it very clearly, Mr. Hickman." Jeff said. "But you are assuming that my navigational radio is working and that your ATIS is in service. How do you know I'm not in trouble up here? In which case, you would be wasting critical time.

"Now, since you don't seem to understand your function in the tower, let me enlighten you. Your mission is to provide information to pilots upon request and to safely and efficiently track and direct air traffic within your control zone. A condescending manner is counterproductive. A nervous student could get flustered to the point of losing control of his aircraft. It takes less time to give me the information I requested than it does to be an asshole, so I submit that you are confusing your authority with expertise. Perhaps you and I and your supervisor need to sit down together and review the recording being made of this conversation to see how we might improve your performance, Mister Hickman. Over."

A moment passed before there was a reply. When it came, it was a different voice on the speaker. "Niner-Niner-X-ray. Buffalo Valley Airport runway two-six is the active. Winds two-eight-zero at twelve knots. Barometric pressure three-one-point-seven. This is Buffalo Valley FSS manager Bill Farrell. You are correct, Niner-

Niner-X-ray, our ATIS is down. Thanks for pointing it out. Sorry for the inconvenience."

"Roger, Buffalo Valley. While you're fixing things, you might want to do some remedial work on Mister Hickman's mic-side manner."

"Your observation is duly noted Niner-Niner-X-ray. If there's anything we can do for you while you're here, please stop in."

"Thanks Buffalo Valley. We'll be there shortly."

"I'll bet that felt good," Pete said after Jeff hung up the mic.

"Things haven't been the same since Ronald Reagan fired nearly 12,000 federal air traffic controllers back in 1981 after they refused to end their strike. He ordered that those who were went on strike could never be rehired. Reagan hired strikebreakers to replace them.

"You mean he sent the jayvees in to play varsity?"

"Exactly. Before that, a guy like Hickman wouldn't even have gotten an interview for an ATC job.

"Don't get me wrong. most of the replacements eventually got to be as good as the old team. But by that time an entirely different culture had formed among controllers. There is still an aggravating number of individuals scattered around the country with a bad attitude."

"Maybe they don't have the self assurance that comes with knowing what the hell they're doing."

"Courtesy used to be the rule at controlled airports. But some of them have this irritating air of superiority. I don't like it personally, but it's potentially unsafe for students who may lack confidence."

A large white dome sat a hundred yards from the Buffalo Valley tower. The building looked like an enormous golf ball. It was part of a guidance network for planes in flight.

After landing, Pete and Jeff taxied to transient parking adjacent to the airport cafe and tied down the Skyhawk. Wooden outdoor stairs led to the Flight Service Station directly above the eatery.

The men were struck by the number of cars and pickup trucks in the parking lot. More than one might expect to see at a small town facility.

A cluster of young Native American men hung around the entrance to the restaurant. None in the little group looked directly at Pete and Jeff as they passed by. There was the strong smell of alcohol in the air.

Life outside the tower reflected the pace of a typical small town; unhurried and unstressed. When Pete and Jeff stepped inside the FSS, however, the facility was an energy capsule bustling with intensity not to be found for a hundred miles in any direction.

The air conditioned center gave those inside a 360-degree view of the sky through its ten-foot-high glass sides. Controllers could see everything coming and going. The place was well equipped and staffed by any measure, but especially for such a relatively small airport.

Jeff said, "This place is so big because it is directly below some major flight routes. That makes it a key facility for commercial and private aviation."

Current weather facts came across a line of computer monitors at each controller's station.

An array of devices on the roof sensed and relayed wind direction and velocity, temperature, and barometric pressure to the men and women in the center. They, in turn, exchanged the local information and winds-aloft reports from passing pilots with weather forecasters and with flight service stations throughout the country.

An uncommonly large man who looked to be in his early forties stood at the far end of the glass-walled room. He was wearing aviator sunglasses, a white shirt with epaulets and a conservative necktie held down by a miniature pilots' wings tie tack. His stomach hung out over the belt that held up a pair of dark summer-weight pants. In the shirt pocket was a plastic pocket protector full of ballpoint pens. On his wrist was a military type watch with all the aviation bells and whistles. Pete and Jeff could feel the hostility from across the room.

"That's gotta be Hickman," Pete said.

At well over six feet tall, they guessed the man weighed in at more than 250 pounds of glaring brawn.

A thin, balding man with glasses came over to greet the visitors.

"Gentlemen. I'm Bill Farrell, chief air traffic control officer at this station. You the fellas from Niner-Niner-X-ray?"

Jeff nodded. "I'm Jeff Burke, Mr. Farrell. This is my partner, Pete Sunderland."

"Sorry about what happened," Farrell said, lowering his voice and leading the men to a far corner of the room. "Being out here in the boonies has some real advantages. A nice place to raise kids and all. But finding qualified help locally is not one of the benefits."

"Where do you get your people from?" Jeff asked.

"A lot of them relocated to here when we first set up the place. This is also a training center for air traffic controllers who will eventually be sent to other locations around the country. And we hire a few of the local folks on a part time basis to fill in the gaps. Ben Hickman's one of them. Most have worked out just fine. But, quite candidly, Hickman has been my greatest challenge since I got here six months ago. I believe in working with an employee to help him get straightened out, but he routinely stretches the limit."

"Mr. Farrell," Jeff said. "I've logged more than three thousand flying hours in fixed wing aircraft and helicopters. II've talked to a lot of controllers over the last two decades. That man has the worst attitude I've ever experienced."

"I remind him about it now and then, but the reprimand soon wears off and he goes right back to his old ways. I get a lot of complaints, but I've never heard it said better than when you reamed him out over the big speakers for all to hear. I don't believe you exchanged more than a dozen words with him before you had him sized up perfectly."

"That must have made him squirm," Pete said. "A guy like that wouldn't like witnesses when he's being put down."

"He tried to cut it off, but I jumped in and took over. I'm as patient as they come, but today's little display may have been the last entry in the file I've been putting together on him."

"I think I know his story just by looking at him," Jeff said. "Most likely he hangs out with people like himself, but has no real friends. When he was a child, the other kids probably always called him by his last name. Probably still do. And he'd be one of those who has to check his manhood regularly to make sure it's still there. Certainly not a licensed pilot. I'd bet a month's pay he wouldn't know an empennage if he fell over one, or a tetrahedron if it bit him on the ass."

"You called that one right," Farrell said. "All but one of us is a college graduate and a pilot. You can guess which one is neither. It's easier to strut than to study."

"Our chief mechanic back at Santa Monica, calls them 'shortcutters'," Jeff said.

"Every high profile group has its wannabes," Pete said. "Some people settle for appearance over substance."

Farrell looked across the room and raised his hand.

"Hickman," Bill Farrell said, motioning the man over to where the visitors stood. It was obvious the supervisor had instructed him to apologize. Hickman was slow to respond to his boss's order to face the two men.

"I guess I got here in a shitty mood," Hickman said as though that explained and justified his attitude. "Me and the old lady had a go-round this morning. Then, when you didn't check with ATIS it pissed me—"

"Ben," said his supervisor. "This was supposed to be an apology."

"Hell, Farrell, it's been a bad day."

"Mr. Hickman," Jeff said. "Some occupations don't allow for a bad day. Yours is one of them. The safety of my student is my primary concern and it ought to be yours. You are in a responsible position with no room for moodiness. If you can't leave it at home then maybe you need to find some other line of work."

As expected, Hickman did not take Jeff's words well.

"Who the fuck do you think you are, man?"

"I'm one of the people who pay your salary and I'm not getting my money's worth."

Hickman reached for Jeff, but suddenly found himself lying on the floor. Pete, without removing his hands from his pocket, had swept the big man's legs out from under him.

Looking up at Pete, Hickman said, "This doesn't have anything to do with you."

"Yes it does," Pete said calmly, his hands still in his pockets. "I'm the nervous student who could get flustered to the point of losing control of his aircraft."

"Hickman." Farrell said. "Go back over there and wait for me."

Rising from the floor, Hickman said, "I don't have to take shit from him."

"Well, you have to take shit from me. Either go back to your station or hit the bricks right now."

A macho code as old as masculinity hangups required that Hickman give Jeff and Pete one final threatening look before he could allow himself to go to his communications console as ordered.

"You did say you were a patient man didn't you Mr. Farrell?" Pete said.

"My supply just ran out." Farrell said. "Air traffic control does not include physically attacking a visiting pilot."

"I can't say I'm sorry for what will happen to him," Jeff said. "But I hate to be the one to bring it to a head."

"Tomorrow will be a brighter day because of it," said the supervisor. "You fellas have a good trip."

Hickman gave them a final black stare over his shoulder as they left the center.

Since they were already on the ground they decided to break for lunch at the airport restaurant. It was right below them, on the ground floor beneath the control tower.

The young Indian men were still standing around near the entrance to the eatery.

The small, smoke-filled cafe was jammed with locals and pilots passing through.

They walked past the counter and tables, chose a booth in the back, and settled down to look at their menus.

"After all that excitement," Jeff said, "lunch will probably go down in a lump."

Suddenly, the door to the cafe burst open and an angry Ben Hickman stormed in. He spotted Pete and Jeff and swaggered over to where they were sitting. Loud enough for all to hear, he said, "you bastards got me fired."

Jeff said. "There is some justice in this world after all."

"I'm gonna kick your ass," Hickman said.

Jeff quickly surveyed the space around them. "I've got this," he said and stood. It was less a threat to the man than it was to be in a position to defend himself, if necessary.

Hickman was faster than one might expect a big man to be and swung at Jeff. But Jeff deftly sidestepped as the fist sailed past his head. He grabbed Hickman's arm and, using the man's own weight and forward momentum, caused him to come face first with a steel ceiling support. The post rang like a gong from the impact. Judging from the stunned, vacant look on Hickman's head, his skull must have been ringing, as well. The big man fell backward with a bounce onto his rear in the middle of the restaurant floor.

To Jeff's surprise, a cheer went up from the other customers. Several of the Indian men standing outside had heard the commotion and were pressed against the windows, trying to get a glimpse.

"Do it again, mister," one patron shouted. "Fred here missed it."

The restaurant owner hurried from behind the cash register to where the dazed man was still sitting on the floor, trying to recover his full faculties.

"Sorry," Jeff said. "I tried to keep everything as neat as possible."

"No problem," the owner said. "Hickman's had that coming to him for a long while. I'm just glad I was here to see him get it."

The big man turned over onto his stomach and struggled to his knees. Then he fumbled around for the post to help him make the long, blurry trip to a standing position. Blood trickled from both nostrils to his upper lip. From there, two bloody lines rolled down from the corners of his mouth, causing Hickman to resemble a ventriloquist's dummy.

"You want me to call the sheriff, mister?" the owner asked.

"That depends on what he does when he gets up," Jeff said. "Maybe the sheriff, maybe an ambulance, maybe the coroner."

"Hey buddy," another customer called out to Jeff. "Make Hickman ring the bell again." He was drowned out by laughter.

The owner helped the severely disoriented man to the exit. On wobbly legs, Hickman flung open the front door to the restaurant, roughly pushed two Indian men aside, got into a pickup truck, and sped away, showering the front of the restaurant with gravel.

"I'm amazed," Pete said. "That was as smooth a takedown as I've ever seen and I hold a couple of black belts in a mix of martial arts."

"Judo," Jeff said. "None of that fancy Asian crap for me. Just disable them and get it over with."

"And you hardly touched him."

"Judo is defensive rather than offensive," Jeff explained. "Karate relies on blows and counter blows, he swings at you, you respond. In judo, the opponent defeats himself. You just use his weight and momentum against him."

The two men refused the owner's offer to buy them lunch. They finished their meal with great difficulty. Some of the lunchroom patrons stopped by their table to shake hands with Jeff and thank him for teaching one of the region's renowned bullies a well deserved lesson.

"He'll be a terror for a few days," one man told them. "I feel real sorry for his poor wife and some of the local Indians."

"How will they be affected?" Jeff asked.

"Hickman always goes for the helpless ones. That's the way it is with bullies."

"Shit," Jeff said, slamming a fist down on the table. "Some people are going to suffer because of me."

Another man said, "If it wouldn't of been this, mister, it'd of been something else. People like that fly off over nothing. If he can't find a real enemy, he'll make one up."

It was small consolation.

Jeff felt genuinely depressed as the Skyhawk lifted off the Buffalo Valley Airport runway once again. Any thought of staying the night in that place was forgotten. Neither would have been able to rest. Jeff would agonize for a long time about having played a role in grief that might be inflicted on another.

Chapter Twenty-One

Once aloft, Jeff said, "This was a fine day until we ran into Hickman.

"My grandfather once said 'it takes all kinds to make a world' and my grandmother said 'it doesn't *take* all kinds, but we have all kinds just the same'. I think Hickman proves grandma's point."

The days trials were not over yet.

At altitude, with Buffalo Valley barely out of view, a shadow flashed over them like a dark strobe. It was followed by a light thump at the front of the Skyhawk.

"What was that?" Pete said.

"I think something hit us," Jeff said. "I heard it and I swear I felt it."

The sound had hardly been noticeable above the roar of the engine. But any sound that should not be there and comes without warning can give a pilot a bad moment while cruising high above the earth.

Whatever the case, it had both men's instant and undivided attention.

"I am not enjoying this day," Jeff said.

The engine held its monotonous hum for nearly a minute before they heard a distressing change in the sound. The tachometer registered a slight drop in RPMs. It seemed no more than a minor slowing. At first the engine began to run unevenly. Then it sputtered and threatened to quit altogether. Jeff grabbed the sectional chart and Pete quickly took the checklist down from the sun visor.

"What do you think it was?" Pete said as his training kicked in. He pulled the carburetor heat control part way out to melt any ice that may have formed. When there was no improvement in the engine's performance, ice was eliminated as a suspect. A quick check of the Skyhawk's dual ignition system showed the magnetos were not the problem either.

"We have plenty of fuel," Pete said, checking the gauges.

The Cessna was not completely without power, but could not be depended upon without first locating a mechanic.

"At least the Rockies are behind us," Jeff said, looking down at South Dakota below them. Both were scanning the land for possible landing sites.

Jeff estimated their current position on the sectional chart.

"Buffalo Valley is ten minutes behind us," Jeff said, looking at the aeronautical chart. "An uncontrolled airport near the town of Red Creek is another ten minutes in front of us if we can hold this speed. The book lists some services on the field."

"I hope they include a mechanic," Pete said, turning the Skyhawk slightly off to his left toward Red Creek.

The engine continued slowing, speeding up, slowing, speeding up, at least consistent in its unreliability

The rough, rolling landscape looked hostile. Pete had already spotted several relatively flat, straight possible emergency landing areas between an occasional gully and plateau—if it became necessary.

"Don't waste your safety margin by bleeding off altitude too soon," Jeff said. "You can always descend without power, but you can't climb without it."

Pete held the altitude as best he could until a safe landing could be assured, but the Skyhawk was slowly descending.

"I'll call Red Creek Unicom and see what they've got down there," Jeff said.

The engine continued its eccentric pattern, rising and falling. After each nerve-jangling decrease, Pete and Jeff feared the engine might not recover again, that they would be left with no power at all and find themselves colliding with the rocky maze below.

If they could have run the engine on adrenaline, they would have been in fine shape.

"Where the hell are they?" Jeff said, irritated at the lack of response from the airport.

Finally it came.

"Aircraft calling Red Creek Unicom. Please repeat."

Jeff grabbed the mic again. "Red Creek Unicom, this is Cessna Niner-Niner-X-Ray. We are about two miles west-southwest of the airport, having engine trouble. Do you have a mechanic on the field?"

"We don't have a repair shop, as such, but Chris Hutchins is a licensed Aircraft Maintenance Technician, one of the best. He runs the FBO and restores vintage aircraft. I'm sure he'll have a look at it for you."

"Would you let him know about our problem? We're headed your way. No way we can continue on at this rate."

"Roger, Niner-Niner-X-Ray. I can hear it over the radio."

As they struggled toward Red Creek, Jeff was relieved to see the nearly two-thousand-foot-long dirt strip just ahead.

"We have you in sight, Red Creek."

"Runway two-six is the active. Nobody else is incoming, so just get down any way you can. We are standing by to assist."

With the runway well within gliding distance and altitude to spare, both men breathed a tentative sigh of relief.

Pete reduced power and let the Skyhawk sink toward the runway.

"One consolation," Jeff said. "You're getting some real emergency landing experience."

"I'll try to look on the bright side," Pete said, continuing his descent.

Personally, Jeff would happily have settled for those times when he would reach over and surprise his student by shutting down the power, letting him handle it like a real crisis. But, practicing emergency landing approaches on rural roads, inactive drag strips, and remote fire trails was not the same as being forced to deal with the pressures of an actual emergency. Authenticity meant giving up the luxury of being able to pull up at the last moment.

"Think you can handle this okay, Pete?" Jeff said, although he no longer had any real doubts about his student's skills or how he would react under white-knuckle conditions.

"I'm fine," Pete assured him. If anything, Jeff thought, the student was calmer than the instructor.

"When you're on final, I'd pull the power all the way back, Pete. Better to have a reasonably steady idle than an unreliable rising and falling of the engine, causing the plane to bob up and down like a porpoise."

Pete accepted the suggestion and reduced the power to idle on the final leg. The Skyhawk settled onto the runway with a slight bounce that was no less graceful than some of Pete's early landings at Santa Monica.

"As the old-timers say," Jeff said with a nervous laugh, "'any landing you walk away from is a good one'."

They taxied toward the flight office at the opposite end of the sleepy little airport's runway as awkwardly as it had flown, surging forward with each increase in engine speed.

"Pull up to the office," the Unicom operator said.

Pete did as he was instructed.

A tall, weathered-looking man in his late fifties, wearing greasy coveralls and a Desert Storm Veteran baseball cap, waited for them at the front of the dusty green Korean war-era Quonset building. A classic Stinson taildragger was parked next to them. Parts and tools sat on a workbench at the front of the plane. Pete let the Skyhawk's engine run for a few more seconds so the mechanic could hear the problem. At the man's signal, Pete shut it down.

"Doesn't sound electrical. Gotta be in the fuel system," he said as Pete and Jeff climbed out of the plane. "Howdy boys, I'm Chris Hutchins."

The men introduced themselves and described the mysterious bump at the front of the plane and the unsettling minutes that followed. Hutchins raised the cowling for a look. He reached through one of the front air intakes, pulled at something, and wrenched it free.

"This might be the problem," he said, holding up a clump of feathers and gore that looked as though it had been run through a blender. "What's left of a red-tailed hawk was plugging up one of your air intakes."

"That's all?" Jeff asked.

"I'd better check the system to be sure there is nothing still jammed in there," he said. "No telling how long that will take. Not long, I'd guess."

"I think we're done flying for the day," Jeff said, wiping the sweat from his forehead and looking at the remains of the bird Chris placed next to the nose gear. "Chris, is there any place we can camp?"

"Pick your spot. I'll leave the restroom open for you. There's a shower in there, but go easy on the water. It's scarce hereabouts."

Jeff had wondered many times since they left Los Angeles whether people were becoming nicer as they got farther from the city, or whether he had become too withdrawn and self-involved since his divorce to recognize goodness that was there all the time. Whatever the answer, he was enjoying the openness he found in nearly everyone they met. The renegade air traffic controller at Buffalo Valley was far outnumbered by those who had shown them kindness.

They settled on a flat area between the flight office and the Cessna's parking space to set up their campsite. Meanwhile, Hutchins searched the Skyhawk's air passages and fuel system. He found nothing likely to give them further trouble. He started the engine several times and it ran as smoothly as Jeff and Pete had ever heard it.

"Good as new," Chris said as he shut the cowling.

Hutchins would not accept any payment, claiming he was behind on his quota of good deeds. "The way I see it, all I did was pull a bunch of feathers out of your air vent. But, if you think it was more than that and you really want to pay me back, then you can satisfy the debt by doing something nice for someone else."

"We'll stay alert for the very next good deed opportunity," Pete said.

"I should warn you, though," Chris said with a twinkle, "repaying people isn't a one-shot deal. Once you start, you can never stop."

"Is that written on the wall of an ancient Egyptian tomb or something?" Pete asked.

"It's written on a sheet of paper tacked to the bulletin board in the flight office. The words of my grandmother. She used to say, 'Repayment for a good deed received, is a lifetime of good deeds given'."

Jeff said, "My wise old grandma had a saying, too 'If someone does you a favor it is the giver who gets to decide how it will be repaid'."

"I like that idea," Chris said. "If I plow your field for you, you can't give me a jar of homemade dill pickles and call it square. That being the case, the repayment I require is for each of you to help someone who needs it. Fair enough?"

"A bargain if I ever heard of one," Jeff said.

"We'll get started on that right away," Pete said.

Jeff checked his cell phone and was surprised to find four bars on the reception indicator. Thinking of Stephanie, he excused himself and went to a quiet place to make a call.

Pete also called Melanie.

"There are some coffee, soda, and junk food vending machines at the far end of the office," Chris said, climbing into a restored World War II military jeep. "I'm done for the day. In case I don't see you before you take off in the morning, have a good trip."

The men thanked him and he drove off across the harsh countryside.

Pete picked up two intact feathers from the debris that had once been a hawk. Handed one to Jeff and stuck the other in the band of his baseball cap.

They watched Chris Hutchins' dust trail fade in the distance. "Karma," Jeff said, "is the belief that you get back what you give, good and bad. If everyone repaid debts of kindness, sooner or later their own good deed would come back to them."

"Yeah," Pete said, "but it seems like some people do all the giving, and some do all the getting."

"The chain gets broken."

"Well, we can't start any sooner than now."

As it turned out, *now* would be soon enough.

CHAPTER TWENTY-TWO

When the last aircraft owner had gone home and night descended on South Dakota, the men had the airport to themselves.

Their campfire light flickered against the buildings and was absorbed into the cool blackness around them.

Pete got the aeronautical chart from the plane. "We are southwest of the capital city of Pierre. And we are roughly midway at a point east of Rapid City and west of Sioux Falls." He squinted to see the map by the light of the campfire. "We're near a couple of Indian reservations."

"We can motor to Red Creek tomorrow for supplies," Jeff said, holding the sectional chart closer to the firelight. "We need a few things and—"

Suddenly both men looked up to where the firelight met the darkness and were astonished to see a young Indian boy standing there. He appeared to be about ten years old. They had not heard him approach.

"Hello," Jeff said, relieved that it wasn't a marauding animal. "Come on over by the fire, young man."

Very slowly the boy inched toward them. He stopped a good dozen paces from the fire as if to give himself a head start on a retreat if the strangers turned out to be hostile.

Sensing the boy's caution, Jeff said, "This is Pete. I'm Jeff, what's your name?"

"Jimmy Jeeters," he said quietly. Even from that distance both men could hear deep, rattling lung congestion. He was dressed in ragged clothes too thin for adequate protection against the cool night air.

"What are you doing out here this late, Jimmy?"

"Saw the fire. Thought somebody could help" The bronchial ailment gave the young boy's voice resonance.

"What's the problem?"

"My mother is having a baby."

"Right now?" Pete said.

"Soon, I think."

"Come over and warm yourself by the fire," Jeff said, spooning soup from the pot on the campfire into a metal cup.

Pete offered the boy a seat and handed him the cup. "Kind of late for you to be way out here, isn't it, Jimmy?"

"I live over there," he said, pointing to the west," he said, attacking the soup as though he had not eaten in awhile.

"I'll get some things together and we'll see what we can do."

"Where's your father?" Pete asked the boy, as he quickly pulled the scooters from the back seats of the Skyhawk.

"Don't know," Jimmy said. "Maybe Sioux Falls."

"Are there any relatives or friends nearby who could help?" Pete asked.

Jimmy just shook his head, hungrily finishing the last of the soup.

While Pete assembled the scooters, Jeff grabbed the first aid kit and a small sewing kit from the plane and put them in a daypack with the flashlight, a blanket, and some towels. In moments they were ready for the road.

"Put this on, Jimmy," Jeff said. He handed the boy his windbreaker jacket and helped him into the daypack so there would be room for both of them on the scooter.

"I had pre-med in college," Pete said.

"Good. You're elected," Jeff said.

"But I don't know nothin' 'bout birthin' no babies," Pete said in his best Butterfly McQueen imitation.

"Okay, then I'm elected. I've had a little experience with farm animal births," Jeff said as he readied the gear. "Better than nothing. Is there a doctor in the area, Jimmy?

"One in Red Creek."

"Does he know where you live?"

The boy nodded.

"Pete, why don't you go see if the doctor can come out here."

"We don't have no money for a doctor," Jimmy said.

"Don't worry about that," Pete said. "We'll take care of it."

The motor scooters were removed from the Skyhawk and unfolded.

It was a tight squeeze, but Jimmy was small and they were soon putt-putting side by side down the dark, deserted stretch of road. At a crossroad, Pete took a right turn to the east, toward Red Creek. Jeff and the youngster made a left turn and rode westward for what seemed like a long way for a young boy to walk at night, with only a sliver of the moon to light the way.

"Turn here," Jimmy said at last, tapping Jeff on the left shoulder.

Jeff pulled the scooter onto a flat dirt area. The small headlight revealed what Jeff at first thought was a shed. But the ramshackle building was apparently the family's residence. As they got closer, Jeff could see a dim light coming from inside.

The walls of the makeshift dwelling appeared to be a hybrid affair. The foundation was made of adobe; squares of local earth mixed with water and straw to form into blocks. The roof and several walls were made of materials that had been other things in other lifetimes: metal sheeting, plywood, wooden pallets, shipping crates. All manner of discarded items had been picked up and pieced together to stand between a harsh climate and people with few resources. A tiny ancient camper trailer was attached to the back end of the flimsy structure. It apparently served as the kitchen.

"This way," Jimmy said, leading Jeff into the shack through a thin plywood door on hinges made of leather straps. Years of dragging the door open and shut across a floor of mismatched plywood and rough planks had worn a semi-circular groove.

Faint illumination in the single room came from a kerosene lantern hanging at the end of a length of wire fastened to the ceiling. The place was filled with the smells of kerosene smoke, soured food, and odors generated by people caught between pride and circumstances.

"Ma, I got somebody to help."

In a corner, a woman lay on a torn mat, propped against dirty sofa pillows with the stuffing showing in places. She was half covered by a ragged comforter. The lantern's light was reflected in the perspiration on her face. She looked too old to be having a baby.

"I'm Jeff, ma'am," he said, helping Jimmy remove the daypack. "My partner went for a doctor. Meanwhile, I'll do what I can."

"I am Jaleen Jeeters," she said, wincing in pain as she spoke.

"How far apart are the pains?" Jeff asked.

"Maybe one minute," she said. "Don't have a watch."

"That's close. It should be coming pretty soon," Jeff said. "Jimmy, you have any brothers or sisters?"

"Got an older brother. He ain't here. Had a sister, but she died."

Small wonder, Jeff thought. Bad enough in this place on an early summer evening. What must winters be like?

"Where is your brother?"

"Rapid City. Trying to get work."

"How long will he be gone?"

"Awhile."

Time seemed an alien concept to the boy, as though the dark and light of night and day were merely abstract dividing lines between events.

"A day, a week, a month?" Pete pressed the boy.

"Maybe a couple of days."

"Ma'am," Jeff said to the woman, "Do you remember when your other children were born how long it took after your pains were this close together?"

"Like now," she said, her face twisting in pain. The contractions had begun again.

"Jimmy," Jeff said, "Why don't you wait by the road for Pete and the doctor so they don't miss the turnoff."

The boy did as he was asked. He seemed to understand that Jeff wanted him out of the way while his mother went through this very personal ordeal.

Jeff sat the flashlight on the floor and aimed its beam where he thought it would be needed.

"Mrs. Jeeters, my experience is limited to calves and pigs on my grandparents' farm when I was younger. But, until the doctor gets here, it looks like I'm the best we could come up with on short notice. I'll do what I can."

"It's okay," she said, squeezing her eyes tightly shut. "I think it's coming now."

Jeff opened the daypack and spread one of the towels on the blanket he had brought along. Taking a bottle of iodine from the first aid kit, he poured some of it slowly into the palm of one hand. With the other hand, he rubbed the brownish-red liquid over every surface of skin up to his elbows, repeating the process, just to be sure.

The woman's face was contorted in agony, tears mixed with perspiration on her cheeks. Jeff felt helpless to bring her any immediate relief, so he concentrated on delivering the child.

He could see the very top of the baby's head had begun to emerge. At least there would not be the complication of a baby turned around the wrong way. Jeff tried as much as he could to assist, yet not put too much pressure on the infant's head and neck.

"Push, ma'am," Jeff cried. "Push."

As he shouted encouragement, Jeff could see her trying to help. With each push, the baby emerged more. Finally, he was able to get his hands under its arms. With one great final effort, a new little boy was pulled into the world.

The baby's face looked as though he were crying. All that was missing was the sound. Jeff carefully turned the slippery newborn upside down, as he had seen done so often in the movies, and gave the child a vigorous pat on the back. Almost at once, the newborn gave forth a cry.

"Some welcome, huh, young fellow?" Jeff said. "Mrs. Jeeters, you have another son."

Jeff laid the child on the small bed he fashioned of the blanket and towel. He twisted the umbilical cord at the baby's red, wrinkled belly. Using heavy thread he had dipped in iodine, he tied the cord in two places; the first where he had twisted nature's lifeline at the baby's navel, the second a few inches farther out. With a pair of scissors, he cut the cord between the two points. Then he swabbed the area around the baby's tummy with the remaining iodine. Finally, he wrapped the child in the largest of the towels against the chill of the room and carried him to his mother, who lay exhausted on the pillows. The doctor could deal with the more clinical details when—and if—he arrived.

Jeff had warm memories of helping his grandfather deliver a new calf and a litter of pigs. But the feeling he got from being part of the human birthing process was far more intense and satisfying than anything he had ever experienced before. At the same time, he was troubled by the family's surroundings. He wondered what kind of existence awaited the life he had just helped to start. He determined that being born may have been the easiest part.

"I'll give Jimmy the news, Mrs. Jeeters," Jeff said.

"Wait," she said.

Jeff went over to where the Indian woman lay holding her child.

"This is for you," she said, handing Jeff a small talisman; a hawk carved from a blue stone and strung on a leather thong.

"It has been in my family for a long time. We believe it protects the person who wears it from evil spirits."

"Ma'am, I can't take this," Jeff protested, trying to give it back to the woman. "This is a treasure that you should keep for your children."

"It is our custom to give a gift of something of value to someone who has helped me as you have. Please take it. This is all I have."

Jeff thought about it for a moment, torn between what the object must surely mean to her and her obligation to conform to custom.

"I'm honored to have it Mrs. Jeeters," he said, finally. He dropped the gift carefully into the breast pocket of his shirt and patted it softly, as though it were something precious and fragile.

"I'm just sorry we couldn't find a woman to help you," Jeff said.

"No Indian woman would help me."

"Why not?"

"They say I am a woman of low morals."

Jeff thought for a moment about how, despite the shabby surroundings, the woman seemed to have done the best she could to provide for young Jimmy.

"Somehow I doubt that," he said, deciding to drop the subject.

Jeff stepped out into the cool night air. "Jimmy," he called, "you have a new brother."

The boy showed no emotion at the announcement. Never had Jeff seen anyone so devoid of visible feelings, especially one so young.

"Who's going to take care of you, Jimmy?"

"Don't need nobody. I can take care of myself."

"You're a kid, you need—"

"Car coming," Jimmy said, his breathing deep and rumbling.

Jeff saw headlight beams in the distance and hoped it was the doctor. He could not rest easily until a professional checked his work to make sure nothing was forgotten, and that he had done nothing seriously wrong.

Pete was the first person out of an older model red Chevy pickup truck. He was followed by an elderly man whose white hair and beard were clearly visible, even by the dim light of the moon. He carried a medical bag and hurried toward the house.

"Jeff," Pete said, "this is Doctor Henry."

"Everybody calls me Doc, son," the man said, shaking Jeff's iodine-stained hand as they walked back to the house.

"It's a boy, Doc," Jeff said.

"Good God, man," the doctor said. "You mean it's all over?"

"Yes sir, but I'll feel better after you have a look."

They went inside the little shack.

Examining the child and his mother, Doc gave Jeff a high passing grade and an offer for him to stay on as the permanent, official Red Creek midwife.

"Once in a lifetime is enough, thanks," Jeff said. "I don't think I could stand the pressure."

The old man put a hand on Jimmy's head.

"Young man," Doc said firmly to the boy, "I want to see you at the clinic tomorrow. We have to do something about that cough."

Jimmy simply shrugged.

Beyond the boy's hearing, the doctor said, "If he actually does show up, I've got a bunk at the clinic. I'll keep him there for awhile. He can help out around the place and I can be sure he takes his medication every day and get some decent meals. And it will be one less mouth for his mother to feed."

Only minor post-birth duties remained. Pete, Jeff, and the boy waited outside until Doc finished and joined them there.

"She'll nurse the baby tonight," Doc said. "Then, he'll be in the same cycle as most everyone else in these parts. It will be a constant fight for nourishment and the basic elements of preserving life and health. Those are hard to come by in these parts. It will be a miracle if he survives his first year."

"Doesn't the government offer any help?"

"Health care is available through the U.S. Department of Health. It used to be overseen by the Bureau of Indian Affairs," Doc said. "But the way these folks have to live, and as spread out as they are, it's impossible to keep ahead of it."

"Doc," Jeff said. "Mrs. Jeeters told me no one would help her here because she is 'a woman of low morals'. What, exactly, does that mean?"

"First of all, she's not Mrs. anything. If you understand how people in small towns think, that ought to tell you something. A tribe is like any small town in that way, but the gossip is more vicious among Indians than in most places. Talking about people behind their backs is part of the culture. The threat of that keeps everyone in line and following the rules. This woman has been with many men. She has another older son. Lost a little girl a couple of years ago. Her children probably had different fathers. It's likely even she isn't absolutely sure who some of the fathers are."

"You mean she's a prostitute?" Jeff asked.

"No, she's a survivor. She can't make it alone. If that means making herself available to men now and then, that's the way it has to be. She does what she has to do even when the unfortunate by-product of providing for her children is having more children. She's in her early thirties and so worn down she looks fifty."

"Why aren't the men taking some responsibility?" Pete asked.

"The complete answer to that would take hours to explain," Doc said. "The short version is that when the Indians stopped fighting the U.S. Army they were transformed from warriors and hunters to men without purpose or occupation. In their own minds, the treaties made 'women' out of them. They have never made the transition."

146

"Jimmy seems in pretty good shape, all things considered," Pete said.

Doc shook his head. "He is malnourished, has head lice and chronic bronchitis. He's thirteen-years-old, the size of a ten-year-old with the eyes of a hundred-year-old. He doesn't get any schooling and there's no food in the house. If that's 'good shape' I'm a gopher's grandmother."

"We have some things back at camp that should give them a start," Jeff offered.

"Then what?" Doc said, shaking his head wearily.

"Well, Doc," Pete said, "I thought about that on the way to town to get you. If you have some time, I'd like to run some ideas past you."

Pete and Jeff arranged to meet the old man in Red Creek early the next morning, before the people who would fill his waiting room started to file in.

Back at camp, Jeff's natural sensitivity kicked in when he noted Pete was much quieter than usual.

"Want to tell me about it, Pete?"

It took a moment for Pete to gather the words.

"I was thinking about what Charlie Benson told us that first morning after we started out. He said the only way things will change for the better is to help bring everyone into the winner's circle."

Jeff said, "To have something for themselves that they won't risk losing. Pretty smart guy for an old hippie."

Pete poked at the campfire's embers and added a few small pieces of scavenged brush.

"Jeff, I hope you won't think this is a stupid Pete Sunderland project-of-the-moment, but I want to help the Indians."

"After what we've seen tonight, I certainly don't think it's 'stupid'."

"I was touched and appalled by what we saw and what Doc told us." Pete said. "I want to do something."

"What do you have in mind?"

"I don't know yet."

Both men looked off into the darkness. Neither spoke for several minutes

Finally, Jeff said, "Maybe you should let Doc be your guide."

Both slept fitfully that night, the events of the day replaying in their dreams.

00

They awoke to the sounds of birds singing and squabbling and a bright, sunny sky that seemed to go on forever.

Jeff had an ache in his side and realized that he had been so tired when he went to bed that he had not noticed his sleeping bag was positioned on a rock and that was how he slept the entire night.

"I've got to find a softer sleeping place," Jeff said.

"Come on Kemo Sabe," Pete said, rubbing sleep from his eyes. "We've got deliveries to make and shopping to do. We can get breakfast in town."

Jeff filled a collapsible two-gallon plastic container with fresh water. Pete gathered up all the food that might be useful for the family, including powdered milk, and canned and dried foods and fruits. He loaded them into two daypacks and a cardboard box he found in a dumpster behind the flight office. They fastened the cargo to carrier racks on the backs of the scooters.

The two men motored their way toward the Jeeters home. The impression they had of the terrain from the previous night's ride was dramatically different from the land as seen in full daylight.

The region had more ups and downs than was evident in the dark. Occasionally they would come upon a gorge that may have gotten its start with the glaciers. The land was further etched out by thousands, perhaps millions, of years of wind, rain and flash floods.

Had it not been for dry wild grasses covering the ground, a blue sky above them, and a spindly tree here and there, the white walls of a ragged ridge in the distance might have been mistaken for a moon crater.

Jimmy was not there when they arrived at the shack. They dropped off the food. After a brief explanation of how to prepare the dried food packets, the two men headed down the road toward Red Creek.

Chapter Twenty-Three

Red Creek sat many miles from any major highway in a parched region between the South Dakota badlands to the west and the Iowa and Minnesota borders to the east. It was not so much a town as it was a collection of wood frame buildings backed up against a dry creekbed. If not for the post office and a church it could hardly be described as a town, at all.

As with most settlements, Red Creek got its start because of the availability of water sufficient to support a population. A well supplied the town with drinking water since nineteenth century settlers first gave the place its name.

Even the creek that Red Creek took its name from was at odds with the facts. It was neither red, nor did it seem to be much of a creek. Brown was the prevailing local summertime color. But brown lends itself poorly to the poetic dispositions of those who name creeks, so red won the day.

In the late winter and early springtime the rains would create picturesque marsh ponds and tall plains grasses. Snow runoff from the higher elevations would cascade down to fill the depression behind the town and renew its status as a creek. Red Creek's creek was distinguishable as a waterway only because it was a dry, flat spot that lay slightly lower than the dry, flat spot the town was built upon. When the rains stopped, the landscape changed dramatically.

The hot sun had turned the region arid, transforming it into the kind of land given to Indians when no other uses could be found for it.

A hitching post along the row of the town's buildings, a relic of an earlier time, still did occasional duty for ranchers who rode in on horseback. More than a century of leather reins tied to it had worn the wood smooth.

149

Main Street could have been called "Only Street," since there were no others. On one side of the rutted road running between the sleepy settlement's buildings was the post office, which was also the general store with two vintage gas pumps at the curb. On the other side of the street was a small restaurant, which was also the town saloon. They had been told by Doc Henry that Red Creek was too small to have anything that could enjoy the luxury of serving only one purpose. That included the Lutheran minister, who was also the justice of the peace, and Myra Mae Foster, who waitressed at the Red Creek Bar and Grill—among other things.

"Not many life signs," Jeff said.

Several older model cars and pickup trucks were parked along the street. A dog slept outside the post office, too lazy to object to flies that had gathered on his nose.

"I'll bet a dust devil swirling through town draws a crowd," Pete said.

"Moseying is probably a big activity here," Jeff said. Almost as he spoke, a local citizen came out of one of the buildings and moseyed to the opposite side of the street.

The Lutheran Church, a wooden cross on its white steeple, stood at one end of the town. It was the only building that had been painted in recent times. At the opposite end was the structure that housed Doc Henry's clinic and his second-floor living quarters. The weathered wood edifice matched its neighbors in faded paint and uncomplicated design.

"Buddy boy," Pete said, "I do believe we are standing on the windswept outer edge of nowhere."

Compared to the rest of the town, a small group gathered on the porch outside Doc's office seemed like a crowd. The clinic would not officially open for another hour, yet they had already begun to file in for whatever relief Doc could offer.

A handful of white residents wearing their afflictions like neon signs distanced themselves from several Indians who had come in from the reservations. The Indians offered few clues beyond an unavoidable limp or muffled cough as to why they waited in front of Doc's medical practice. At least, no complaint reached Pete and Jeff's ears.

The two men fell into line behind a pair of boys who stood together in the ragged column. One was in his late teens and somehow looked familiar. The smaller boy turned toward them and Jeff realized it was Jimmy Jeeters.

"Jimmy," Jeff said. "You took Doc's advice. How'd you get here so fast?"

"Clarence got home and we hitched a ride," the boy said, gesturing down the street to a rusty, beat up Ford pickup truck that had once been blue.

The older boy was about eighteen.

"This is your brother?" Pete said.

"Yeah," Jimmy said. "These are the guys that helped with the baby."

Jimmy would look like his older brother in five years or so, both in physical features and the anger that burned beneath the surface.

"You feeling any better this morning?" Pete asked Jimmy. When the boy started to respond, his elder signaled him to be quiet.

"Sorry," Pete said. "I'm not being nosy, just interested."

The older boy eyed Pete and Jeff with suspicion. He was obviously not accustomed to sharing his troubles with white people. It was likely there had been few who cared enough to inquire about any aspect of their lives. Now that one had, he seemed wary.

"If you were a blue-eyed blonde female paleface with big tits, maybe we'd talk about it," he said, avoiding eye contact with either of the men.

"Where would you find a blue-eyed blonde around here?" Jeff asked.

"We get some," the boy said. "They mostly come from eastern colleges to do charity work among the lowly Indians. When they have enough brownie points to get into heaven or get a job with a big company, they're outta here."

"You think I could earn a few credits with God or General Motors by asking about your brother?" Pete said with a smile and a friendly pat on the younger boy's shoulder.

"Maybe some little ones," said the older brother, softening slightly.

The ice had been chipped, if not broken.

The older boy kept looking at the hawk feather in Pete's cap.

Finally, he said, "we have to earn our feathers here."

Pete took the cap off and looked at the feather. "I doubt that I earned it in the way you mean. But I hope you'll believe me when I tell you I worked hard for it." Pete explained briefly about the hawk incident and the source of the feather.

"Are you interested in airplanes?" Jeff asked, knowing perfectly well that all young boys are interested in airplanes.

"I took aeronautics in college."

"You went to college?" Pete said, a little too quickly, then felt a little ashamed of himself for being surprised that an Indian might have gone on to higher education.

"Got a scholarship and went to junior college in Rapid City for part of a year."

"What did you learn there?" Jeff asked.

"How to sit in little rooms for many hours without moving."

"A valuable skill in today's world," Jeff said. "Why didn't you finish?"

"I didn't do very good. I couldn't keep up."

"You're not dumb."

"The others didn't have no trouble," he said, looking at the ground.

"Gotta be something else," Jeff assured him.

The young man seemed to appreciate that Jeff had rejected lack of intelligence as a possibility. Such an attitude was apparently not within Clarence Jeeters' range of experience with white people.

"How did the job search go?"

"Didn't find nothing."

"Why did you go all the way to Rapid City to look for work?"

"Nothing around here for an Indian."

A tap on the window from inside the office attracted Jeff and Pete's attention. Doc directed the men to go to the back of the building.

"We have an early appointment with Doc," Jeff said. "Good luck guys." A quick survey of those in the lineup and they decided there were no pressing emergencies that demanded immediate attention.

At the rear door, the old man motioned them into a dark, cluttered office that smelled of disinfectants and medications. Every sound echoed against the hard surfaces of the walls and wooden floors and the white enamel cabinets and equipment. The furniture was sparse and of many eras, not including any recent ones. If not for some electrical devices plugged into wall sockets, they might well have stepped into a scene from the early twentieth century.

"Quite a crowd gathering out there, Doc," Jeff said. "You're a pretty popular guy."

"Not only am I the best non-federal government doctor in these parts," Doc Henry said, "I'm the only one."

"Why aren't there more?" Pete said, leaning on a dented dark green file cabinet.

"The rest went to Beverly Hills where there is already one physician for every fifty people. The population there is happy to pay through the nose for all those big words doctors had to learn in medical school."

"It's obvious you aren't here for financial security," Jeff said. "How do your patients pay you?"

"Pay me?" The old man broke out in laughter. "That's funny," he said, smacking his knee. "If someone actually paid me I'd need a doctor myself for a stroke or heart attack from the shock. Those who can afford it pay a little something. Some bring in a chicken now and then, a few eggs. My real payment is in feeling useful by taking up some of the slack. Out here I can occasionally believe that my existence is actually of value."

An ancient refrigerator clicked on with a heavy whir.

"But you have to have some kind of cash flow to operate." Pete said.

"I had a good practice in Albuquerque. After my wife died ten years ago I sold everything I owned. I bought this place and put the rest of the money into income investments. The interest and dividends keep us going and keep me in beans. It's never enough, of course, and it's getting worse as the population increases, prices go up, and the dollar's buying power goes down. A few volunteers from the reservations and a couple of local church ladies who actually practice their religion keep us operating."

"What made you leave the city?" Jeff said.

"It was coming on for a long time. Over the years I found myself getting farther away from the reasons I got into medicine in the first place. I was sick to death of hearing pampered people bitch about trivial ailments that the Indians wouldn't even think to mention."

"Your respect for them seems to put you in the minority. I notice some of the locals kept their distance from the Indians waiting outside."

"We're a multi-cultural land. I'm apparently one of a handful of white residents who see that as interesting rather than threatening.

"It would be pretty dull if we were all the same," Jeff said.

"Sure it would," Doc said. "But, human nature being what it is, people are suspicious of anyone different from themselves. Some think they need to keep someone around they can feel superior to. They don't have confidence to believe that customs that don't match their own is no skin off their asses. What's the difference if a person chooses to pray in the quiet of the Lutheran Church down the street or if they dress in feathers and skins and dance around in a circle of fellow believers. If there is a God, I'm sure He or She cares more about how we treat each other than about how we worship."

"It sounds as though medical needs are only part of the problem here," Jeff said.

"Rampant alcohol and drug abuse, a high infant mortality rate, constant exposure to the elements, mass unemployment, poor diet, low self-esteem . . ."

"We witnessed some of that just now," Jeff said. "A bright young Indian kid who dropped out of college because he says he couldn't keep up with the others. He thinks he's stupid."

"Competition is the big factor in that," Doc said. "Indians grow up learning to work as a team, helping each other, supporting each other through their common misfortunes. Individual effort is tolerated only insofar as it advances the tribe. In the white world, everything is a game where people work against each other to excel. That is completely against the Indian culture. A white college curriculum swamps them before they can adjust to it. They never catch up.

"If they start out at an Indian college and later switch over to a white university, they tend to do much better than if they began at a white school."

"Are there many Indian colleges?" Jeff asked.

"Not nearly enough," Doc said. "The ones that exist are underfunded and have a hard time attracting competent teachers and getting accreditation. The people who most need the education can't afford one. The people who could afford to help either can't see the problem or aren't interested."

"Don't the Indians have any political muscle?"

Doc huffed and smiled.

"Every four years the politicians stop by. They put on feather headdresses and have their picture taken with tribal leaders for the newspapers and television. They make a lot of promises and then you don't hear from them for another four years. Meanwhile these folks are trying to get by day to day just trying to feed their kids. If you ask me, the Indians would become more self-reliant if they got neither help nor promises.

"Occasionally you hear talk about emancipation, but it never goes anywhere. Some say cutting them loose would free the Indians to improve their lot. Others say it would amount to abandoning them after having made them completely dependent."

"Which one is correct?" Pete said.

"Both," Doc said. "With the help of land-hungry 19th century settlers the U.S. Government destroyed the Indian culture beyond any hope of complete repair. Federal efforts to help have been pathetic at best, lost in a bureaucratic mire like everything else government touches."

"What made you come to this place in particular," Pete asked.

"I heard about the dismal health problems here so I checked it out, found it was far worse than I'd heard, so I set up shop."

"Why not on the reservation?"

"I didn't want to be on Indian land because it would fall under Bureau of Indian Affairs and tribal regulations. Red Creek is between two reservations and close enough to a couple of others for me to do some good. I can do things my way here without the BIA or tribal leaders shining a flashlight up my ass."

"Your clinic is not exactly Johns Hopkins," Pete said, "but it seems to have the basics."

"There's never enough of anything. My X-ray machine is a castoff. Still, I'm lucky to have it. My antique Underwood typewriter would make a good boat anchor. An old friend and colleague in Albuquerque sends me medical journals so I'm able to stay only slightly behind on the latest developments. Mrs. Caruthers comes in twice a week to keep my records straight."

"Doc," Pete said, "I want to help improve things.

"I figured that's what you had in mind when you said you had some ideas. Look son, I know you mean well, but the problems here are pretty complex. It would take a lot of time and money to get anything started."

"I have plenty of both," Pete said as he took out his checkbook, wrote a check and handed it to Doc. "This is payment for that house call you made last night. Maybe it will give you some breathing room."

"A thousand dollars?" Doc said, wide-eyed. "You sure know how to get my attention."

"It's only money, Doc. But I didn't come here to do the easy thing. That's the last check I'll write. No amount of money can buy what these folks need most. You must have known that when you came to Red Creek. Until last night, I didn't realize it, but that's why I'm here, too."

Jeff sat silently by, seeing Pete in an entirely new light.

The old doctor looked over the top of his reading glasses at the face of the earnest young man.

"Pete, I look at you and think of the legion of well-intentioned idealists who have come here and gone. They made some kind of effort, became intimidated by hard-case anti-government militants, or disheartened by the sheer volume of the poverty. They finally left and the people are no better off than before they arrived."

"I think I'm tougher than that."

"I wonder if you have any real idea what you'd be getting into," Doc said, sagging into an elderly wooden swivel chair behind a scarred desk that had long ago lost most of its veneer.

"A certain element hereabouts enjoys keeping the Indians dependent so they can continue to hate them for their dependence."

"Now there is a sick pattern of logic," Jeff said.

"It comes down to power," Doc said. "I theorize it's a birth defect that shows up every so often in the population. You never know which one of us will be predisposed to cancer or heart disease or emphysema, who will be left-handed, blue-eyed, or a genius. I believe it works like that with some personality quirks, too. A certain percentage of live births turns out one of those goddamn control freaks. They take over some unimportant corner of their little universe, turn it into a personal fiefdom, and take perverse pleasure in terrorizing anyone who comes within their area of imagined authority."

"See, Pete," Jeff said. "You thought your father was a nasty old bastard, when the poor man just has a birth defect."

"There are oppressors everywhere," Doc said, "and that's only part of what you'd be up against."

"I already know about oppression, Doc," Pete said. "Candidates for national office come to my father for advice and money and to touch the hem of the kingmaker's garment. The power they give him in return provides him with an even larger club to beat them over the head with in the future. I lived in that man's house for twenty-five years, so I have been worked on by the best. The experience did give me an advantage. It helped me develop a pretty thick hide. Maybe I can make a difference here. I sure as hell haven't made much of a contribution anywhere else."

The old man searched Pete's face for some clue to his sincerity and his strength. The only sounds that could be heard were the ticking of an antique Regulator schoolhouse clock on the wall and the whirring of a 1960s model Philco refrigerator.

After a thoughtful pause, Doc said, "I take it you're asking for my help?"

"I'm asking you for direction," Pete said. "They need your medical skills and your advocacy more than anything else you can do. What I'd like from you is some idea of what the next step should be."

"You fellows came in by airplane, didn't you?"

"Jeff and I have been traveling while I work on getting my pilot's license. The plane is out at Chris Hutchins' airport."

"Think you can land that thing on a graded dirt road?"

"Doc," Jeff said, "You just described every small town air strip between here and California"

"I'll meet you at the airport around three o'clock this afternoon," Doc said. "I should be finished here by then."

CHAPTER TWENTY-FOUR

After their talk with Doc, Pete and Jeff decided to walk down to the Red Creek Bar and Grill and have some breakfast.

The saloon half was separated from the dining area by a chest-high fake bamboo planter with dusty, faded plastic ivy hanging over its sides; a failed 1950s attempt at modernization. The smell of food being prepared in the kitchen mingled with the smell of beer from the bar.

When the floor covering was first laid down on top of the original plank flooring forty years earlier, the manufacturer would have called the material 'linoleum'. Local residents still did. The vinyl had been compressed by many generations of customers walking on it, squeezing it into the cracks, knots, and wood grain of the underlayment. Clearly showing through were the outlines of nail heads hammered into rough sawn boards by carpenters long since consigned to the little plot behind the Lutheran Church at the end of the street.

At a time of day when most folks still have doubts about whether they can get a normal breakfast past their palates without nausea, a half-dozen habitual boozers and local riffraff had already lined up noisily at the bar, drinking straight liquor and boilermakers. Diners were outnumbered at least two to one by saloon patrons.

Layers of accumulated kitchen smoke from thousands of mealtimes that wafted into the dining room had turned the tin tiled ceiling an unappetizing brown. When it was first painted over, the ceiling had been something close to white.

Covering the walls were faded photos of the townspeople's forbears dating back to when photography was a young art.

It was doubtful that the red-and-white-checkered curtains at the windows had ever been washed. After years of hanging there, permeated by kitchen grease and cigarette smoke, then baked brittle by the sun, they would certainly crumble at any attempt to launder them now.

If the restaurant was a conflict of styles and eras, so was its only waitress.

Myra Mae Foster was a living monument to late nights and smoky places. In her late fifties, her makeup was too vivid and too amply applied. Instead of hiding her deep facial lines and misplaced features as she had apparently intended, Myra Mae had accented her flaws to the point of caricature.

Her dress was too short for someone her age and with legs that heavy. The blouse was cut too low to suit the local corps that established and monitored the town's moral standards and who did their own drinking in private and their carousing out of town. Myra Mae's hairstyle was only slightly more modern than girls wore when the restaurant's linoleum was new.

Myra Mae probably considered the nametag on her blouse a professional touch. It was completely unnecessary, however, since everyone in the region knew her. Many quite intimately.

She would get off work at seven o'clock, go home to her simple one bedroom upstairs living space down the street that barely qualified as an apartment. There she would change into one of the four dresses she owned, not counting her waitress uniforms. By seven o'clock each evening she would be back, seated at the bar in the next room. There she would remain until closing time when someone would have to help her home. Odds were good the Samaritan would still be with her in the morning. There had been a lot of half-remembered nights for Myra Mae Foster over the years, as the lines in her face deepened and her hopes for a bright future dimmed further.

"I'll have the number four breakfast," Pete said, ordering from the menu. "Be right back, Jeff. Gotta find the little boy's room."

Jeff was alone at the counter when the door flew open, startling most of the patrons.

Ben Hickman had made a grand entrance. His nose was covered with a bandage.

"Draw me a beer Abe," Hickman shouted. The demand was for the benefit of cronies and customers as much as for the bartender. He laid down a cloud from the cigarette that hung out of the opposite side of his mouth from a snaggle-toothed smile. He had some crude remarks for Myra Mae, with no consideration for the more refined sensibilities of restaurant patrons. The waitress ignored him.

When he got around to scanning the room to see who he had been putting on his show for, Hickman spotted Jeff.

"Well, now," Hickman said, leaning in close and blowing smoke into Jeff's face. "Look what dropped out of the sky like bird shit."

"Hello Ben," Jeff said, barely looking up from his coffee.

"Hey, fellas," Hickman called to his bar buddies. "This is one of the guys I told you about. The ones sucker punched me and got me fired."

"Did you tell them the whole story, Ben, or did you leave out the part where you cried for your mommy?" Jeff remained seated and turned his back on Hickman.

Hickman took advantage of Jeff's contemptuous inattention to swing a well-leveraged arm and balled up fist at the seated man, striking him on the back of the head. The blow spun Jeff off his counter stool, face down on the floor.

Hickman had lost all pretense of a smile. "You got lucky the last time, prick." he said. He reached behind his back, under the shirt that hung out over his jeans, and pulled out a large handgun. He aimed the cheap knockoff of a Colt .45 semi-automatic directly at Jeff's head.

Jeff rolled over on his back and looked up at Hickman towering above him.

No one noticed that when the gun came out that Myra Mae had made a quick phone call.

"I'll give you thirty seconds to put that thing away, Hickman," Jeff said.

"What are you gonna do about if from down there, bird shit."

Jeff did not want to alert Hickman to the fact that Pete had returned and was standing directly behind the armed man.

Pete crept to within inches of the bully, cupped his hands to his mouth to amplify his voice and shouted, "Look out behind you, Hickman!"

Hickman spun around in awkward surprise. Pete gave him a quick punch to his already-injured face, jamming the lighted cigarette against the startled man's bare skin. The stunned bully relaxed his grip on the gun just long enough so Pete could snatch the weapon away with a quick twist of the wrist.

"And you don't get this back until the end of the school term, young man," Pete said, holding the gun between his thumb and forefinger.

"One of those birth defects we were talking about earlier," Jeff said, rubbing his aching head and struggling to his stool at the counter.

"Nothing smells worse than a mouth-breather with buzzard breath." Pete said.

Pete sized up Hickman as a man who, more than most, hated to have his manhood or his intelligence questioned. Which, of course, made those things all the more attractive to use on him.

"I can't believe that even a mental peewee like you fell for that old 'look-out-behind-you' trick, Ben," Pete taunted. He pressed the button that released the magazine on the huge handgun and let it slide out into his hand. "Sorry I took so long, Jeff," Pete said.

Hickman growled, "You talk pretty big when there are two of you and a gun."

"Well, that's odd," Pete said. "When you had the gun and a bar full of fellow rednecks, you were a 'big man'. When it's me holding your gun, I'm a 'big talker'. What is it with you and restaurants, anyway, Ben? We never seem to get through a whole meal lately that you don't show up."

Pete leaned toward Hickman. "I'm going to have to punish you for that, Benny," he said, a dark, demented look coming over Pete's face in a comical blend of Peter Lorre and Jack Nicholson. "Would you *like* me to punish you, Benny?"

"It ain't over yet, asshole," Hickman said, blood trickling down onto his upper lip from beneath the bandage.

"Oh, Ben, it is so close to being over that you wouldn't believe me if I told you," Pete said, aiming the gun at Hickman. With his free hand, Pete suddenly pulled back the slide assembly. Hickman jumped as though he had been shot, but the action had merely ejected the remaining bullet from the gun's firing chamber and sent it flying upward. Pete caught it in midair. He slipped the cartridge into the magazine, which he dropped into his pocket. Without taking his eyes off Hickman, Pete began to disassemble the gun and toss the individual parts onto the floor.

"What are you doing, man?" Hickman said.

"I'm taking it apart," Pete said quietly. "And when I'm done, Benny, unless you're a very good boy, I'm going to do the same thing to you."

"Aw, come on, Pete," Jeff said. "I wanted to take him apart."

"You got to beat him up the last time, Jeff. It's my turn."

"Oh, all right," Jeff said, going back to his coffee. "But I get the next one all to myself."

Several of the men in the saloon were on their feet and had moved toward the restaurant, a move that did not escape Pete's notice.

"Now, in the unlikely event that Benny starts winning, Jeff, you must promise me you won't jump in unless those bozos in the bar do something stupid."

"Certainly not," Jeff said, casting a threatening look at the men that stopped their lame advance. "We don't want it to be said we ganged up on old Ben. We want everyone here to know exactly what happened. So there's no mistake—this time."

While most of those present probably hoped the tyrant would be humbled, few had any reason to believe Pete was capable of pulling it off. Hickman was a full head taller than Pete and close to a hundred pounds heavier.

"Hey, Benny," Pete said, flipping the stripped frame of the weapon to the floor and moving closer to Hickman. "It's not a gun anymore. Now it's a pile of metal. And I'm making a citizen's arrest."

"For what?"

"Being ugly without a license," Pete said.

By the time Ben Hickman's fist reached the spot where Pete's face had been, Pete no longer occupied that space and Hickman was doubled from a painful punch to his sternum.

"Oh-for-one, Sunderland," Pete said, a silly grin on his face, dancing around with his fists in the air like an old-time prizefighter. "Want to try again?"

As it happened, Hickman did want to try again. But when he lunged, Pete nearly destroyed what remained of the man's face with a series of quick punches that ended with kicks to the groin, midsection and head, sending him crashing onto a pinball machine in a fiery shower of sparks and flying glass. When the legs of the machine collapsed, Hickman fell forward at Pete's feet.

"Sunderland scores the extra point," Jeff yelled, "and the crowd goes wild!"

And the small Red Creek Bar and Grill crowd did go wild as one of the region's major tormentors lay bleeding in the rubble of broken wood and glass and scattered gun parts. If any of Hickman's bar buddies had considered taking on Pete or Jeff, they had changed their minds and went back to their drinks.

Pete took a high five from Jeff as he hopped onto his stool at the counter.

"Karate," Pete said. "Unlike judo, you get to actively kick the shit out of your opponent. It's a lot more fun."

To the astonished waitress, Jeff said, "Whatever my friend is drinking and a couple of aspirin for me."

"Coffee, please."

"Don't forget," Jeff said, "The very next guy who comes at us with a gun is mine."

"Absolutely," Pete said apologetically.

Hickman stirred and tried to rise.

Without getting up, Pete spun around in his stool and kicked the bloodied and dazed man to the side of his head, knocking him completely unconscious.

"That didn't count," Pete said, "I had already started on him."

The sheriff's deputy who answered the call put handcuffs on the badly disoriented Hickman. It took some time to convince the deputy that a man the size of Ben Hickman could have suffered so much damage at the hands of a man the size of Pete Sunderland. But witness after eager witness came forward to testify as to who started it and who finished it.

Hickman was arrested for battery on Jeff, attempted assault with a deadly weapon, and reckless endangerment. On top of that, according to the deputy, Hickman was carrying a concealed firearm without a permit. Plus, he was carrying it in a business establishment where alcohol was served. That alone could get him some jail time.

With Jeff's help, the lawman located the gun parts scattered about. Pete gave him the loaded clip. Myra Mae found an empty bread wrapper to carry everything in.

"That ought to hold him for awhile," Jeff said, as Pete paid the tab. It included the cost of a new pinball machine and something extra to the waitress for cleaning up the mess.

"He'll be out on bail in an hour, hon," Myra Mae said with neither regret nor enthusiasm. She had few remaining illusions. Years of expecting nothing and getting what she expected had conditioned her so that she never suffered disappointment. She was a woman who had gained control of life's ups and downs by eliminating both.

Indeed, the deputy did not have to drive Hickman to the jail in the county seat. He was free in the time it took his fellow low-life to pool enough cash to pay the bail to the Lutheran minister who wore his black Justice of the Peace jacket for the occasion. Hickman was free until the next time the circuit court judge came through.

But Hickman may as well have been in jail that day for all the more movement he was capable of.

After Doc Henry patched him up, Carolyn Hickman came to pick her husband up at the clinic where his pals had taken him for treatment. Doc noticed she had a swollen eye and a split lower lip.

"I slipped and fell against the kitchen table," she said.

Doc knew better, but didn't press the issue. She refused his offer to dress the injury.

"Those broken ribs will have Ben's chest tender for awhile, Mrs. Hickman," Doc said.

The swollen testicles would mend themselves in their own good time. Or not.

"He'll need to be awakened every two hours throughout the night because of the concussion."

Having said that, Doc knew Carolyn Hickman would not lose an opportunity to get an uninterrupted night's sleep.

Chapter Twenty-Five

Chris Hutchins was grinning broadly when Jeff and Pete pulled up in front of the flight office and parked their scooters beside the Skyhawk. "I hear you fellows performed another valuable public service this morning."

"Good news travels fast in these parts," Pete said. "How'd you hear about that so soon?"

"We have telephones here now, you know. They're faster than most motor scooters. I thought you boys would be gone by this time, not hanging around torturing the locals."

"Trying to get rid of us, Chris?" Jeff said.

"Are you kidding? Before you fellas got here, all we had for entertainment were one snowy television channel and a poker deck with the eight of diamonds missing. Stay as long as you like."

"Pete," Jeff said. "Are you up for yet another good deed?"

"If you count this morning's activities, we're running way ahead on our quota, aren't we?"

"Not according to Chris here."

"That's right," Chris said. "You can never overdo good deeds."

"Those two kids at Doc's office should be finished by now," Jeff said. "It's a long way to walk on a hot day."

"You drive," Pete said, tossing the Cessna's keys to Jeff.

They had no trouble locating the boys. They had barely taken off when they spotted the boys.

"There they are," Pete shouted as they cruised a hundred feet above the dirt road west of Red Creek. Taking care to avoid power poles and lines that ran parallel to the road, Jeff sat the Skyhawk down just ahead of the boys. He kept the engine running and waited for Jimmy and Clarence to catch up to them. The boys jumped into the rear passenger seats, as near to excited as either was ever likely to be.

167

The Cessna climbed quickly to several hundred feet above the road. At 140 miles an hour the Skyhawk was at their destination in much less time than it would have taken the boys on foot.

"That's our camp," Clarence shouted as they passed over the cluster of buildings.

"Which one is your place?" Jeff shouted.

"There," Charlie said, indicating a grouping of flimsy structures below.

Jeff had not realized on his first visit in the dark that there were other buildings in the area. He put the Cessna into a steep banking turn around the settlement. People streamed out of the houses to see what was happening above them. Then he circled wide to land toward the buildings from about a half mile down the road. As the craft touched the surface, they could see children running toward them in the distance.

"Not much of a ride for you guys," Pete said as the two jumped down from the Skyhawk. "We'll do better the next time."

The two brothers waved to the pilots as the Cessna turned around, rolled down the road and took off again toward Red Creek Airport, leaving the boys and the running children behind in the prop wash.

Clarence and Jimmy would be the village heroes that day, telling everyone about their brief adventure.

Chapter Twenty-Six

Doc Henry arrived at the Red Creek Airport just minutes after Jeff and Pete and brought his old pickup to a stop in front of the office.

"You fellas made some extra work for me," Doc said. "I haven't seen anyone in such bad shape since there was a twelve-car pileup on the interstate a couple of years back."

"I guess working on Hickman was kind of recreational for you, Doc?" Pete said.

"Doctors are not allowed to take pleasure in such things, son," Doc said with a straight face. "Now, speaking as a citizen of Red Creek—"

"I think Hypocrites just flipped over in his grave."

Once in the air, Doc gave them directions and narrated the tour, reeling off a long list of problems experienced by the Indians: diseases, a predisposition to alcoholism, drug addiction, a far higher incidence of theft, murder, spousal and child abuse, and the prejudices they faced from whites they came in contact with.

"On top of all that," Doc said, "they are susceptible to all the other troubles visited upon citizens of this century, regardless of skin pigmentation or economic status."

"What do they do for a living," Jeff said.

"Whatever they have to to get by. Hell, these people were hunters. When the white people killed off the buffalo, they may as well have killed the Indians, too. A lot of them did. Then the government came along and forced a whole new way of life on them. The United States of America, with its freedom of religion, shoved Christianity down the throats of a people that had a religion thousands of years older than any other. Then the government expected the Indians to stop fighting and ease right into this new lifestyle. That was well over a century ago and most still haven't adapted. They just got ground up in a malignant welfare system.

The average annual income here is less than a thousand dollars. A county within one of the reservations is listed as the poorest in the United States."

The old man pointed out the windshield.

"There's your airfield," Doc said, indicating a dirt road that led to a few buildings.

Jeff made one pass over the cluster of wooden shacks and old trailers to check the road for obvious hazards. Seeing none, he sat the Skyhawk down, rolled the plane to a stop in front of one of the dilapidated buildings, and cut the engine.

A woman and several small girls peeked out at them from behind curtains made of material that looked like it may originally have come from flour sacks. Some of the buildings appeared nearly as bad as they remembered the Jeeters place.

"Folks out here don't get much medical attention," Doc said. "It's too far to town. I try to ride a regular route, but there're just too many of them."

"I thought you said they were provided with health care," Pete said.

"It's there," Doc said, "but these folks don't trust anything run by the federal government. Their attitude is not entirely justified, but you can see how they might feel. They use the facilities only when they have to. By that time their condition or disease is usually so far advanced that there isn't much help for them. Besides, living conditions are so bad that it's impossible to keep ahead of their health problems. They come to me because I don't judge them or give them any hassle. Most of all, I think, because I'm not with the government."

"Aren't you under Bureau of Indian Affairs and tribal control out here, Doc?" Jeff asked.

"When I come here I'm a guest of the people who invited me. Neither the BIA or the elders and tribal police can argue with that."

Pete and Jeff stayed with the Skyhawk, surrounded by children of the settlement as Doc finished his rounds. Then the three men shooed the kids to a safe distance, climbed into the aircraft once more and returned to Red Creek.

Back at the airport, Doc stepped from the Skyhawk and said, simply, "Walter Lonetree."

"Who's that?" Pete asked.

"There are two basic Indian factions here. There are those who figure the white man is here permanently, so they may as well resign themselves to being part of the twenty-first century. Then there are those who want to return to the old ways, with no influence from the whites. Walter Lonetree and his traditionalists cause most of the local ruckus. He and his anti-government sidekicks sandbagged themselves in an old shack a couple of years ago and held off federal agents with guns for six days. The whole bunch of them will be on probation for a long time. He's crude, he's rude, he's a pain in the ass, and he's the man you ought to see first."

"If he's all that, why talk with him?" Pete asked.

"Because, not only is everyone afraid of him, no one knows better than Walter Lonetree what needs fixing. And, once you get past the macho bullshit, you will see that nobody cares more about his people than he does."

"Where do we find him?" Pete asked.

"Billy Iron Feather's general store is where they usually hang out," Doc said, pointing at a small dot in the road west of the airport on the sectional chart Jeff handed him,.

"Is that road anything like the one we just landed on?" Pete asked.

"Yep. It'll take you right up to the store," Doc said, setting his finger on the chart where two lines crossed at an intersection of county routes designated as unimproved roads.

"It occurs to me that an airplane might come in handy around here," Pete said.

"A fleet of airplanes," said the old man. "And a battalion of doctors, paramedics and midwives. Pete, we need so many things I'd have trouble deciding which should come first."

"In that case," Jeff said, "anything we do will be right."

"Jeff," Pete shouted. "You said 'we'. Doc, did you hear that? Jeff said 'we'. You're my witness."

Shaking his head, Doc said, "God save us from white guilt." He got into his truck and drove off in the direction of his clinic.

CHAPTER TWENTY-SEVEN

There were no moving vehicles in sight when Pete sat the Skyhawk down on the bumpy dirt stretch leading to the crossroad.

As Doc predicted, they found a ragtag renegade band leaning against a store in the middle of a remote, treeless area where the store's porch overhang offered the only shade.

Several old pickup trucks were parked in front. A half-dozen Indian men in their twenties and thirties were trying their best to look cool, even though an airplane was driving down the road toward them.

Pete nosed the Cessna toward the row of weathered buildings. The two pilots quickly sized up the small gathering before shutting down the engine and stepping out of the plane. Some of the men had the classic features of Native Americans they had seen in old photos. Others were a mix of hair and skin coloring and might have gone unnoticed on any city street corner in America, the result of nearly two centuries of white presence.

The smell of liquor too fresh to be left over from the night before blended with body odor and cigarette smoke that hung heavily over the group.

One man stood next to a pay phone, slightly apart from the rest. Although no taller than the others, there was a certain presence that made it seem so. No one would ever have mistaken him for anything but the leader.

"You Walter Lonetree?" Pete said.

Lonetree's immediate response was a sideways look of silent disdain; a favored stratagem of those who use intimidation as a defense.

"Doc Henry told us to look you up."

Still the man said nothing. But Pete refused to be cowed and walked without caution to well within Lonetree's comfort zone.

173

Almost unconsciously, all six of the men placed their feet more firmly on the ground in a defensive stance.

Turning to Pete, Lonetree said, "What the fuck you want Wasi'chu?" The term roughly translated to "greedy person" and was a favorite pejorative as applied to whites.

Tactics that worked so well with everyone else were having no effect at all on Pete.

"Your people need help," Pete said.

Lonetree slowly turned his gaze to Pete.

"No shit. And the great white warriors of the sky are going to make everything just fine, right?"

"No. There's no pride in a handout. The people need to take care of themselves. What we—the great white warriors of the sky—are prepared to do is to help them to help themselves."

"Why come to me?"

"Doc Henry says you have a handle on what goes on here. He thought you might be interested in working with us to make some improvements."

"The biggest improvement would be for white people to go away and leave us alone. We did all right for thousands of years before you showed up."

"Yeah, well we're not leaving and there are more of us than there are of you, so do you want to help or not?"

"Why would I want to be part of a system that keeps my people down?" said Lonetree.

"You wouldn't. Neither would I. That system doesn't work for Indians. We want to help invent a new one."

"Talk. We don't need more talk. We've had enough speeches for ten lifetimes. We need to keep our traditions alive, to speak our own language, to practice our own religion, to be who we are."

"And you need jobs, decent housing and health care," Pete said. "Tradition doesn't mean squat if your people are all dead."

"Whites have been here for more than two hundred years. What makes you think things will be any different?"

"Because we're going to go around the system," Pete said as he walked down the row of men, looking directly into their faces. He was neither intimidated nor threatening.

"Of course you want to get rid of government," Jeff said, breaking his resolve to stand back until Pete called on him. "That's understandable. But a lot of your people are at the other extreme, waiting for government to do everything for them. If they keep that up, their great-grandchildren will be no better off than they are."

"They've got to get started on a better life," Pete said.

"Then what?" Walter Lonetree said. "We solve the problems and the politicians move in and take the credit."

Jeff's impatience began to show. "Why should you give a damn who takes the credit if it helps people," he said.

"Because after they take credit, they take control and make money from the misery."

"That's where I come in," Pete said. "It will be my job to hold back the exploiters."

"Come on man," Lonetree said, with disgust. "I seen it all before. When you dance at the white man's campfire, you dance to the white man's drum. Government money comes with government rules."

"No government money," Pete said. "We finance it ourselves, shut out the feds and call our own shots."

"Let me have a puff of what you've been smoking man. Where the fuck we gonna get that kind of money?"

"Let me worry about that."

A short man wearing torn jeans and a faded plaid shirt said, "You mean no more Indians gonna go to welding school?"

His companions hooted in support.

"Welding school is a sacred tradition among my people," said a man with a tobacco bag string hanging out of his shirt pocket. "You show me an Indian man and I'll show you a welder."

Doc had told Pete and Jeff of the enormous numbers of Indian men who had been sent to government-sponsored welding programs. Despite a glut on the market, the training continued because a Washington desk jockey decided that, facts aside, if it seemed like a good idea, then it must be a good idea.

"We don't have to fight the white man anymore. We just weld the doors shut on their Cadillacs and they starve to death."

Pete waited for the laughter to subside.

"Who makes the decisions in the tribe?" Pete said.

"Important decisions are not made *by* Indians, they are made *for* Indians," Lonetree said. "Whatever you want to do, it would have to be off the Res to keep it out of federal control."

"I thought the bureau was created to help your people?" Jeff said.

The reaction of the men might have been compared to that of parents to a child who has said something naive and there is no simple explanation to set them straight.

"Let's put it this way," said Lonetree. "One story goes that before General Custer left for Little Big Horn he told the head of the Bureau of Indian Affairs not to do anything until he got back. And they never have. Got the idea?"

"Got it," Jeff said. "Is there a central governing body within the tribe?"

"There is the council and the tribal chairman, but they cave in every time BIA snaps their fingers. A lotta things they decide gotta get the okay from the Great White Asshole in Washington."

"Maybe the council just wants to keep people from getting killed or hurt," Pete said.

"There are worse things than dying," said Lonetree. "And there are a lot of ways you can get hurt."

"Does the council have any real influence?" Jeff said.

"It's like anyplace else," Lonetree said. "People get used to things and they don't want to change. Even a bad habit feels right after awhile. The council don't have a lot of real muscle, but if the leaders ain't with you, the people ain't with you."

"And what about you, Lonetree?" Pete said. "Where do you stand?"

"If it's good for the people, it don't matter to me who don't like it."

"And if the council approves?" Jeff said.

"So much the better?"

"Could you set up a meeting for us with the council?" Pete said.

"Why would I want to do that?" said Lonetree.

"Doc Henry told me you care about your people," Pete said. "If we can help, they'll be better off. If we're full of shit, you'll find out soon enough."

"There are some who don't want the Indians to better themselves."

"We ran into a couple of them at Red Creek."

"Did you change their minds?"

"Pete changed one guy's face," Jeff said. "Does that count?"

"We heard there was some trouble there yesterday," said Lonetree. "Was that you?"

Pete, his hands in his pockets, just shrugged.

"The way we heard it, a white motherfucker named Hickman is wearing his nuts where his adams apple used to be."

"It's like they say about training a mule," Pete said. "First you've got to get his attention."

"White men fighting white men," Lonetree said. "Why didn't I think of that? If we just leave them alone they'll kill each other."

"We're not all brain dead rednecks like Hickman," Jeff said. "You have more white friends than you think."

"Come on, Lonetree," Pete said, turning on a double-barreled blast of Sunderland charm. "Are you going to help or are you going to stand there and prop up that building?"

"I ain't the most popular guy with the council. A lot of them don't like the way I do things. They call me a militant because I want to kick the government out and go back to the old ways."

"How about if I take over the diplomacy department," Pete said.

"You mean the bullshit department, don't you?"

"Call it whatever you like. There's a time to use your methods and a time to use mine. Maybe if we work together we can get the whole job done."

Lonetree thought about it for awhile.

"We'll take you around the Res," he said, looking to his followers. "I don't guarantee they'll listen. Hell, I ain't sure I like the idea myself."

A cloud of dust rose from the road to the west as a vehicle approached the crossroad at high speed. A pickup truck the same dull color as the land blasted through the intersection, ignoring the stop sign. Its driver slowed and leaned forward in the cab to get a look at the group of loiterers. At the same time, they could see his bandaged face. Then he sped off, stones and dust flying behind him.

"Speak of the devil," Jeff said, as the truck disappeared down the road. "That was Ben Hickman."

"He'd like to go back to the old ways, too, Lonetree." Pete said. "Back when his kind killed Indians for sport."

Jeff and Pete started toward the Skyhawk. "Think about what we've said and get back to us, Pete said. We're staying at the Red Creek Airport.

CHAPTER TWENTY-EIGHT

Lonetree showed up at the airport to say he and his band of rowdies would take them to meet with the tribal council.

Pete's flight training was put aside. The Skyhawk sat in its parking space at Red Creek Airport as Walter Lonetree and some of his closest followers accompanied Pete and Jeff in Doc's borrowed pickup truck to observe some of the problems first-hand. When they weren't touring, Pete was doing a lot of reading.

Only once did tempers flare between the men. Lonetree took exception to Pete's ranking of priorities. Pete insisted that providing jobs was priority number one. Lonetree's number one priority was to get the U.S. Government out of the tribe's affairs immediately. Pete continued to assure him that by making themselves independent of the federal government, everything else would take care of itself. The argument got heated.

Pete quickly settled the prickly matter by unbuttoning his shirt in comical pseudo macho fashion and doing an exaggerated swagger to within inches of Lonetree's face.

"All right," Pete said. "Let's settle this once and for all. Now, the way I understand it from all the movies I've seen, we both strip to the waist and slather bear grease or olive oil or something all over ourselves so we look all shiny in the light of a campfire. I know all about that shit. Then we take knives or tomahawks or a burlap bag full of horseshit, or whatever, and fight to the death, right?"

Even Lonetree, who was known to interpret a raised eyebrow from a white man as a challenge, had to laugh.

"No, man," said Walter Lonetree. "I was thinking more of flipping a coin for it."

"Your coin or mine?"

"It'll have to be yours," Lonetree said. "Nobody in this crowd has money."

179

In the days that followed, Lonetree lowered his guard to a less combative level and eased into the role of active, though wary, participant. He helped the visitors get a sense of the problems and their possible solutions.

"I still got my doubts about this," he said. "But we'll see."

It quickly became clear that, in addition to experiencing the same difficulties shared by all members of the human species, the Indians suffered an excessive gap between their needs and their means. Worse, the conditions they lived under seemed designed to keep it that way.

As in all poverty situations, its victims are too occupied with their immediate needs to give much thought to long range solutions. What most people everywhere considered as the basics of life, many of the Indians had come to regard as luxuries. Anything beyond food and shelter got bumped down the list as they lived one meal at a time, one winter at a time, one ordeal at a time.

In every residence, whether a newer modular structure or patched-together hovel, there was always a television set. What might have served as a valuable window to the wider world became, instead, an unwavering reminder of their inadequate resources. Disguised as entertainment, the appliance that sat in every living room inundated them with images of the unattainable and deepened their sense of hopelessness. Before television, they only had each other for comparison.

Pete Sunderland and Jeff Burke each wondered whether their own strength could outlast the despair they were seeing all around them.

CHAPTER TWENTY-NINE

Pete and Jeff borrowed Doc's old truck again to get to the meeting at the tribal chairman's home. The chairman's dingy mobile home was an eight-foot-wide model built in the days when they were still called trailers. The leaders gathered under a primitive gazebo, a pole structure covered with dried branches and dead leaves to shade them from the hot sun.

Women and children hovered nearby and peeked out at the strangers from behind buildings and shrubs.

Walter Lonetree had already briefed the group about his conversations with the two pilots. It became quickly apparent that convincing tribal leaders of the proposal's value would be a challenge nearly as large as the project, itself. The body language of some of the council members was plainly saying 'no' to suggestions not yet put forth.

After awkward introductions between the visitors and their suspicious hosts, Pete decided to charge forward.

Speaking softly he said, "If you want to improve the lives of your people, you will have to do some things different from the way you've been doing them." He looked at the faces of the men gathered around him. "Your people are suffering today because of what began centuries ago. It doesn't have to continue. Jeff and I believe that by working with you, by putting all of our heads and our resources together, we can come up with a plan that will make things a lot better for you and your families.

"I know a lot of you are angry. You have a right to be. But you don't have a right to stay angry if your anger keeps you from getting ahead. White people have brought unimaginable, unforgivable grief down on you. But it's time to move forward. We're here to help if you'll let us."

"What if we don't want your help, Wasi'chu?" called out one of the men.

181

"Are you serious?" Pete said, as calmly as possible, considering the strain on his sense of logic. "We're offering you a chance to have decent homes, better health, good jobs and profitable businesses of your own. But that won't happen unless you redirect your energies and become productive."

"Here it comes." said one of the men, slapping his forehead. "We're gonna have another Indian jewelry factory so some New Jersey Jew can pay us pennies and he can live in a big house and send his kids to fancy colleges."

"No," Pete shouted so loudly that even Walter Lonetree was startled. "No stereotypes. No jewelry, no pottery, no fur and feather artworks. We'll study the needs of mainstream America and find things consumers would buy no matter who made them."

"Other tribes have casinos," one of the men said. "How about that? Everybody would get a fat check every month."

"A lot of those casinos are run for the Indians by organized crime," Pete said. "And there is no pride to be had in getting money for doing nothing. Just another form of welfare."

"What do you get out of it?"

Caught off guard, Pete thought about it for a moment and said, "That's a fair question. The short answer is that after almost thirty years of having made no contribution to the betterment of mankind, I will finally have a chance to do something useful. I need that as much as you need the skills I can put to work on your behalf. It's also to partially make up for what my father and grandfather have done to people not too different from yours."

"Yeah. You could make a lot of money off this," said one of the men with a sneer.

"Look. I inherited more money than a lot of small countries have in their treasuries. I don't need any more. My father and grandfather made their fortunes and mine selling weapons to governments of poor nations to use against their own people. Sound familiar?"

"If you have all that dirty money, why not just give it to us and we'll call it even?"

Pete had to nearly shout to be heard above the laughter. "Because it would only take care of today, and you'd have nothing left for tomorrow."

"We always lose the things we get," said a man called Running Bear. "White people make sure of that. When gold was found on our old reservation in the Black Hills, we got pushed aside by the Great White Asshole in Washington, may his puny dick drop off. Custer was at Little Big Horn in violation of the treaty so he could kill our people and get the gold. We kicked his ass, for all the good it did us. When the gold was gone we got the land back because nobody else wanted it. Then they found uranium and we got bumped into this rocky hell hole. If you find some diamonds laying around, don't say nothing or we're gonna have to move again. Every time we get anything, white people come and take it away."

"So, you're saying you don't want to own anything because someone might steal it," Pete said. "Do I have that straight?"

"Hey, man," shouted one of the younger council members. "We don't need another white man putting us down."

"Then let's not talk about how we can't do it," Pete said firmly. "Any one of these mouth-breathing rednecks who live around here can think of ways something *won't* work. We have to work together to figure out what *will* work."

"Our people are tired," said Running Bear. "They have been fighting this battle since white people got here."

"Let me ask you a question," Pete said very quietly. "If I blindfolded you and a group of your friends and dropped you off a hundred miles from here without any equipment or weapons, where do you think you would be tomorrow night?"

"We'd be standing right here, really pissed at you, man."

"That's right. But not just because you know how to find food and water and what direction to travel. It would be because the instinct to survive is in your genes. You know how to work together for the common goal. When you are in a situation like that, you don't lie down and die. You work your way out of it together. BIA may have cut off some parts of your culture, but a lot is still there. What I propose is that we bring that social structure indoors and apply it to business for the survival of your tribe.

"Look, one of the most important elements of your tribe's ability to endure has been flexibility. It's built right into the culture. Your people have always worked together to protect each

183

other. You have tribal laws and traditions that must be followed but, when those get in the way of the welfare of the people, change has always been permissible. That goes back for thousands of years.

Pete stayed quiet for a moment and let his words sink in before continuing.

"Many of you want to go back to the way things used to be. Good. But remember, one of the old ways is to accept the new ways as they make sense, as they are needed to benefit all of your people. I'm sure we can sit down together and come up with a plan that will make everyone's lives a lot better. Anybody willing to try?"

"Whatever we do," Lonetree said, "it takes money. Where we gonna get money?"

"I'll find the money," Pete said. "You just worry about what we're going to spend it on."

"Let's party," one man shouted.

"No. You don't eat your seed corn. You plant it to grow food and more seed for the future. You don't eat the goose that lays golden eggs. You cash in the eggs and you take real good care of that goose. We let the money make more money. Then we party."

"You want us to forget what white people have done to us?" Running Bear said.

"Do you think revenge will help you get a job," Pete said. "Will getting back at those who have harmed you put food on your table, buy a color TV, guarantee your children a future? You're outnumbered. You're outgunned. And even worse, there are some white people who hope you will do something violent so they have an excuse to destroy you."

"We're ready for them."

"Then what? You can't prosper if you don't survive. Why give these people what they want. By refusing to play into their hands, you can get what you need."

Lonetree raised his hand to stop the shouting so he could address the group.

"You know me as a man who wants the government to get out. I still want that. But these men are offering us a way to tame the beast. Nothing we have done so far has worked. Maybe it's time to try something else. Give them a chance to talk."

"I'd rather see this in positive terms," Pete said. "Not as a way to get back at white people, but as a means of improving your lives."

"But it sure would piss them off," Running Bear said with a smile. "Nothing a redneck would hate worse than seeing an Indian driving a Cadillac."

"Hey, Pete," Jeff said. "You have to admit that's a pretty good kind of revenge."

"Yeah," Pete said. "Okay then, let's piss off some rednecks."

"It could be fun," Jeff said.

"Please consider what we've said," Pete said. "Talk it over among yourselves and let's get together tomorrow and take it to the next step."

As they walked back to the truck, Pete asked Lonetree, "How did we do?"

"Some are willing to give it a chance," he said. "Others would rather kill all the white people for what they've done to us. Part of me feels that way too."

"You know, Walter" Jeff said, "we're probably alike in more ways than we are different."

Lonetree stopped abruptly and looked straight into Pete's eyes. "Anybody take a shot at you lately? Somebody put a .44 magnum slug through my living room window a couple of nights ago. The bullet went through a wall and hit a lamp next to where my two-year-old son was sleeping. That ever happened to you? It happens to my people all the time, and sometimes they aren't so lucky. People don't die of old age here as much as they do where you come from."

"People take shots at you in different ways," Jeff said. "Not always with a gun."

"We get shot at that way, too," Lonetree said. "An Indian can't walk down the street in town without getting hassled. You're telling us to forget about all that?"

"We're telling you the cycle has to be broken any way you have to do it," Pete said. "The people have to find the strength for one final battle. Not with bullets or hatred, but with imagination, cooperation, and hard work."

"You're saying we have to pull ourselves out of a situation we didn't get ourselves into. And we gotta do it all by ourselves."

"As unfair as that is, that's exactly what it means."

"You ask a lot."

"I'm not asking anything, Walter. You have to ask it of yourself. Our role in this, if you want our help, would be to work with you to figure out how to pull it off. Let me know what you decide."

Pete and Jeff drove away, leaving Walter Lonetree standing by the side of the road.

OO

In camp that night, Jeff and Pete were too stimulated to go right to sleep.

"How did you know all that stuff about tribal structure, Pete?"

"I talked to a lot of people and read some books. Anyone who calls the Indians 'savages' doesn't know what they're talking about. Before the feds came along the Indians had a far more organized and complex civilization than our own. Thousands of years before there was a United States of America the Indians had a national government. They had a Supreme Court and an intricate system of local governing bodies that kept everyone orderly and working for the benefit of all. They had a religion and moral code that rivaled anything that has ever existed. Then, along came the white man and, in just a few years, destroyed that magnificent structure.

"How can it be put back together again?"

"You know Jeff, there are some elements of that old system left. I can see it in the way the Indians treat each other and the way they do things. With the bits and pieces of the culture that still exist inside every tribesman, I think we can help them rebuild a lot of what they've lost."

"Maybe you ought to call the organization 'Humpty Dumpty'," Jeff said. "You'd think the white business community would jump on something like this as a practical matter, if nothing else."

Deep in thought, Pete poked at the campfire and added some fuel for warmth through the night.

"For every person pulled out of poverty, a new consumer is created. Businesses spend millions to attract more customers. Yet here is an untapped supply of potential new buyers of their goods and services that is being completely ignored."

"And for every person taken off the welfare rolls, a new taxpayer is born." Jeff said. "That's a saving on one end and income on the other.

"Maybe people just need something to hate. If they didn't have Indians, they'd find something else.

Jeff said, "A black friend in college told me once that every social group has its 'nigger'. In Pennsylvania it's the coal region Polish. You'll find it in little backwater pockets throughout the country where the people aren't quite up-to-date."

"Yeah. When there are no ethnic groups around, some people focus on other differences. Intelligence is a favorite target. Innocence is another. Pity the poor secretary or sales clerk who isn't very sophisticated. If I can make you look stupid, then I must be pretty smart, huh?"

"There's something about the human animal that makes him take the easy way out," Jeff said. "It's easier to keep others from succeeding than it is to stand out on their own. It takes less effort to criticize than to perform."

"If someone tells you often enough how worthless you are, you believe it of yourself."

"We have our work cut out for us, my friend," Jeff said, as they crawled into their sleeping bags, the events of the day still racing through their minds.

"Did you say 'we', Jeff?"

"Dear God. I did, didn't I?"

If a single day had been exciting, the possibilities for the future seemed electrifying--and terrifying.

CHAPTER THIRTY

Lonetree told Jeff and Pete the tribal leaders had agreed, if not to actively participate, to at least not stand in their way.

"How'd you do it, Walter?" Pete said.

"I gave them the same argument you gave me; if you're full of shit we'll know soon enough."

Chris Hutchins volunteered an empty Quonset at the airport as a temporary home for what was to be called Sky Warriors.

Within two hours Lonetree and his group were moved in.

Pete wasted no time in getting them to hire a capital city law firm. He made the tribe a no-interest loan to cover immediate expenses and told them it would have to be paid back. After the tribal leaders elected a board of directors, the lawyers began to rush non-profit incorporation through the process.

It would be at least several weeks before Sky Warriors could officially start raising funds as a non-profit.

"This is getting big," Walter said. "Where's the money coming from?"

"I'd like to know that myself, Pete," Jeff said. "Who's going to pay for it?"

"In the end, the people will pay for it," Pete said. "What they don't need is for an outright handout, but they do need some help in solving their problems. We already know welfare doesn't work and that's what a casino would amount to. There has to be an element of personal pride and accomplishment. If there is no satisfaction through participation it will fail. These folks' lives have been hard enough already, but it's very important that they do this for themselves and pay their own way, with interest. Not cash interest, but 'sweat' interest—their personal involvement in helping each other. That shouldn't be hard. Generosity is part of the Indian culture."

189

"That part's good," Walter said. "But it still don't tell me where the money's coming from."

"Most of the initial financing will come from the big corporations," Pete continued. "You see, the federal government makes the big boys put some of their profits into worthwhile projects. There are foundations out there looking for us. I'm going to help them in their search."

"How do you keep the government out of it? You know how they are in Washington. If they can't control it, they destroy it. They're gonna be all over us."

"Why?" Pete said. "The project is off the Res, out of federal jurisdiction and not operated with tax money. If it works as well as I think it will, it will get people out of the welfare cycle."

"I still think the government will stick its nose in," Lonetree said. "Some of the local whites, too."

"We're far enough from population centers so we're not throwing it in anyone's faces. We'll try to avoid direct competition with existing businesses that might put pressure on us. We'll spend money with local companies that are nice to us. Everyone's a winner here. Where's the problem?"

Seeing a chance to play devil's advocate and make the point for Lonetree at the same time, Jeff said, "Now you're being logical. The problems will come for the same reasons the religious impose their beliefs on atheists, and politicians try to regulate private enterprise? They believe they have a mandate from a higher authority, whether it's God or the voting public. They'll tell you it's for the good of all. They interpret the law as it suits them, or rewrite the law if it doesn't."

"We'll beat them with strong lobbies in the state capital and in Washington and a regional public relations program. And, if we can't win them as friends, we'll squash them as enemies. God, I love violence."

"You're your father's son, all right," Jeff said.

"Except that we're protecting the rights of oppressed people instead of trampling over them."

Taking on projects of their own, the three men did not see much of each other for the next few days, though they were in constant contact on cell phones Pete bought for each of them.

CHAPTER THIRTY-ONE

Clarence Jeeters stood nearby as Jeff made a phone call.

"Buffalo Valley Flight Service," Bill Farrell said at the other end of the line."

"Bill? Jeff Burke. You may remember my partner, Pete Sunderland and me from a few weeks back. We were in Niner-Niner-X-ray. Had a bit of trouble with one of your people."

"It would be hard to forget you boys. They'll be telling stories around the campfire about you for a thousand years after the way you flattened Ben Hickman's face. What's on your mind Jeff?"

"We're over in Red Creek and I wondered if you had filled that spot we helped you vacate?"

"I have a couple of applicants, but I'm not real impressed with any of them."

"I have a young fellow here who could be your man," Jeff said, looking at Clarence. "He lives out your way."

"Send him over," Farrell said.

"I'll do better than that, Bill. I'll fly him there myself. How about if I take you to lunch tomorrow and give you a chance to meet Clarence?"

"I'm looking forward to it. See you then."

When Jeff hung up, Clarence said, "You didn't tell him I'm an Indian."

"Is that important?"

"It might be to him."

"It won't be."

"You know this guy a long time?"

"About a half hour." Jeff said.

"Oh shit."

"That's long enough for some people, Clarence. If Bill Farrell doesn't hire you it won't be because you're an Indian. You're an

191

intelligent young man. You do have to do some work on your attitude, though. Not all white people are your enemies."

"They have been so far."

"Hey. There's no guarantee that life will be perfect from now on. But you have a chance to make things better for yourself.

"You think I can do it, huh?"

Jeff could see it took a lot of courage for Clarence to even ask such a question. "You'll do the lot better than a jerk named Hickman did before he got canned."

"Ben Hickman? Big motherfucker from Red Creek?"

"Yeah. You know him?"

"Shit! I am one dead aborigine." Clarence said. "Hickman don't need a reason to abuse Indians. How do you think he's gonna feel about somebody who took his job?"

"You won't be taking his job," Pete said. "His big mouth lost it for him."

"You explain that to Hickman when you see him over at the Red Creek Saloon every night, boozed up and ready to kick redskin ass."

00

Jeff flew Clarence to Buffalo Valley for their meeting with Bill Farrell. Even by the next day, the young man's concerns had not been entirely put to rest.

Farrell needed nothing more than Jeff's recommendation and a favorable impression of Clarence to give the young man a chance.

"Young fella, if Jeff Burke says you're okay, you're okay," Farrell said. "You'll have a three-month probationary period, same as everybody else. If you do as good as I think you will, you'll have the job permanently if you want it."

"And Pete and I will make a pilot out of him."

Jeff shook Clarence's hand and asked Farrell, "what are the chances of full-time work?"

"After his probation he'll be first on the list for the next step up the ladder to a full-time position."

Jeff knew Clarence would not have his usual problems with white people because all of the air traffic controllers at the FSS were from places that did not have the prejudices against Native Americans that the local population had. They would be more likely to see him simply as a fellow employee.

Clarence was quiet on the flight back to Red Creek. Although he did not say the words, Jeff understood.

He would need transportation to his new job. Pete had already agreed with Jeff to give the young man one of the motor scooters. Pete filled the gas tank and gave Clarence a five-gallon can of fuel that should last him until he got a paycheck.

Walter Lonetree was also well-schooled in stoicism, but did acknowledge what Jeff had done.

"Thanks for helping the kid," Walter Lonetree said later.

"All we did was help him find an opportunity," Jeff said. "The rest is up to him."

Chapter Thirty-Two

By the end of the week Pete had more than a hundred-thousand dollars committed to the project. Just as important, he had the blessing of the Sky Warriors Corporation's Native American board of directors to put together a committee to locate a piece of off-res property on which to build the future Indian center.

Pete insisted on including some of the better-educated women to serve on the board. Walter Lonetree's wife was one of them.

Jeff looked at the list of priorities and said, "It should probably be at least five-hundred acres; big enough for an airport, a medical clinic, elementary and high schools, and a future Native American university. Maybe even a shopping center."

"Now you're talking," Pete said.

Over the next several weeks Pete discovered that by standing back from planning sessions, giving only occasional suggestions and encouragement and by asking probing questions, the planners did very well on their own.

Sometimes it was challenge to keep everyone focused on issues, rather than personalities and old hatreds.

"This is bullshit," Harvey Stone Face shouted. "Why the fuck we digging ourselves out of the hole white people put us in?"

Some of the younger men were too damaged and disruptive to be of much value. Many dropped out almost immediately. Where possible, dissidents who remained were assigned to areas where they would be out of the way. They could still be involved without their negativity spilling over onto the larger group.

Everyone was encouraged to challenge ideas. However, once the arguments had all been heard, a vote was taken, and a decision was made by the leadership, continued opposition was met with what amounted to shunning.

Compromise was difficult in an atmosphere where the disagreeing parties insisted on getting everything they demanded.

To avoid even the appearance of white people controlling the program, Pete and Jeff refused to have a vote on the issues.

Peer pressure had an enormous effect on agitators. Most were won over through patient discussion. The rest went along with the program largely because of the sheer numbers of those who would oppose them.

One serious episode threatened the relative calm. Stone Face led a group of young men. He was tired of the regimentation and finally exploded in frustration.

"I'm outta here." he said. "Lonetree, you can stay here and dance at the end of the white man's string. I'll go back to being what I am."

"And what are you, Stone Face?" Walter Lonetree asked.

"I am a man."

"You are a man who spends his whole life leaning against the wall of Iron Feather's store. Yes, go. Be what you think you are, Stone Face. When you decide to become what you could be, let me know."

Then Lonetree and those loyal to him turned their backs on the rebellious tribesman and changed the subject as if he were no longer there.

Several fellow agitators had apparently also become tired of the project—and the restrictions on them. Seeing no immediate reward in it, they went to Stone Face's side, as though a line had been drawn in the dirt. Some of the others hesitated, but did not join him.

"Cowards," Stone Face shouted at them. "Stay here with the women and children and do tricks for the white man."

Lonetree still did not respond. The self-appointed renegade chief and those who chose to take his side climbed into a pickup truck. The wheels spun on the gravel driveway as they sped off in the direction of Billy Iron Feather's to take up their old loitering spots.

"Shit." Lonetree said, shaking his head. He regretted the loss, but had no time to grieve.

"This is nothing new," Pete said. "There were dropouts in the old days, too. If their differences were too great, tribesmen would go off and form their own hunting and war parties."

"Defectors are not exclusive to Indians," Jeff said. "Religious organizations do it all the time. When a denomination seems too strict or too liberal for some of its members, they split off and start their own church."

"I get it." Pete said. "The United Evangelical Dissident Brethren of Billy Iron Feather's Storefront Church."

Pete accepted the role of unofficial interim co-director with Walter Lonetree until a real one emerged. Because of Pete's light touch, no resentment was evident. Everyone seemed to accept assignments approved by the board and issued through Lonetree. They were carried out without major complaint, though not always as completely or efficiently as Pete would have hoped.

Pete offered encouragement and acknowledged individual contributions, while emphasizing that the overall outcome would be a group effort.

They were reviving ancient tribal ways and transitioning them to a modern setting. Running Bear, who began as a major objector to the project, seemed to be emerging as a co-leader. Pete saw the big man as a likely future co-director.

The dynamics that had kept a Native American system of generosity and selflessness in motion for the greater good had been seriously damaged by the U.S. government in the latter half of the nineteenth century.

But now, deeply encoded behaviors appeared to be rekindling the fire.

CHAPTER THIRTY-THREE

"Walter," Pete said into the cell phone. "I have an idea for a project if you want to consider it."

Walter Lonetree stood on top of a hill, twenty miles from where Pete was standing.

"Do you think you could set up an organization to survey the needs of the population?"

"Are you kidding? My people invented bureaucracies a couple thousand years before the white man got here."

"Then you're the guy for the job. We have to find out what the people believe are the major problems that need solved?"

"Hell, I can tell you that."

"I know you can, Walter, but wouldn't it be valuable to get everyone's input. We want the people to feel like they had something to say about all of this. Plus, you might find out some things you didn't know about."

"I'll get some people together and go around the res."

"Plenty of women, children and old people, too," Pete suggested. "And not just the people you *like*."

"I'll make a list of what they say."

"You'll hear a lot of the same things over and over," Pete said. "But that will tell us how important everyone thinks a problem is. When you finish we can add to the record anything you think they missed and start working on solutions."

"Me and Running Bear will get right on it," The two men were in their vehicle almost the instant the conversation ended.

Doc's pickup truck had more miles put on it in a few weeks than the old doctor had run up the entire previous year. Pete took Lonetree with him to buy a new truck at a Chevrolet dealership in a town nearest the reservation. They made certain the dealer knew that Lonetree was making the purchase. They had it registered in Doc's name. They also let the dealer know that the tribe was organizing itself. If treated well, he told them a rich future customer base would be likely to bring them more business.

"I hardly know what to say," Doc said. "My old heap was just about ready for the scrap pile."

"Call it a thank you gift for your service to the tribes. If you don't want the old one anymore," Pete said, "we'll fix it up and use it on the project."

"It's yours," Doc found the pink slip, signed it, and handed it to Pete.

"Now that you have a new truck, can we borrow it?"

Doc laughed until tears ran down his wrinkled face.

Pete asked Walter Lonetree to locate a capable mechanic on the reservation to completely rebuild the old truck. A week later it was finished and pressed into immediate service.

Pete spent his time shuttling between meetings with the committees and board members and having animated telephone conversations with corporate foundation executives, pacing back and forth with the cell phone constantly at his ear or chirping in his pocket. He used the phone so much that Pete had to install a cigarette lighter in the old truck to plug in a cell phone charger.

00

"Pete, you are a surprise," Jeff said on one of the rare occasions he got to see him.

"I am, aren't I?"

"Maybe you're not the sniveling little snot everyone thought you were."

"Until I hear otherwise, I'll take that as a compliment," Pete said, and raced off to his next appointment.

A few days later, Walter Lonetree tossed an armload of papers onto the table Pete used as a desk.

"Here's that information you wanted," said Lonetree. "Is this enough?"

"Jesus, Walter. You must have talked to every man, woman and child for a hundred miles," Pete said.

"And damn near wore out a pair of boots doing it," Lonetree said, poking a finger through a hole in the sole.

"Shoe repair," Pete said, grabbing a pencil to add another occupational group to his growing list of needs and career training opportunities.

Pete leafed through Walter's stack of papers, choosing some at random to get a sense of the problems the people felt needed the most attention.

Looking over the lists Walter noted, "one old lady says her most important problem is her TV don't work. I didn't know how to list that one."

"How about 'Services for the Elderly' or 'Appliance repair'?" Pete said.

"One guy said his new false teeth don't fit right."

"Why didn't he take them back where he got them?"

"He don't want trouble."

"Okay. Let's call that one 'Consumer Problems'."

Pete added "shuttle service." Those without transportation were going to need a reliable way to get around. They would buy a bus right away and hire a driver.

With a little imagination and some sensitive interpretation, the two men were able to fit each identified problem and suggestion into one of dozens of recognizable categories. As Pete suspected when he came up with the idea, a lot of the Indians' problems, though generally more extreme, were not much different from those found elsewhere in America.

At Pete's urging, and with Lonetree's backing, the board appointed a committee to make recommendations for the elements of a master command center they would build. Implementing everything was a slow process. Most of the participants had never held a regular job. They did not have the discipline that comes with—as Clarence Jeeters had said—the ability to "to sit in little rooms for many hours without moving." Pete and Jeff had resigned themselves to accepting the unhurried pace and dealing with it.

"We see it taking shape," Fast Elk said. "We just can't figure out what the shape is."

"That's because it's a flexible shape," Pete said. "It can change with the people's changing wants and needs.

"If I were designing it there would be a central place run by volunteers. People could go there to get answers to every aspect of their lives: food, shelter, jobs, health, child day care, programs for the elderly, job training; the works. And they need to pay for that in some way to preserve their own pride. If everyone pulls together, I expect the corporation will change a lot of lives. Probably even save some."

"It shouldn't get too big," Lonetree said, "or it will be like government. Better the people depend on themselves and each other."

"Amen," Pete said. "We don't want to create another institution that takes away personal responsibility. That's one of the things wrong with the rest of the country. If parents get old, we send them to the senior citizen's home instead of taking care of them ourselves. When we get old, we draw Social Security. Instead of having family and friends help us. When we get sick, we use Medicare or public assistance benefits. If our house burns down, insurance pays for it instead of neighbors pitching in to rebuild. Pretty soon, everybody is out of the habit of helping each other. Government and big business have let people off the hook. People need to take back that responsibility."

"We have to get some money flowing into the Indian economy," Jeff said.

"Create jobs and pay them," Pete said.

The committee scanned the list of occupations, chose those most immediately needed, and hired people to fill the jobs at a standard minimum wage. Everyone was paid the same hourly rate with bonuses for recognized contributions above and beyond the job description. Salaries came out of the general fund. Doc's helper, Mrs. Caruthers, and several other volunteers from the church did the books until someone in the tribe could be trained to handle it.

Many of the people on the reservation lived in shacks with no running water or indoor plumbing. Fighting a lifelong habit of buying everything he needed, Pete begged and borrowed from a multitude of sources to fill the need.

A team assembled to implement the program was comprised of the better educated, more creative, and more motivated in the tribe. They designed and produced detailed drawings for solar hot water heaters and affordable home water purification and sewage systems. Anyone who wanted plans got them at no cost. Anyone who needed help to do the work would get it in exchange for assisting on someone else's project.

The group would not allow anyone to fail to live up to a commitment to repay in labor. Even Walter acknowledged that if someone received a service before they paid for it they would never show up to pay the debt. Payment was always to be in advance.

Jeff called on his experience working summers on his grandfather's farm. "Everyone from farms around the area would come to Pappy's place and help with harvesting," Jeff said. "Then Pappy and everyone else would go to the next farmer's place to bring in the corn, hay and such. It was the perfect no-cost co-op system."

Pete seemed to be everywhere, offering guidance rather than authority. He worked from before sunup until well after even his most enthusiastic supporters were too tired to continue. Rather than becoming exhausted from the effort, Pete seemed to grow stronger.

If a planning session threatened to go too far afield, or ideas detoured into the realm of the impractical, Pete gently brought the participants back on track. No proposal, no matter how large or small, ever got less than everyone's full attention. If a suggestion seemed unrealistic at the outset, they brought everyone together and brainstormed it into a workable form, never allowing any contributor to feel his input was not important.

As the weeks went by, the core participants were coming to view the project as bigger than any individual. Making it work became a project within the project. Patience was elevated to an art form, diplomacy a competitive sport whose mechanics were catching on.

While the women kept the workers at a worksite site fed, children filled canteens with water and kept them coming. Everyone had a particular job and each took his responsibility seriously, as part of a functioning mechanism. Pete and Jeff rolled up their sleeves and worked side by side with the others on labor projects, so as not to appear like bosses.

Where Pete had feared ego problems, he was delighted to find that, from the moment they began their work, most came to feel they were part of a system that could not survive without them and failure would be a personal disgrace. Nothing they could do about those who didn't buy into the program, but they could not allow that element to get in the way of what was being accomplished.

The undertaking was not entirely without disputes. There was still some time-consuming bickering and macho posturing. The project's most important resource in neutralizing hostilities was Walter Lonetree.

Without Lonetree's support, the project would doubtless have ended before it began. When conflicts arose, Walter was able to effectively prevent them from escalating into full blown confrontations and bring them back to the goal.

The most unendurable sanction that could have been applied to a disrupter was the disfavor of those held in high regard. Walter knew it well and worked the concept to maximum impact. Doc Henry had been correct beyond even his own expectations about Lonetree's dedication to his people.

No volunteer had ever experienced tribal life such a level of efficiency before. But there were apparently enough bits and pieces of tradition, Indian law, and native common sense remaining in the makeup of each individual so that the best of what once had been had a real chance of being reassembled.

"You've done it," Doc said, shaking his head at what he was seeing.

"We didn't do it," Pete said. "The people are doing it. They just needed some organization."

Those directly involved began to allow themselves to believe that the lives of their tribesmen could improve, that they could take some control of their lives, and that they would have done it themselves. Until the plan actually became a reality, its forward momentum was powered by the growing conviction that it would succeed.

There were some occasional hitches, however.

"We're being sued," Pete said, spreading some papers on his table.

"That's it," Running Bear said. "We're fucked."

"No we're not," Pete said calmly. "Being sued just means someone disagrees with us and wants the courts to settle it. It also means our lawyers will have to work for the retainer fee we're paying them."

"Why are they suing us?" Walter asked.

"They're citing land use restrictions," Pete said. "But the real reason is they're afraid we might take some business away from local companies. They think they're entitled to all the business because that's the way it's always been. They want to legislate or regulate us out of their way."

"What are we gonna do?" said Running Bear.

"We're going to sit back and let the lawyers and the lobbyists do their jobs. Meanwhile, we'll keep doing our jobs."

CHAPTER THIRTY-FOUR

Outside resistance to the project had a price. Every moment Pete had to spend on the telephone with lawyers was a moment away from more productive activities.

"We've got them on the run, Pete," attorney Hal Lunsford said when he telephoned. *"I think the judge will probably throw the whole thing out of court."*

"Thanks, Hal," Pete said. "If you pull this off, I might just have to start liking lawyers."

"Thanks. I'll send you my bill," Lunsford said.

"In that case, forget what I said about liking lawyers."

A top lobbying firm at the capital used its influence in the back rooms and hallways of government on behalf of the Indians. With the help of a public relations firm in the capital city at Pierre, Pete set up some meetings with major business owners and community leaders throughout the region. He and Jeff traveled around to explain the project and to dilute concerns of business people and the major players in the lawsuit. They wanted to assure everyone that, not only did Sky Warriors not have any intention of hurting their businesses, the Indians would become some of their best customers.

Jeff and Pete attended one particularly critical meeting with influential representatives of the business community nearest the reservations. They didn't take Walter with them because they were afraid the people they were talking with might not fully express themselves. Pete began with the simple statement, "Gentlemen, you will lose this court case."

After the initial outrage subsided, Pete went on to tell the group of political, business and religious leaders, "We are going to win in court, but it is not our intention to rub your noses in it."

"You sound very sure of yourself, Mr. Sunderland, said Will Geistman, a local Ford dealer.

"I am very certain, Mr. Geistman." Pete said. "We understand the judge is ready to toss the case as a frivolous use of the courts."

"If that were true," said the Reverend George Masterson, an Episcopal minister, "it is unlikely you would even bother to come and talk with us?"

"Not at all pastor," Pete said. "We don't want to simply clobber you in the courts. We want your help and your whole-hearted support of the project. In return for your blessing and assistance we will trade you a very large group of working, voting, taxpaying consumers who will reward you for your foresight. Not only will they no longer be a drain on the public treasury, which will save tax money, they will be wage-earners with money to spend with firms that have earned their loyalty by offering them friendly support."

"But these people don't want to work," said Ed Champion, a Rapid City CPA. "They're lazy and they sit around their shacks all day getting drunk."

"Mr. Champion," Pete said as patiently as possible, "please don't make the mistake of judging all Indians by the worst of them. Keep in mind that the Indians were once hunters and warriors. When the buffalo were gone and the war was over, their men no longer had a role in their society, at great cost to their pride. They have never gotten over it. We can help to clean up that mess and do all of this state's citizens a great service at the same time."

"What makes you think they even want to improve themselves?" said Ed Magee, manager of a local insurance agency.

"I have been working side by side with people who want the same things for their families that you want for yours and they're willing to work for it. It won't happen overnight, that is for certain. But the investment in time and patience will pay big dividends.

"A couple of months ago, some of them hated my guts for no better reason than that I am white. Today we are building something together. That feeling can spread beyond the reservations, beyond the project, and can benefit all of you. If you can't think of it in human terms, think of it in business terms. A brand new group with spendable income will be shopping around to buy the elements of the American Dream. Doesn't it stand to reason that they will think kindly of those who helped them when they most needed it when it comes to buying insurance, Mr. Magee, and new pickup trucks, Mr. Geistman?"

"But they're heathens," said the Reverend Masterson. "They have never accepted Jesus Christ as their Savior."

"Reverend Masterson." Pete said, "I don't want to get into an involved theological discussion with you, or get too deeply into American constitutional guarantees of freedom of religion. However, I would like to point out that the Indians' religion dates back long before Christianity and, if you examine it as I have, you will find they are not dissimilar."

"Preposterous," said the Reverend. "They don't believe in a single God."

"Those who still practice the old religion believe in Wakan Tanka, The Great Spirit and sixteen lower gods that represent such entities as the wind and the waters of the earth. Very much like angels, don't you think? What could be purer than that?

"You prove my point, Mr. Sunderland. They don't even believe in the holy trinity."

"Father, Son and Holy Ghost, or sun, moon, earth, wind and sky? Who's to say your three and their sixteen don't come down to the same thing. Both serve to bring order to societies and meaning to the lives of the people, Indian or white. They even have a devil."

"Is that right?"

"Iya personifies evil to the Indians. Iya is an outcast God," Pete said. "Does that sound familiar, pastor? Lucifer, the fallen angel of Christianity."

"I was not aware that the Indian religion was as intricate as that," said the preacher.

"Most people think it's a lot of dancing around a campfire or wailing to the skies," Pete said. "It is so much more. Beyond the meaning of the Indian religion to the individual practitioner, it is a moral code, a set of rules for living. It can be compared with the teachings of Confucius, Allah, Buddha and Jesus Christ."

"They have no bible," the preacher said.

"They have no written language, pastor," Pete responded gently. "But the stories they tell—parables, if you will—are handed down verbally from generation to generation. They serve as examples of the benefits of living right. They are a constant reminder of the perils of getting off the path."

"Mr. Sunderland," said Dr. James Gorman, a psychiatrist, "how does bathing naked in a heated hut compare with sitting in church with your family on a Sunday morning?"

"It equates wonderfully, if not precisely, Doctor Gorman. A sweat bath is a purification rite. A sinner asks to purge himself of his transgressions. By declaring his sin to his community, he is acknowledging that he did wrong and knows it. How is that so different from Catholic confession or the Baptists coming forward to repent their sins? Not so different from talking things over with a mental health professional."

"I don't see it as the same at all," Reverend Masterson said.

"Pastor, if you are looking for exact comparisons: reading the Sunday paper together, going to a quiet church and taking a nice drive in the country afterward, stopping off for ice cream on the way home, you'll be hard pressed to find them here. But if you look at the overall concept, you will find that the religion of the Indians, just as in Christianity and the other great faiths, is the conscience of a civilization."

"Conscience," said Dave Murphy. "Those people murdered Custer at Little Big Horn and a great many white settlers, as well."

"Custer was viewed as a trespasser in the Black Hills in violation of the treaty," Pete said. "I don't deny there was savagery on both sides, but then and now the good people outnumber the bad ones. There were Germans who helped Jews escape Hitler. There were southern whites who helped black slaves escape, and there were good men and women who held onto properties on behalf of Japanese-American citizens who were unfairly imprisoned during World War II. History is full of good people among the bad. What we need to emphasize is that, regardless of all that happened during and after the Indian wars, the important thing now is to move forward. Don't you agree, Dr. Gorman?"

"I can hardly argue with that, since that's what I say to my patients.. I tell them that nothing can change what has happened to them in their lives. All they can do is to go on from where they are at that moment."

"The healing of a single mind or the healing of a society," Pete said. "The mechanics are no different.

"Look, I'm not harboring any illusions that the hurts, prejudices, and philosophical differences will disappear immediately. But look at us. Strangers who started out hostile when we got here are now talking. We've learned from you and you have learned from us. What we're asking is that you give it a chance."

00

Of one thing Jeff and Pete were certain. Most of the community leaders they spoke with had moved a little closer to their point of view; or had become a little less certain of convictions they had held for a lifetime.

Those who could not be won over suddenly found themselves in the minority, despite the long-standing tradition of repressing and manipulating Indians. Support dwindled among initiators of the lawsuit. The sheer magnitude and the expense of the response to the court action put the entire matter on shaky ground.

A few days after their meeting with the leaders, the suit was dropped even before the judge had announced his decision.

There was cheering around Sky Warrior headquarters when Pete broke the news.

CHAPTER THIRTY-FIVE

Jeff completed his preflight and had started the engine to leave for Rapid City to get some equipment for the project when Chris Hutchins hailed him from across the transient parking area.

"Could you pick up a NavCom radio for me at Ed's Avionics in Rapid City?" Chris shouted above the hum of the idling engine.

"Glad to. Anything else? A pizza maybe?"

"Sounds good. Make it a large one with everything except those little fish."

After a few more moments of good-humored banter, Jeff taxied to the end of the runway and completed his run-up. Seeing no incoming traffic, he turned onto the strip and shoved the throttle to the firewall. The Cessna accelerated quickly as it moved down the runway. In seconds, the craft reached takeoff velocity and rose to about 100-feet off the rough surface.

Suddenly, without warning, a pilot's worst fear was realized. The engine simply stopped running and there was no sound but the whistling of air passing over the wings.

With less than three-hundred feet to the end of the strip and the rocks and rough scrub growth that lay beyond, Jeff's mind raced through his mental catalog of everything he had ever learned in twenty years of flying. Instinctively he let the craft settle solidly on the ground until he was certain the plane's full weight was down. Then, with all his strength, he hit the toe brakes. When the craft slowed some, he released pressure on the right brake, causing the craft to go into a whiplashing ground spin to the left. The plane continued to skid forward on the runway, as though on ice.

The force of the sudden change in direction caused the craft to begin to tip over. The right wing might have touched the ground and cartwheeled the craft end-for-end, completely out of control if Jeff had not had the presence of mind to tap the opposite brake lightly, causing the Skyhawk to stop its rotation and slam down onto the nose gear.

When it did, Jeff could feel the gear buckle. He watched as the front end of the plane sank and skidded a final few feet, into the dirt and rocks by the side of the runway.

Jeff was shaken, but uninjured except for a little stiffness from being flung around the cockpit when the plane spun violently.

The moment Chris Hutchins heard the engine quit, he started to run down the airstrip. His heart was beating wildly as he ran toward the cloud of dust still hanging over the field. He was the first to reach the plane.

"You okay Jeff?" Chris shouted.

"Yeah, but you're going to have to wait for your pizza," Jeff said, stepping down from the Skyhawk.

"What happened?"

"The engine was working just fine and then it wasn't working at all."

The men pushed the plane off to the side of the runway where Chris could check under the cowling and find out what went wrong.

"Here's the problem," Chris said, holding up something that looked like white BB shot.

"What is it?"

"Someone cut the ignition wires and rejoined them with wax. When it got hot during the run-up, the wax melted, the wires came apart, and the electrical connection was broken, instantly killing the engine."

"You mean somebody did this on purpose?"

"No doubt about it. Whoever did it knew something about aircraft dual ignition systems."

"No pilot would do that to another pilot?" Jeff said. "Chris, it's a good thing you came over to talk to me before takeoff. If the engine had failed a minute later, it could have been much worse than a bent nose gear."

00

By the next day a National Transportation and Safety Board investigator named Marvin Eubanks had flown in to look over the site and the evidence Chris had gathered. He examined the engine carefully, so as not to touch anything that might point to the guilty party.

"Whoever did this bought a world of trouble for himself when we catch him," Eubanks said. "I found a couple of clear fingerprints that survived the heat of the engine. Several were on the cowling. They could belong to the last mechanic who worked on it, or it could be the saboteur."

"Let me help you narrow the possibilities, Mr. Eubanks," Jeff said. "Not to accuse anyone, but you may want to check that print against a fellow named Benjamin Hickman. He lives in this area."

"Do you have reason to suspect the man?" Eubanks asked, writing Hickman's name in his notebook.

"We've had a couple of run-ins with him," Pete said. "He's not a pilot, but he probably knows just enough about airplanes to be able to cause something like this to happen."

"I'll need his fingerprints."

"You probably already have him on file. He was a part-time air traffic controller at Buffalo Valley until recently. We had a hand in his being fired."

"So, his prints will be in Washington," the NTSB investigator said. He turned to the airport owner. "Mr. Hutchins, is there anyone else who works here who might have seen something."

"There's my helper, Sammy Bodine. But he went to Sioux Falls to pick up an engine part for me. Hard to say when he'll be back."

"Have him give me a call just as soon he returns," said Eubanks. "Thanks for your help fellows. Where are you staying until the Skyhawk is fixed?"

"In a tent right next to the plane," Pete said.

"No you're not," Chris said. "You're moving into that other empty Quonset behind the flight office. It's safer."

"Mr. Eubanks," Pete said, giving the investigator a slip of paper with some telephone numbers on it, "if you need us, give us a call. Or you can leave a message with Chris or with Doc Henry in Red Creek."

When Jeff considered the potential for disaster that might have occurred, he felt extremely vulnerable. Worse, it depressed him considerably that anyone would do such a thing to another person. The blue mood stayed with him for the rest of the day.

00

Sammy Bodine arrived at the flight office just before three o'clock.

"Sammy," Chris said, "did you see anyone near the Skyhawk in the past couple of days?"

"Not that I noticed."

"Anything out of the ordinary? Anything that didn't fit in?"

"No. Well, there was one guy. I didn't think much about it at the time. It was three days ago. Monday, my first day back from vacation."

"Was he hanging around the plane?"

"Not when I saw him. He was leaving when I got here. It was just getting daylight and people aren't usually here that early."

"Do you know who it was?

"I couldn't tell."

"What was he driving?"

"A tan pickup truck. A Ford, I think. Nobody I know, but I live on the Res, out near Buffalo Valley, so I don't know many people over this way."

"And you didn't get a look at him?"

"No, his face was hidden."

"What do you mean 'hidden'?"

"It was covered up."

"A mask?"

"More like bandages."

"Holy shit," Jeff exploded. Within moments, the NTSB investigator was on the other end of the line.

"That's right Mr. Eubanks," Jeff said. "Chris Hutchins' helper, Sammy Bodine, says he saw a man with a bandaged face drive away from here early Monday morning in a tan pickup truck. Hickman drives a tan Ford pickup and he has a face full of bandages."

"That is good news," Eubanks said.

"The bad news is that nobody actually saw Hickman tamper with the plane."

"It doesn't matter. Placing him near the scene within that time frame should give us enough."

"How?" Pete asked. "It's his word against ours."

"Not quite. I emailed that fingerprint to Washington and just got word that it's a match with Hickman's. With that and the testimony of you and your witness we probably have enough to put him away for quite awhile on federal charges."

When Pete and Jeff called Melanie and Stephanie that evening, neither said anything about the incident.

00

Word of the near calamity at Red Creek Airport spread quickly through the area. By the next day, it had also slipped out that there was a suspect in the case.

When an FBI agent accompanied the federal investigator to pick up Hickman at his house, they discovered that the suspect had evidently put two and two together and bolted for parts unknown.

"That means the sonofabitch is out there somewhere," Chris said. "No telling what he'll do."

"He'll leave the area if he's smart," Pete said, looking at Jeff.

"Right," they said, almost in unison.

"Exactly," Chris said. "And he has a lot of supporters here. They may not like him, but they think the same way he does. It would be real important to Ben Hickman to get even. If I were you boys, I'd watch my back until they catch him."

Pete and Jeff flew to Rapid City in a Piper Cherokee they borrowed from Chris. The trip was ostensibly to pick up the research materials related to the project, a NavCom radio for Chris, and a pizza with no anchovies. It also served to keep them out of harm's way until they could map out a plan, or until Hickman was in custody.

When they returned to the airport, there was a message taped to the door of the Skyhawk. One of Chris Hutchins' employees had apparently taken the call.

Pete & Jeff:

Meet at shack 1 mi. west of Culpepper Road and County Road 17 crossroad at 4 o'clock.

<u>Doctor Henry</u>

"Odd that Doc would ask to meet us someplace other than his office," Pete said.

"It's almost four o'clock now. I've got to go to the meeting place," Jeff said. "You stay and give Chris a hand with that landing gear."

Without hesitation, Jeff jumped in the truck and took off down the road.

"I don't like it," Chris said, looking at the note again. "Why would he say it was from 'Doctor Henry' instead of just 'Doc'?"

"That's a real good question, Chris," Pete said, punching out Doc's number on the office telephone.

"He's not here," Mrs. Caruthers said. *"He had to go look in on a patient on the reservation."*

"He didn't say anything to you about meeting us at four o'clock?"

"There's no way he could do that. His appointment was at four and that's a half-hour drive from here. I'm sure he would have told me if that was his plan."

"Thanks Mrs. Caruthers. When you see Doc, tell him we'll check with him later."

A call to Jeff's cell phone went straight to voice mail.

"Jeff is headed straight into trouble, Chris," Pete said, hanging up the phone. "He'll need some help. I'll head for there."

On his way out, Pete asked Chris to call Marvin Eubanks in Pierre. "Tell him what's going on and see if they can get the FBI out here."

CHAPTER THIRTY-SIX

There was no vehicle in the yard when Jeff pulled up in front of the old shack. Doc had apparently not arrived yet.

The front door stood open. There was no one inside. Jeff stepped back outside to wait on the porch. When he did there was a sudden pain in his head and the world turned blazing white just before everything went completely black.

By the time his mind cleared somewhat Jeff found himself face-down in the dirt and tied in such a way that he could not stand up, let alone defend himself. A man stood over him holding a shotgun, the barrel of which was apparently the same blunt instrument used to put a throbbing knot on the back of Jeff's head.

"I got you this time bird shit," the man said.

Ben Hickman's scarred and broken face looking down at Jeff filled in the details. He grinned through broken teeth and a bandage that covered most of his face above the upper lip. Jeff was tied up in such a way as to make it impossible to defend himself. Hickman was taking no chances that he would be made to look bad again in front of his fellow losers.

"Look over there," said Hickman. "We got your boyfriend, too. He was trying to sneak up on us."

Jeff turned his head. Pete was lying about ten feet from him. He was conscious, but trussed up in the same manner. A thin line of blood trickled down the side of his head.

"I've got to work on my sneaking technique," Pete said.

Three men of the same rough ilk as Hickman stood idly by. Two of them had rifles. One had a semi-automatic handgun stuck in his belt. Hickman carried a twelve-gauge pump shotgun.

"You okay Jeff?" Pete called to his partner.

"Tolerable. Remember that promise you made not to get involved the next time someone comes at me a gun?"

"Yeah."

"I'm releasing you from your promise."

"Great. You take the four on the left."

"There are only four guys altogether, Pete."

"Are you sure. I counted eight. My aching head."

"Shut the fuck up," Hickman shouted.

"Hey, Ben, buddy," Pete said. "You can't fool me Benny. I know it's you behind those bandages. I'd recognize that sparkling smile anywhere you handsome rascal."

Hickman answered the taunt with a vicious kick to Pete's side, almost turning him over.

"How do you like that you cocky little bastard?"

"I could say I hated it, Ben," Pete groaned, "but a guy who enjoys pain as much as you do would know I was lying."

Pete was able to take some of the power out of the second kick by rolling with it. Still it knocked the wind out of him, so he lay quietly on his side for a few minutes before moving again.

"We got some big plans for you boys," Hickman said. "And when we're done with you we're gonna take care of that little prick who stole my job."

"The kid didn't steal your job," Jeff said. "Your big mouth lost it for you."

Hickman seemed to be considering whether to give Jeff some of what he had given Pete, but apparently had a different idea. "Boys, why don't you drag these two Christmas packages up the slope so they make better targets," Hickman said.

"I don't know about this, Hickman," one of the men said. "I figgered we'd knock 'em around a little, is all."

"Let me make it easy for you Wilson," Hickman said, flipping a lighted cigarette butt into "Chub" Wilson's face. "Do you want to be behind these guns with us or in front of them with these assholes?"

"I didn't mean—"

"I'm waiting," Hickman said, bringing the shotgun up under Wilson's chin.

Wilson nodded, and did as he was told. One of the men helped him drag Jeff up the rocky incline. The other dragged Pete roughly behind him. Hickman took the lead.

Pete thought he saw something out of the corner of his eye, but dismissed it as random shadows or an optical trick caused by the blow to his head, and from being dragged along the bumpy ground by Hickman.

Then a pair of the shadows reached out and grabbed the two men at the rear of the column. They put their hands over the surprised men's mouths and knocked them both out cold.

Almost soundlessly the two thugs slumped to the ground, their heads dented with clubs wielded by Wild Elk and Lonetree. They picked up the men's weapons.

When the next man forward in the line turned to investigate what sounded like someone thumping a melon, he got his own melon thumped by Wild Elk. Lonetree caught the lever-action rifle before it hit the ground. He took the man's handgun from his waistband and tossed it to Wild Elk, who passed it along to one of the others.

By taking the last man first, Hickman had no idea the others were being neutralized one at a time.

His cronies strewn along the path behind him, only Hickman remained.

Lonetree jacked a cartridge into the chamber of the rifle he had taken from the fallen man. He aimed it at the widest part of Ben Hickman's considerable bulk. Hickman stiffened, tightened his two-handed grasp on the shotgun, and appeared to be considering a quick turn.

"Go ahead Hickman," Lonetree said quietly. "Turn around with that shotgun and give me a legal reason to send you to meet your low-life ancestors."

If Hickman had turned suddenly he would surely have died where he stood. Four tribesmen filled beyond capacity with hatred for his kind had also aimed their confiscated weapons at the big man's vital parts. Hickman slowly laid the shotgun on the ground beside him and did not resist as he was tied up.

"Walter," Pete said. "You are one stealthy sonofabitch. I think I love you."

"If you kiss me, I swear I'll cut your heart out," Lonetree said as he untied the ropes on Pete's hands and feet. "That was really stupid to come out here alone."

"How did you know we were here?"

"Jaleen Jeeters found out. She was in town and overheard some white men talking about getting revenge on some white pilots. You are the only white pilots she knows. She went to the clinic and told the lady who works there. She called Chris Hutchins and he called me."

"We owe Jaleen big time," Jeff said.

"What the hell were you thinking, Pete? You couldn't take on that pack of dogs by yourself. These guys are crazy and Hickman is third generation nuts."

"I guess the planets were aligned and the winds were just right," Pete said.

"Don't try that spooky Native American bullshit on me. You're lucky you're still breathing."

"That is so sweet," Pete said, patting Lonetree on the cheek. "You really do care about us."

Walter swatted Pete's hand away. "I care about the project, man. It would go to hell if something happened to you guys."

"You hear that, Jeff? Walter believes in the project."

"I believed in the project almost from the beginning," Walter said. "It took this to make me see how easy it could fall apart."

Running Bear had bound the captives and thrown them, with no regard for their comfort, into the back of Hickman's pickup truck. Clifton Kamach collected the rest of the weapons and stacked them on the porch of the old shack.

"I rounded up my guys right after we got the call," Walter said. "Got here as soon as we could."

"I'm sure glad to see you," Jeff said. "Thanks for dropping by."

"Don't thank us. It gave us a chance to be the winners for a change. That hasn't happened since Big Horn."

"Yeah," Kamach said. "When we were kids we played cowboys and Indians. I always wanted to be a cowboy. Maybe now my kids will want to be Indians."

The lighter moment caused the group to take their eyes off the prisoners momentarily. Ben Hickman took advantage of their inattention. Though his hands were tied behind him, Hickman was able to reach into the top of his boot and retrieve a small .22-caliber revolver his captors had overlooked when they searched him. He brought the weapon up awkwardly and squeezed off a single round. The shot barely missing Pete's head and struck Running Bear in the shoulder.

Walter Lonetree was on top of Hickman before a second shot could be fired. Walter pulled Hickman to the ground, ripped the gun out of his hand, and tossed it to Pete. Walter had the big man by the hair, his knife drawn back to strike.

"Walter. Don't," Pete shouted. "Please don't kill him."

A lifetime of anger was concentrated in a single moment. Walter Lonetree was shaking with rage. He had become a force of nature bent on destroying the embodiment of everything he despised.

"Please, Walter," Pete pleaded.

There was no doubt in Ben Hickman's mind that he had spent his last day above ground. Now he waited for Lonetree, who was poised to drive six inches of high carbon steel into his throat.

Pete put his hand gently on Lonetree's shoulder.

"Listen to me, Walter," Pete said. "Before you kill him, think about this. He caused the crash of an aircraft. That's a charge that will get him a long stretch in federal prison. Plus he almost killed Running Bear just now. Add another couple of decades for attempted murder. Toss in a bunch of civil rights violations and you can say bye-bye Ben."

Perspiration poured from Walter's face. His need to exterminate the man was at war with Pete's logic.

"If you kill a man who's tied up they'll put you in jail," Pete said. "Walter, there's too much to be done. Please don't. You said the project needed us, but you were wrong. If it's gonna work, you're the one it needs. You can't do it from prison."

The ferocity in Lonetree's eyes did not diminish.

"Remember when you told me there are worse things than dying?" Pete said. "If you kill him, he'll only die once. If he goes to prison he'll die a little every day. Think about that, Walter."

Lonetree kept a firm hold on Hickman's hair, his gaze riveted to the terrified man. "You okay Running Bear?" Lonetree said.

"He just creased me."

"Did you say this ugly motherfucker will probably spend the rest of his useless life in a federal prison, Pete?"

"For sure."

"Can I kill him if he ever gets out?"

"I'll pick you up at the old folks home and wheel you over there myself."

Lonetree's face contorted savagely. "I don't want to wait that long," he said, rearing the knife back. With every ounce of strength in his body, the angry Indian rammed the blade into the dirt beside Hickman's neck.

"But I guess I will," he said, relaxing his grip on Hickman who, by that time, was sobbing uncontrollably. The terrified man had voided his bladder.

"Okay, Hickman," Lonetree said, returning his knife to the scabbard hidden under his shirt. "We'll let it slide this time."

When Chris Hutchins arrived at the shack with an FBI agent, the NTSB crash investigator, and a half-dozen sheriff's deputies, six Indians were sitting quietly on the bed of Running Bear's pickup truck.

"We'll take these men to Pierre for arraignment," Marvin Eubanks said. "Take a good look around you Hickman. You won't be seeing open spaces from now on."

Jeff tied a handkerchief around Running Bear's wound and turned to the lawmen. "We have these fellows to thank for saving our skin."

The sheriff's deputy looked sternly at the group of Indians. "You boys didn't use any firearms did you?"

"Firearms?" Lonetree said. "You mean like guns? No, man. That would be a violation of our probation. We were just on our way out to my camp to play some baseball when we saw the trouble."

"Baseball?" said the deputy, holding up a fire-hardened oak two-by-four that had been carved to fit Running Bear's hand.

"We lost our equipment funding," Running Bear said.

CHAPTER THIRTY-SEVEN

For every story a tribesman had to tell of personal and family hardship, there was at least one account of another tribe or individual who had experienced even harder times.

"If this works as good as we think it will." Pete told the leaders, "We owe it to others to help them do the same thing."

Had Pete been coaching a sports team, they would surely have been headed for the finals. One of his greatest successes, and the one that pleased him more than any, was watching the changes in Walter Lonetree. He had evolved from unfocused rabble rouser to gifted corporate executive.

To help bring Doc's clinic up to date Pete ordered a full set of current medical books from the old man's list of priorities. To save time, Pete quietly paid for them himself.

When Jeff finally had a chance to talk to Pete, he said, "How's the fundraising going?"

"Well, we've got enough money to keep us going for six months at the projected rate. That probably translates to three months, because nothing ever goes the way you think it will. If we can hold this together we should be self-sufficient in a year."

"Look partner," Jeff said. "Chris has finished repairs on the Skyhawk. We've already been here longer than we originally thought. We need to think about moving on."

Pete looked shocked.

"We can't leave now."

"If you can't leave now, you can never leave," Jeff said. "You've helped build a great organization. Walter can hold it together for another month or so, if not indefinitely. It is very important for him to do that. You can only do so much on the telephone. Then you have to go belly to belly with the corporate people. Let's wind it down, take a little rest break along the way, and then do what we have to do in L.A."

"You're right," Pete said. "We can suggest some projects and step back from it for awhile and give everybody a chance to realize they don't need us looking over their shoulders.

"Let's figure on being out of here by the end of next week."

Pete nodded.

"I didn't mention it before, Jeff, but when we get back to Los Angeles I have to make a deal with the devil."

"I don't follow you."

"My father has always wanted me to be involved in the Sunderland enterprises."

"Ohmigod!" Jeff erupted. "You're not going into the firm."

"Not exactly," Pete said. "I'm going to compromise. Except it will be my father's kind of compromise where I double my demands and then settle for half. I get what I want, he thinks he gets what he wants. He's in no position to argue if he wants his son involved at all."

"How can you be committed to Sky Warriors and work for your father too?"

"Some of the more respectable Sunderland corporations are subject to the same government rules as everyone else to spread the goodies around. I will propose that we set up the Sunderland Foundation. With me in charge, of course, to direct cash to various projects. Someone may as well benefit from the ill-gotten gains."

"Isn't that going against family tradition?" Jeff said.

"You're right. Usually we arm the side that is already in power and wants to stay there."

"How will bankrolling the project help the Indians become self-sufficient?" Jeff asked.

"Because they're getting loans, not gifts, to set up businesses of their own. Each individual enterprise will have two years to succeed. After that, they're on their own. Second, if they do happen to succeed—and you and I will make damn sure they do—they must pay the money back, in cash or sweat, to finance similar projects in support of others."

"What if your father changes his mind at some inconvenient time," Jeff suggested. "That would leave a lot of people in the deep end of the cesspool."

"I've considered the possibility. The Sky Warriors Foundation will cover it."

"The Sky Warriors Foundation?"

"Seed money would come from any place we can scrounge it, with zero reliance on my old man. Sky Warriors will collect the money and distribute it to worthwhile projects like infrastructure, education and such. Anything we get from the Sunderland Foundation would be put aside for projects that won't die if he pulls out. I'm not too worried about that, though. With the old man's name on it his ego won't let it be shut down. My father is very concerned about looking good. In this country, at least. He won't risk what I would do to the good reputation he lets people see. After this is in motion, I'll be sure to let him know that if we get any shit from him I will do the biggest reverse public relations campaign in history."

"He'll be pissed at you for not getting into the business end of the business."

"What have I got to lose? It has cost more than a hundred thousand dollars for psychiatrists over the last fifteen years, but it has only taken these past few months to realize that I don't have to hate him. I have never felt so free in my life. That won't change, regardless of anything he says or does from now on."

That morning the board approved the purchase of nearly six-hundred acres of scrub land one of Walter's committees had located. It was in a spot central to several reservations, but outside of any of them.

The leaders gathered around a plot plan that was spread out on a table in the temporary airport headquarters. "This is all yours," Jeff said.

When Pete got the airport owner off to the side he handed him a check and said, "This is for you, Chris."

"A thousand dollars? Chris said. "You gotta be kidding. You don't have to do that."

"I lost track of all the work you did on the plane, the phone calls, electric bill, and everything else. I hope that more than covers it and I insist you take it."

"I'll find a good use for it," Hutchins said.

"Everyone appreciates what you've done, Chris," Pete said. "It's important that the tribes build their own place now. They're setting up a temporary office at the new site in a used mobile home donated by a Rapid City dealer."

As a truckload of equipment and office furniture pulled away from the airport, Chris Hutchins said, "It's going to be lonesome here."

To demonstrate to all, including himself, that things would not fall apart without him, Pete faked a broken cell phone. After two days of working out problems on their own, Jeff knew the time was near to move on.

CHAPTER THIRTY-EIGHT

"What now, Kimo Sabe?" Jeff said.

Putting his arms on Walter and Jeff's shoulders, Pete said, "I reckon we've got to find us some more Indians."

"Plenty more where we came from," Walter said.

The next major stop would be St. Louis where Pete could take his private pilot test and both men could get a few days rest. They had already spent more time in one place than they intended. They would have to abandon their plan to tour the northeastern states and head back to Los Angeles.

"I guess the rest of America will have to wait until the next time you need to go find yourself," Jeff said.

"Then I guess I'll never get to see it," Pete said.

"Funny how your priorities can get changed right out from under you," Jeff said.

"We have some research to do," Pete told Walter. "Then I'll make the rounds to squeeze money out of corporations."

"And, if they turn you down?" Lonetree said.

"Hey Walter. I'm a spoiled rich kid, remember? I don't take 'no' for an answer."

"And they call *me* a militant."

By Friday afternoon everything had been organized to the best of Pete's ability, without actually remaining with the project.

The three men were standing on the land they had bought. Pete unfolded the plot plan and drew a pencil line across part of the area spread out before them.

"There's something else you could do while we're gone, Walter." Pete said.

"Name it."

"Build the air strip and taxiway right here."

Walter looked at both men in the way someone might if they had asked him to bench press the truck they had driven to the site.

"It has to be asphalt covered, five-thousand feet long by fifty feet wide," Jeff said, ignoring the stunned look on Walter's face. "It has to be absolutely seamless, as straight as an arrow, east to west, as flat as Kansas."

"You trust me to do that?"

"We trusted you with our lives once," Jeff said. "After that, an airport ought to be easy. And don't be afraid to bring in some consulting experts, even if they happen to be white."

Pete handed Walter a list of names of firms experienced in building airports. The list included the outfit that built the runway and taxiway at the Stafford ranch.

"Get a couple of bids before you settle on one company. Tell the winning bidder very diplomatically that the only way they get the job is if they use local Indian labor and pay them at the same rate as they would pay anyone else. Here's the telephone number for the law firm we're using. Run everything past the lawyers and get everything on paper up front.

"Hire as many people as you need, make sure they are each paid the same hourly rate, including yourself as foreman. Keep good records of every dime you spend. Oh, one more thing. You're on a budget, so use your imagination in place of cash."

"Not to make trouble," Walter said, "but what do I use for money till the fat cats come across? I can do a lot with not much, but I can't do everything with nothing."

Pete handed Lonetree a white card attached to a clipboard.

"Sign your name on this line, right above mine."

"What is it?"

"It's a signature card from the bank where I opened a checking account. There's fifty-thousand dollars in there. That should hold you until I continue my raid on the capitalist pigs," he said, handing Lonetree a book of checks.

Lonetree looked slightly embarrassed holding the checkbook.

"What's the matter, Walter?" Pete asked.

"I—I never wrote a check before."

"No problem. I'll show you how it's done. Mrs. Caruthers in Red Creek volunteered to help keep things organized if you need her. Now don't scare the hell out of the poor woman."

"I never saw that much money in my life." Walter said. "A cousin of mine had a hundred dollar bill once."

"The money will be gone before you know it." Jeff said.

"What if we run out before we get more?"

"Then you'll have to turn on that famous Walter Lonetree charm." Jeff said.

"No, man, I'm the 'kick-ass' department. Pete is the 'kiss-ass' department."

"The practice will do you good." Pete said. "I'm sorry to put this all on you, Walter, but there's a lot to do in the city."

"It beats the hell out of hanging around Iron Feathers store."

"It pays better, too," Jeff said.

Lonetree looked out over the empty land they hoped would one day be filled with the elements to once again make the tribe self-sufficient.

Walter reached out his hand to Pete. "You done real good, paleface," he said. "When are you coming back?"

"We have a few more stops to make. Then to L.A.," Pete said, unclipping the map and giving it to Walter.

"Pete will head straight back here after he runs his raid on corporate America," Jeff said. "I'll set up a Los Angeles branch and pop in and out with equipment and supplies a couple of times a month.

"Figure six weeks or so." Pete said. "Think you can have the airport underway by then?"

"I hope so," Walter said. "We were both right, you know."

"About what?"

"I was right that our old ways are best. You were right that the future is here and we have to deal with it."

"Like the death of someone you love," Jeff said. "You can't change it. You can only move ahead."

Lonetree nodded. "It's like my grandfather used to say: 'you have to know who your enemies are before you can defeat them'."

"A wise man, your grandfather," Pete said. "Did he give you any other words to live by?"

"Yeah. He said 'beware of white men carrying clipboards'."

CHAPTER THIRTY-NINE

"There's a powwow tonight," Walter Lonetree said.

"What, exactly, is a powwow?" Pete asked.

"It's the people getting together to sing and dance, socialize, and honor our culture. You want to come?"

"The last party I went to was at Pete's parents' house," Jeff said.

"That wasn't a party." Pete said. "It was mud wrestling Bel Air-style."

"This is more than a party," said Lonetree. "It brings the people together with the ancient traditions."

"Is it a religious event?" Jeff asked.

"Not enough to get in the way."

"Will we be welcome there?" Pete said.

"A powwow is a time of sharing and acceptance," Lonetree said. "To not welcome my guests would be an offense against me. Nobody would treat another tribesman that way, even if they don't like his politics."

00

Daylight was fading by the time Pete and Jeff drove Doc's old rehabbed pickup truck into the parking lot alongside a long building used for tribal meetings and ceremonies. The lot was already nearly full.

Sounds coming from the hall grew more intense as the men neared the main entrance.

At first the regalia worn by converging Indians seemed to Pete and Jeff an odd contrast with the more modern vehicles celebrants arrived in. But when they stepped from the parking lot into the big room, the current century appeared to fade away. The participants and their surroundings seemed a perfect match.

It soon became evident to both men that a powwow was not just dressup time or reenactment of an earlier era for the entertainment of tourists. They were expressing a society as it had always been.

The only light in the building came from a few tiny windows, flickering candles, and bare hundred-watt light bulbs at the ends of wires that hung from the ceiling. Five men sat around a large, skin-covered drum. They beat a cadence and sang for those who danced in traditional Indian fashion on the huge dirt floor.

Men in colorful regalia representing birds and other animals performed an animated dance along an inner circle. Women wore dresses of deerskin adorned with combinations of feathers, beads, shells, and bone and danced at the outer edge of the room. Each had a shawl over her shoulders. Even small children joined in.

Despite its primitive origins, the music was a surprisingly intricate weave of tone, rhythm, and intensity. Much like modern choral works, but sung within a high, narrower range. If the music lacked tonal variety, the resulting overlay of human and drum sounds compensated for any perceived technical deficiency as hypnotic reverberations filled the hall.

When the dance ended, the crowd grew quiet and a tribal spokesman rose before the gathering.

"Walter Lonetree wants to speak," he said quietly and without ceremony.

A murmur went through the crowd. Lonetree obviously had supporters and detractors among those present, but he had assured his guests that the occasion demanded that animosities be suspended.

Lonetree looked out over the crowd until there was quiet.

"We come to honor those whose deeds make us feel proud of who we are," he began. "Our guests deserve our respect."

"I ask that you honor Jeff Burke and Pete Sunderland. They showed us how we can have a future without giving up our past. I invite you all to come forward now and welcome them as friends."

"These two have given us a gift," Lonetree said. "And one other saved the lives of those I speak of. Jaleen Jeeters, come forward."

Jeff and Pete both smiled at what the unexpected gesture would mean to the person they owed their lives to.

The woman whose baby Jeff had helped to deliver looked shy and hesitant when she stepped slowly out of the crowd and joined Lonetree. Being singled out as one who merited respect was apparently confusing to her after so many years of believing what had been said of her; that she was a woman of 'low morals', and therefore unworthy.

Walter Lonetree spoke once more. "Jeff Burke and Pete Sunderland would surely have been killed by enemies of our people if not for Jaleen Jeeters. She risked her own life by warning the authorities of the danger Jeff and Pete were in. I ask that you honor her."

Jaleen and the two men were nearly overwhelmed by the crush of people who came up to them to shake their hands.

"You did a good thing," Jeff whispered to Walter. "You gave Jaleen status she didn't have before. No one will dare to look down on her ever again."

As the drummers and singers began another song, Lonetree said, "Follow me. Do as I do." Jeff took Jaleen by the hand and followed as Walter Lonetree led them in a kind of slow, rhythmic step that would take them all the way around the dirt and sawdust-covered floor of the lodge.

Men, women, and children continued to come up to them as they walked. Smiling people of all ages shook their hands warmly. Soon, hundreds of people stretched out behind them, the essence of a civilization squeezed into that place and time.

When the two men had completed their circle of honor, arriving at the place where they began, neither could have described what it felt like to be the focus of the gratitude of an entire community.

When it was over, Jeff took Jaleen off to the side.

"Mrs. Jeeters—"

"Please call me Jaleen."

"Jaleen. We would not be here if not for you. I want to give you something."

Jeff reached into his shirt pocket and withdrew the talisman she had given him the night her baby was born.

"It is a custom of my people," Jeff said with a smile, "to give a gift of something they value to someone who has done them a service."

"No, this is yours," she said, trying to push it away. "I gave it to you for helping me."

But Jeff pressed the carved stone hawk into her palm.

"This is my most prized possession," Jeff said. "I treasure it above anything else I have. To give you anything less would be an insult to you. I would be honored if you would accept it as a token of our appreciation for what you did for us."

The woman seemed younger than she had the first time they saw her. Being thought of as someone of value had melted years away from her appearance.

"I hope you will always think of us as your friends."

"Tears had come to Jaleen Jeeters' eyes. Possibly the first she allowed herself to shed in many years of living without emotions.

They waved goodbye as they returned to the truck for the drive back to the airport.

"Pete," Jeff said. "Have I ever told you that money isn't everything?"

"I knew I heard it somewhere."

CHAPTER FORTY

A light rain was falling at Lambert-St. Louis International Airport when the Skyhawk touched down. After the craft was refueled they were directed to transient parking where they secured the plane, grabbed their overnight bags, and slogged through puddles to the terminal.

If they needed to dress appropriately for any mischief they might dream up, Pete had said there were plenty of places in the city to go shopping.

They took the airport limousine to the best hotel Pete could find listed in the terminal lobby's directory. On the way, Jeff phoned Stephanie and Pete called Melanie to let them know they had arrived in St. Louis.

"I feel an overwhelming need to be pampered," Pete said, stretching his legs out to their full length in the roomy limo.

"I can understand that of a man with comfort encoded in his DNA."

"What's your excuse then?"

"Okay, you're right for once. I need a fix of affluence as much as you do."

Jeff looked forward to having hot, steaming water run all over his weary body until he was deep down clean and no longer felt there were weeds in his hair. He also needed desperately to sleep in a real bed. With Stephanie, if given the choice.

As much as both men needed rest, they were also feeling anxious to resume the work when they returned to Red Creek.

"Well, let's put aside guilt and responsibilities for a day or so," Jeff said. "After that we'll jump into the project."

"It'll be hard not to feel guilty about indulging ourselves when you think of the poverty we've just seen."

"We'll be more valuable if we're rejuvenated. Stepping back to look at things from a distance will give us a new perspective. The Indians don't have that luxury."

Despite the occasional strain of making do with just the basics, as they had over the previous months, each had taken some pleasure in living sparsely. Living close to the earth had been a freeing experience. City survival came with constraints of their own kind.

Apparently the hotel staff had not been offended by an unkempt pair severely in need of clean clothes, shaves, and a good scrubbing. They were probably not the grubbiest guests ever to pass through St. Louis, although they may have held the record outside of the 19th century.

A bellhop led them to a large suite that was complete with two baths, a sitting room and a walk-in closet. Any concerns about possible rejection by hotel staff were put to rest when Pete produced his American Express Centurion Card. They were especially welcomed when Pete over-tipped everyone from the bellhop to the young man who came to their room with two bottles of red wine they had ordered from room service. A few well-placed twenty dollar bills instantly upgraded the travelers' status from "smelly clodhoppers" to "affluent eccentrics on holiday."

Pete sprawled across one of the massive room's two queen-sized beds. From his shaving kit he produced a corkscrew and removed the cork from his bottle. "Won't need that little rascal anymore." He scored a mid-court field goal with the cork as it clanked in a metal wastebasket. He tossed the corkscrew to Jeff and, without the formality of one of the tissue-wrapped drinking glasses, Pete chugged several swallows straight out of the bottle.

"Class always shows," Jeff said, as he uncorked the bottle and slam-dunked the stopper into the trash basket.

Jeff looked at the wine label. It made him think of Stephanie. But then most things made him think of Stephanie.

"How are you feeling?" Pete asked.

"Very civilized, thank you," Jeff said, also forgoing the niceties of glassware.

"Look at yourself," Pete said. "You say I'm spoiled. A few months in the boonies and you act like a man who just got out of prison."

"I have to admit it," Jeff said. "I'd gotten soft."

"Well don't get used to it. There are still a few rocks in this great nation that we haven't slept on."

"I can't imagine that," Jeff replied, chugging some more cabernet sauvignon.

By the time they finished the wine, they were in no condition to do anything but sleep. But that was due less to the wine than to the accumulated weariness neither had noticed until they flopped down in a proper bed. The responsibility of navigating an airplane lifted from them, they had only to rest and recuperate.

And sleep they did. Right after Pete saluted his empty wine bottle and did a trumpet imitation of 'Taps' all the way through.

00

The front desk woke them at a reasonable hour the next morning. Room service rolled in a tray covered with the sumptuous breakfast Pete had ordered the night before.

As much as Jeff was enjoying the luxury and quiet of the hotel room and the break from aircraft engine noise, the inactivity once again brought him face-to-face with his aloneness.

He missed Malibu. Not the Malibu where he isolated himself to the point of bitterness, but the Malibu that was filled with sunshine and surf, his little pal, Punkin, and Stephanie Burgess.

When he spoke with her on the telephone the night before, she reported all was well in Buffalo. Her mother had recovered nicely from the surgery and she was ready to go home.

"Sometimes I think I made you up in my mind," she told him.

"Me too. I miss you. We'll be together soon."

Calls every few days throughout the trip had been better than no contact at all. But he missed being able to see and touch her and to smell her perfume.

Pete noticed that Jeff was quieter than usual, spending more time just lying on his bed, hands behind his head, stocking-feet crossed; wide awake, but not really in there.

"I've got to get some post cards," Pete said as Jeff headed for the shower.

Pete found the address book Jeff had left open on the nightstand beside his bed. Once in the lobby he sent some cards to friends they had met along the way. A card would have to do until he could write a more detailed letter to Charlie Benson.

Jeff made an appointment with a Federal Aviation Administration examiner for that afternoon. They spent the time until then shopping for clothes more suited to mingling with city people. Jeff was feeling so refreshed by being back among life's creature comforts that he even allowed Pete to pay for everything.

The FAA flight test was a breeze. Pete's varied experiences on the trip had paid off. He was more than prepared for anything the FAA examiner could throw at him.

"Congratulations," Jeff said when the Skyhawk rolled into the parking area. He handed Pete a small box containing a wings lapel pin he had bought along the way.

Pete had a present for Jeff, too.

CHAPTER FORTY-ONE

It was early afternoon when a knock came at the door of their hotel room.

"Get that, would you Jeff?"

Jeff got up to answer, expecting the maid. Instead he beheld a sight that caused all of the loneliness in him to vanish.

"Remember me?" said an unforgettable Stephanie Burgess, throwing her arms around Jeff.

He had never been so glad to see anyone in his life. If the long, warm kiss she gave him was any gauge, the sentiment was obviously mutual.

"Okay you two, break it up." Pete said, after a decent interval.

"Hello, Pete," Stephanie said, shaking his hand. "Nice to meet you at last. Great idea you had there."

"Pete." Jeff said. "You did this?"

"I'm just a sentimental fool," Pete said. "Besides, you weren't much fun lately anyway, dragging around, sighing every thirty seconds."

Conspiring with Pete on the telephone after she spoke with Jeff two days earlier, Stephanie accepted the airline ticket Pete arranged to have waiting for her at Buffalo's Niagara International Airport ticket counter. She was ready to return to Los Angeles anyway, so the next morning she raced to the airport for the side trip to St. Louis. And here she stood, the loveliest sight Jeff had ever seen.

"Don't I get a kiss too?" Pete said.

"Get your own girl," Jeff said, as another knock came at the door.

"That could be her, now," Pete said, opening the door to a smiling and fashionable Melanie Stafford, who looked not at all like the ranch girl in Levis.

"Hiya, dudes," she said, wrapping her arms around Pete's neck and planting a warm, wet kiss on his lips.

Jeff introduced the two women and quickly filled Stephanie in on their meeting at the ranch.

"You are a truly devious person, Pete," Jeff said.

"Ain't that the truth," Melanie said.

A bellhop appeared with a luggage cart. The suitcases Melanie and Stephanie had left with him in the lobby were on board. Melanie's bags were offloaded, but Stephanie's were left on the cart.

"If Mr. Burke would accompany me," said the bellman, "his room is ready."

Jeff and Stephanie looked at each other, then followed him.

"See you guys later," Pete said.

When they arrived at the lush bridal suite, a magnum of Champagne was on ice.

Jeff hung out the "Do Not Disturb" sign, closed the door behind them and called down to instruct the hotel telephone operator to hold all calls. He was told that someone had already placed that order for their room.

Pete had thought of everything and Jeff realized that the gesture went far beyond money.

That was the last anyone heard from them for the rest of the afternoon, and for most of that evening.

When they rejoined the others for dinner, Jeff pulled Pete off to the side.

"I didn't realize you and Melanie had been, ah—"

"Intimate?" Pete said. "Actually, we hadn't. When I invited her, I told her I'd reserved a separate room for her. But after you left us this afternoon, she said she didn't think she'd need that other room."

"The two of you weren't bored without us, then?"

"We stayed busy, but thanks for asking," Pete said with a howling snort.

Melanie overheard the outburst, but not the conversation that inspired it. "That is the dirtiest laugh I have ever heard," she said. "What are you guys talking about."

"Just guy stuff," Pete said. "Male bonding, you know?"

"I can imagine," Stephanie said.

They looked at the pictures Pete had taken in South Dakota and pointed out the major characters in their adventure. He had sent copies to Walter Lonetree, Doc in Red Creek, and to Charlie Benson.

The couples went to dinner at the fanciest restaurant they could find, dawdled over the meal, and got to know each other better.

"Stephanie and I have agreed," Melanie said. "We want to stay awhile longer and help you with the Indian project."

"When did you decide that," Jeff asked.

"In the ladies room."

Pete slapped his forehead. "You see what happens. It's because women are always going to the ladies room together."

"Why didn't we think of it before?" Jeff said. "All of the problems on the planet could be solved in minutes by sending the wives of world leaders to the ladies room. What do you think, Pete? Shall we let them?"

"They'll probably keep us awake at night." Pete said.

"Another good reason for us to stay," Melanie said, wrapping her arms around Pete's waist.

"I guess we're stuck with them," Pete said.

The foursome spent the next day being tourists. Then it was time to get to work.

They went to a large electronics chain store where Pete bought the best desktop and laptop computers on the market, the Microsoft Office software, an ink jet printer, some cardboard file boxes and plenty of paper and office supplies. The hotel's Wi-Fi allowed them to connect to Pete's Internet Service Provider.

For much of their remaining time together the foursome put down on paper every thought they had for the proposed Indian community of the future. They brainstormed ideas for developing an economic base and compiled a list of CEOs of major American corporation's as potential members of an advisory board. Using Walter Lonetree's list of problems, they came up with possible solutions. They held occasional "what if" sessions, taking turns playing devil's advocate to work out glitches.

Everything was based on Pete and Jeff's observations of the Indians, plus what they could learn about them on the Internet, at the public library, and with a fair amount of educated guesses. They called heavily on their imaginations, sensitivities and personal experiences. They knew the Indians' experiences would come up with things they could not even imagine. But they also knew they had to start somewhere.

"Everything will have to be run past experts in various fields before we present all this to the tribal board," Pete said.

Melanie and Stephanie did much of the legwork, researching laws and government regulations relating to Indians. They culled the names of those most likely to contribute money to Sky Warriors from a downloaded list of foundations.

Pete and Melanie's room took on the look of a command center.

"You'd never believe this place turns into a love nest at night," Pete said, just before Melanie held a pillow over his face and muffled some ribald comments.

Despite all the time they spent working side by side, the two couples continued to enjoy staying together after they finished their work each afternoon. They dined at elegant restaurants and even took in the symphony one night.

On the evening of the fourth day after the girls' arrival, when they had done as much as possible without actually being in South Dakota, they stood back and looked at their work. Orderly stacks of computer printouts and materials from a variety of public agencies and private institutions sat on a table and on the unused second queen-sized bed.

Then Pete packed the computer equipment in its original cartons and filed most of the papers in packing boxes along with the remaining supplies. He put a sheaf of documents in a briefcase to take back to Los Angeles with him. Then he had UPS pick up the equipment and file boxes and ship all of it to Doc Henry at Red Creek. He pocketed a 64 gigabyte flash drive that contained the materials they had put together.

Pete called Doc Henry to say a gift was on its way to replace the old Underwood typewriter in the clinic. He asked the old doctor to hold onto boxes marked "Sky Warriors" for them until they returned.

The two couples had their final breakfast before the girls would head for home and Jeff and Pete would start back to L.A. The only bright spot any of them could identify was that they would soon be together again. Both couples were reluctant to do what had to be done, but they finally packed their belongings, checked out of the hotel, and rode the limousine to the airport.

"This has been great," Stephanie said.

"Yeah," Jeff said, "except for the part where Pete made us go to a symphony."

That even got a laugh out of Pete.

"Melanie and I have decided something," Stephanie said after she checked in at the airline counter.

"Ohmigod!" Pete said. "We took our eyes off them for a second and they went to the ladies room together again?"

"We want to be a permanent part of the project."

"What about your job, Stef?" Jeff said.

"I'm ready to do something more satisfying and worthwhile."

"What about your career as an heiress, Mel?" Pete said with a grin.

"I can be more useful as a Sky Warriors pilot."

"We're never going to get rid of these woman," Pete said.

"Believe it, bucko," Melanie said.

The airline reservation desk called for passengers on the Los Angeles flight.

"Take care of yourself, my love," Stephanie said.

"You too my love," Jeff said, kissing her one more time. They held on to each other for a long while before finally letting go. He watched her look back over her shoulder at him, then disappear through the boarding gate.

Moments later Melanie and the two men walked to the transient parking area. After a reluctant goodbye, Melanie boarded the Stafford family's Lear jet to fly back to the ranch.

"I think I'm in love," Pete said, as they walked to the transient parking area where the Skyhawk waited.

"That's great," Jeff said. "It'll clear up your complexion."

They loaded their gear and did the preflight check. In twenty minutes they were airborne.

Hours later Jeff ran his tongue over his lips and a taste of Stephanie's strawberry lip gloss brought her back to him. He was glad all over again that he would soon be home.

CHAPTER FORTY-TWO

They agreed to finish the rest of the trip home in two relatively short legs rather than make it a grind as they had the previous day.

Stephanie answered when Jeff called that evening.

"It's me."

"Could you be more specific?" Stephanie said, trying to stifle her musical laugh at the Malibu end.

"Ho ho. Did you pick up my mail?"

"Yes. That stuff you ordered from the Department of the Interior came. Also—" Stephanie hesitated.

"Also what?" Jeff asked.

"Also, a letter that smells very nice and was written by a woman."

"Who's it from?"

Jeff could hear Stephanie rustling through the pile of mail she had picked up for him that morning at the Malibu post office. *"It's from Sandra Neilson of Missoula, Montana."*

"That's my friend, Sandy, from the ranch where we met Melanie and her parents," Jeff said. "Open it and read it to me."

"You want me to open a letter to you that smells like this?"

"Go ahead and open it."

Jeff could hear Stephanie tear open the envelope. *"She says: 'Dear Jeff: I took your advice and stopped working so hard at it.' So hard at what?"*

"Finding her true love. Read on."

"And, sure enough, when I stopped looking, he found me. Roger owns a hardware store in Missoula. He's a marriage war veteran, too. As it turns out, I've known him all my life. When I was seven years old he used to squirt me with the water hose when I rode my tricycle past his house."

"So, is she going to marry the dude?"

247

"She says 'I don't know if it's love yet, but it's got a good start on it. He reminds me a lot of you: Kind, sensitive, smart, and gentle'. Jeff. Did you get gentle with that girl when I wasn't around?"

"Why Ms. Burgess. I do believe you're jealous."

"I don't have a jealous bone in my body."

"Nevertheless, I plan to conduct a thorough search when I get there tomorrow."

Pete also called Melanie.

"I've decided to leave home," she said.

"Where will you go?"

"Anywhere you go."

"You know, Mel, in some circles that is known as 'stalking'."

"I want to help with Sky Warriors. You could probably use another warrior. I'm a certified flight instructor. I could teach some of the Indians to fly."

"In that case you can come along."

00

Somewhere over Arizona Pete said, "I've decided not to pay you the agreed-upon salary."

"Okay," Jeff said, apparently unruffled by the announcement.

"I'm making you a millionaire, instead."

Jeff turned to Pete so fast he nearly whiplashed himself. "Wh—why would you want to do that?"

"Call it your 'kiss my ass' fund. With that money you won't ever have to take crap from anyone again. You can put the money to work for you to keep growing. Then you can work for Sky Warriors at no salary."

Jeff was having a harder time breathing than if Pete had physically knocked the wind out of him.

"That's a nice gesture," he was finally able to say. "But you don't have to do that."

"Actually, I do. If you have a lot of money you'll stop giving me the 'rich kid' crap because you'll be rich, too."

"If I have to stop doing that you can keep your money."

Pete ignored him.

"That's a million dollars clear. I'm adding enough to pay the taxes so you will still be a millionaire."

Neither spoke for awhile.

"Our work with the Indians has been the most satisfying of my life," Jeff said. "I don't want to let that go."

"Okay, you're hired."

00

The trip had far exceeded their wildest expectations. As an exercise in perspective, it had been a rousing success for both men.

Beyond the personal gratification, the project could continue to benefit thousands of people for many years to come.

The rest of the trip back to Los Angeles was blessedly uneventful.

"I've made more real friends in the past two months than in the previous thirty years," Pete said as they got closer to the city.

"Same here," Jeff said.

"And you and I have become friends, too."

"That's a filthy, disgusting lie."

"Maybe it's because we're both fed up with bullshit," Pete said.

"But the kind of bullshit you're fed up with comes from Grand Champion bulls."

"There you go again with the rich kid stuff. I thought I just bought you off."

"That would take more than a lousy million dollars."

Both men were silent for awhile, with only the sound of the engine between them.

"You like me," Pete said.

"No I don't. I tolerate you."

"Yes you do dammit. You like me."

"I just find you a little less irritating that I used to."

They both smiled.

Each had learned from the other and neither was certain just when it became unclear as to who was the teacher and who was the student.

CHAPTER FORTY-THREE

Jeff called Stephanie as they passed over Palm Springs. She was waiting for them at Ferguson's Flight Service when they landed at Santa Monica Airport.

"Let's get together sometime next week," Pete said. "I want to buy a fast plane to travel back and forth to South Dakota and I need your advice on what to get."

After they dropped Pete and all the gear at his Westwood condo, they decided there were important things to do before they picked up Punkin and Jeff's car at his mother's place. They headed straight for his Malibu apartment.

00

As the evening sun neared the horizon, Stephanie and Jeff walked slowly along the Malibu sand, their arms around each others' waists.

"I love you, Jeff," Stephanie said.

Jeff stopped walking, faced her, and took both of her hands in his.

"Sure, you love me now when I'm young—ish. But will you love me when all my teeth are gone and there's hair growing out of my ears?"

"Eeeee-oooooooooo. Let me think about it some more."

"How about moving in with me?" Jeff said.

"Why?"

"You could cut your rent in half."

"Is that the best reason you can think of?" Stephanie said, looking at him with her soft green eyes.

"I'm a good cook," Jeff said.

"Do I look undernourished?" she said, her arms upraised, doing a little spin to demonstrate that she clearly did not. "You'll have to do better than that."

"Because I can't play gin rummy by myself?"

"Still not good enough."

"Well then, how about because I love you and I want to get started on being together for the rest of our lives?"

"Oh," she said with a giggle." Okay then."

She squeezed him a little harder.

They walked farther up the beach and held each onto other for a long time.

"You'll probably get tired of hearing me tell the same stories over and over?" Jeff said.

"I'll just do what my grandmother did when granddad hauled out one of his old jokes or a story we'd heard a thousand times before. I'll just look to the ceiling, roll my eyes, shake my head, and say, 'Oh, Jeff'."

The tourists had left the beach for the day.

Malibu residents along the long row of seaside apartments and homes were sitting on their decks, barbecuing their evening steaks, and watching the sun as it seemed to sink into the blue Pacific Ocean.

THANKS

More than 25 years ago I suffered from pain and the near total loss of the use of my right hand after a fall that caused an upper spine injury. I could not type fast enough to continue working as a radio newscaster, so I spent my recovery time writing this book—hunt-and-peck style. It took most of a year. Then it lay in a computer file—the electronic equivalent of a sock drawer—for most of the next quarter of a century; except for an occasional technological update. As each phase of computer technology appeared (every Monday morning, as I recall), I would transfer the manuscript; first from the original hard drive on an elderly IBM PC, to increasingly smaller floppy disks, and to each new generation's data storage vehicle as it came along. Considering the fragility of some of the earlier disks, it's a miracle the manuscript survived at all.

I confess that it is unlikely that the fortunes of impoverished Native Americans could be improved as efficiently, relatively trouble free, and certainly not in the short time period as described herein. I also am aware that I will hear from detractors of the difficulty, if not impossibility, of healing wounds inflicted over the centuries during which the Indians' lands were taken from them, their culture nearly destroyed, and they were forced to comply with the white man's idea of what a people should be.

I hope this story will be seen as I had intended; a tale of two dissatisfied men who go off in search of what is missing from their lives and how others benefit from what they know.

Special thanks to friends, relatives, fellow writers, designers, editors, and all those along the path to publication for their contributions of advice and moral support. It was that combination that got this story from idea to book.

Thanks also to the California Writers Club, Sacramento branch. The organization exposed me to knowledgeable people with expertise in the various aspects of crafting a novel and steering it all the way into the hands of readers.

I am grateful to my wonderful corps of pre-readers who offered opinions and expertise in advance of publication: Author Margaret Van Steyn Duarte, whose Visionary Fiction writings should be on everyone's must-read list; Cindy Sample, whose Laurel McKay murder mystery series is storming the nation, for invaluable advice; Linda Lohman, a fellow writer who honors me with her honesty in letting me know of my literary sins; Kelley Ballard, a supportive friend who is not shy about telling me if I've produced a lemon. Without their suggestions and encouragement I might have given up.

Most of all, to my wife Sherry who has been there through the entire often-agonizing process.

I have a great team and I'm grateful to all who contributed.

Any errors or omissions contained herein are mine alone.

Steve Liddick

www.ingramcontent.com/pod-product-compliance
Lightning Source LLC
Chambersburg PA
CBHW071852220626
47052CB00002B/90